Imperfect Promise

Imperfect Promise

Susanna Lane

FIVE STAR
A part of Gale, a Cengage Company

Five Star Publishing, a part of Gale, a Cengage Company

LIBRARY OF CONGRESS CATALOGING-IN-PUBLICATION DATA

Names: Lane, Susanna, author.
Title: Imperfect promise / Susanna Lane.
Description: First edition. | Waterville, Maine : Five Star, 2021.
Identifiers: LCCN 2021001553 | ISBN 9781432879440 (hardcover)
Subjects: GSAFD: Western stories. | Love stories.
Classification: LCC PS3612.A54993 I47 2021 | DDC 813/.6—dc23
LC record available at https://lccn.loc.gov/2021001553

First Edition. First Printing: November 2021
Find us on Facebook—https://www.facebook.com/FiveStarCengage
Visit our website—http://www.gale.cengage.com/fivestar
Contact Five Star Publishing at FiveStar@cengage.com

Printed in Mexico
Print Number: 01 Print Year: 2022

ACKNOWLEDGMENTS

This book would not have been possible without the support of my family; from the eldest to youngest. Heartfelt appreciation goes out to my dear friends who lent their ears and offered their encouragement. A special shout-out to Monica, from the beginning, and lighting my way. Many thanks to Diane Piron-Gelman for marvelous editing and her capacity for kindness. And so grateful to Tiffany . . . for opening the door. Many thanks to Five Star for giving me the opportunity to write what I love.

AUTHOR'S NOTE

While many of the events regarding railroads and landscape in this book are accurate, some of the locations are fictionalized. Wichita, Ogallala, Emporia, Omaha, and Denton were striving to become prosperous through the cattle industry while railroads crisscrossed the plains. The characters are imaginary and have been placed in the context of the story's events. It should be noted that there is a record of Millie and Wes Hodges and their boarding house in Wichita, Kansas, during this time in Wichita history. Ogallala was a thriving cow town, and Gast's Ogallala House did exist, as did the Cowboy's Rest Saloon. Beyond those mentions, the story is fiction. Any familiar names are coincidental.

Chapter 1
End of May 1876

Lark Marie Garrin nearly tripped on the sloping gangway before catching herself. So desperate to get far away from the boat, she hadn't paid heed to the coiled manila ropes. She clutched her carpetbag, her head held high beneath the old straw hat she wore that served to keep her face in shadows. The *Memphis Queen* bobbed in the rolling wake of a passing sternwheeler, and again she wobbled as Bailey, the cook, took her arm. Beside him stood tall Henry Caster, the kitchen manager, both men wearing solemn expressions. They'd come to see her off and away from this old life.

"Well, now. We'll be missin' you, Miss Garrin." Bailey managed a feeble smile.

"Thank you both for your kindness." She glanced around, taking in the dockhands shoving barrels into place and the dark mud bank beyond, from where a heron took flight. "Can't say I'll miss the smells of the Mississippi muck, the cigar smoke, and all the rest." Mustering a scrap of a smile was impossible.

Henry shook his head, his gaze on the crusted scar along her jaw. She knew the shadows beneath her hat couldn't entirely hide the mean red slice that would forever mark her. Stares and questions would be inevitable.

"My father?" she managed to grit between clenched teeth. Referring to him as her father sent acid to her tongue.

Henry nodded. "That drunken father of yours is still locked in a storage closet, sleeping it off. After what he did, giving you to that man, I'd like to bash him and feed him to the fish. The captain has ordered him off the boat before we sail for Memphis. You best get on that train before we let him go."

"I wouldn't have enough funds if you and Bailey hadn't helped me."

Bailey sighed and cleared his throat. "Just run as far as you can. We should've known Will Cardin was up to something."

"Nothing could've stopped him," Lark snapped. She hadn't meant to sound so disagreeable, and regretted it. Right now, she was lucky to escape.

"Maybe so. Take this salve." Bailey lifted her hand and pressed a small jar into her palm. "It'll help heal that scar. The inside healin' depends on you."

Tears welled in her eyes as she nodded and then turned away. She felt the men watching her until she turned a corner toward the Topeka and Santa Fe Depot, leaving the mighty river behind. As she walked onward, she prayed that Will Cardin would never find her. The outlaw might forget her light brown hair, her voice, and her hazel eyes, but he'd never forget his special mark.

The Santa Fe Railroad train rattled and finally slowed. Plumes of steam curled skyward beside the window. The elderly woman across from Lark had offered friendly comfort and a pleasant distraction, chatting about life in Omaha on the long two-day trip. When the woman went quiet, Lark had stared from her dusty window, mindlessly taking in the endless sea of green and brown grass stretching over the long expanses of short hills. Nothing reminded her of her Ohio roots.

The slowing train told her she was in Omaha at last. Her traveling companion stirred. "Looks like we're here, gal."

Lark lifted her hat and settled it on her head. "I'm so tired, Mrs. Garson. Guess I didn't realize how long a trip this would turn out to be."

"You got a place to stay in Omaha, Lark?"

"I'll find something."

"Just remember to come to Garson's Boarding House if you decide, and we'll figure somethin' out."

"I thank you for the company," Lark said, not committing to the offer.

Mrs. Garson stood, bracing herself against the seat. "Before we go our own ways, I'm curious. That scar. Indians attack you?"

Lark nearly laughed. If only it had been Indians. "That is a story I can't disclose."

"Didn't mean to pry. Just worrisome, is all. But take this with you, honey."

The woman handed Lark a folded page of newsprint, then moved down the aisle and stepped from the train. Lark stood, glancing out the window, and saw Mrs. Garson embracing a gray-haired man. A few seconds later, they disappeared into the crowd.

Once most folks had moved along, Lark stepped down from the train car and made her way to the nearest building. A mercantile. Curious about the paper she'd been given, she sat on the bench beside the doorway. Ignoring the stares of dust-caked farmers and gingham-dressed women, she turned her attention to the words between her fingers.

Women in need of husbands are invited to attend the Ribbon Cotillion to be held on July 8th, 1876, promptly at six o'clock at the Ogallala House. All manner of upstanding men will be in attendance, including farmers, ranchers, shop-keepers, businessmen, and bankers. All are seeking decent, hardy women willing to become wives. If interested, your fare to Ogallala will be provided. Sign for your ticket at the Lost Gold Hotel or at the nearest train depot. Widows with children need not apply.

Lark reread the words. Today was June 5th. The cotillion was a month away. In the meantime, she'd find work here. A husband was her best chance of hiding. A new name on a remote farm. The last place Will Cardin would find her.

A husband. That is, if any man could overlook her disfigurement.

July 3

A sudden loud rumble shook the walls of Mrs. Garson's Boarding House, jolting Lark from her bed and sending her heart pounding out of her chest. Lightning streaked across the sky, illuminating the wall. Breathing deeply, she kept her eyes riveted on the door. At any moment she expected it to burst open. In her mind, she saw the glint of the knife as it descended toward her face.

Her heart still thudding wildly, she rubbed her arms and assured herself that no one held her down. While her breathing slowed, Will Cardin's words came rushing back to her. *"Just stay calm and I'll do this quick. Relax and it'll be over."*

Lark remembered closing her eyes and rolling her head from side to side beneath the man's touch, her screams gagged. With one hand, he'd grasped her chin between his fingers, forcing her to stay still. She'd opened her eyes and stared up at him as he kept talking. *"My friends and I are getting off here on business. You will go on to Memphis. If you aren't there, Lark Garrin, I'll find you and make you regret that you were born. Your pa was short on cash. He offered you. Debt paid as far as I can see. And you sure are pretty as a peach. Too bad I have to mark you. All my possessions are marked."*

Even now, while she stood in a room far from the riverboat,

her stomach roiled. She still heard the chuckles of those men without faces who'd callously held her down. Afterward, they'd left her alone to face the mirror. Now she stood before it again. Lark Marie Garrin looked back. But not the same woman. Never the same.

She turned away from her reflection. In a few days, she would set out for Ogallala. A place she could only imagine.

Ogallala, Nebraska
Late May 1876

Cortland Enders gave the fine people of Ogallala credit. The jail was passable for a jail, and he'd been in a few over the years. Except for roasting alive in this cell, he found the food tolerable. Better than he'd get where he was heading.

Stretching out on the narrow bunk, he studied the barred shadows on the wall, oddly marking his time. At least he had his Stetson to hide his face and pretend to be asleep every time the nosy damned marshal came to chat. Varnum by name, or something like that. He heard gruff voices from the other side of the big door that separated him from freedom. *You really got yourself into a mess this time, cowboy.* No doubt, his next stop would be the prison in Lincoln. He'd heard how most came out of there either crazy or dead. This time, like the last, it had been about a woman. Women were trouble.

Staring at the light streaming through his narrow window, he figured it to be about noon. Perspiration streaked his face and trickled into his beard where he gave it a swipe with his sleeve. The stink of the piss pot mingled with his own sweat. They were pretty lazy about tending to personals here. His stinking sheets were soaked through.

His shirt felt like it had grown to be part of his skin. At night, he took it off, against the marshal's rules. A fly buzzed over his face and landed on his head. He swatted at the fly with his hat. It buzzed in a lazy circle and finally landed on the far wall. The darned insect was probably sizing him up for another attack.

The sound of voices swelled to a louder pitch. A woman's voice caught his attention. Sienna Harris. He'd bet she'd dragged that fancy lawyer along to talk with him. But Judge McKenzie had already sentenced him and there was no going back. He'd shot Mark Tenner and he'd do it again if it meant keeping Tenner from hurting another woman. He'd pulled his shot. Hadn't killed the pissant even though he deserved it.

Mrs. Harris was one tough widow lady. With her husband, she ruled the Circle H with standards that no one crossed or you'd be off the ranch faster than your shadow could follow you. But today was a week too late for her to pull him out of this fire.

The Circle H was home, and as close to good people as he guessed he would ever get. As foreman, he'd been expected to keep out of jail. He'd sure made a mess of things. Wade Harris had taken in a gunslinger when he should have had more sense. The day Cort found Wade lying cold and dead on the ground still felt like a gut punch. They said it was his heart.

"Sonofabitch," he muttered. "Why'd you have to go and die on me? Maybe you could help me get outta here. You listenin' up there or just laughin' your ass off, Wade Harris?"

As though in answer, the clanking of keys and the creak of the outer door announced company. Cort decided he wouldn't be cooperative or listen to another lecture. Instead, he slapped his hat over his eyes and stretched out as comfortably as he could on the miserable bunk. The marshal's worn boot heels scraped against the floor, then came to a sudden halt. Cort swallowed, sensing the man staring at him. He figured he was about to be shackled and carted off to that prison in Lincoln. His cell door squeaked, followed by the sudden snatching away of his Stetson.

"Get up. You got company."

"I don't want to see anybody. Including that lawyer," he mumbled.

"You got no choice. Sounds like you got a good deal on the table and if you don't take it, you're a mule's hind end. Sit up and give a listen."

Cort's gaze followed the marshal as he came closer and hunkered down beside the bunk, setting the Stetson atop it. It crossed Cort's mind to grab for his revolver. He wouldn't get far, though. Besides, he had no interest in killing the marshal.

The lawman shook his head and stood. Waiting. *What the hell?* Might as well get this over with. Cort swung his legs over the side of the bunk and sat up. The sound of quick footsteps approaching caught him completely off guard. He turned his head in time to see Sienna Harris waltz through the cell door as though entering a tea parlor, her lips tight and her eyes narrowed. Disdain was written all over her face.

"Customary for a gentleman to stand in the presence of a lady," the marshal snapped.

Cort knew that. He was just taken aback by her being here and too surprised to move. He stood, trying his best to look indifferent. He tucked in his shirt while Sienna faced him, her eyes raking him from his head to his boots. Unless he misread her, there was a hint of sympathy in the twist of her mouth. Her long, gray-streaked black hair was pulled into a thick loose braid. She wore her usual ranch gear, leather split skirt, fine tooled boots, and a blue shirt that was manlier than most women would wear. He watched as she regarded the cell, her nose wrinkling at the pungent smells.

"Ma'am. Thanks for coming but you shouldn't be here."

"Neither should you, Cort. I'm sorry you didn't get off. If I could've gotten here sooner."

"Don't blame you. Got myself into this. Just so you know, I didn't set out to pick a gunfight. I had a reason."

"I believe you. Got the gist. The judge acted like a horse's rear. Still, after my lawyer, me, and Judge McKenzie had a sit-down, we came to a compromise on that three-year sentence."

Someone behind him cleared his throat. Cort turned to see that pasty-faced lawyer, Marcus Layton, standing just outside the cell with his arms crossed, wearing a gray suit and shaking his head.

Cort looked toward Marshal Varnum for explanation. The marshal stepped back and leaned against the far wall. Watchful. "What kind of deal?" Cort managed to say between his clenched teeth. He looked from the woman to the lawman and then back to the woman, certain a boulder was about to drop on his head.

Sienna addressed the warden. "This cell has got to be aired out, Peter. You can't keep folks locked in a hellhole like this and expect them to stay healthy."

"Mrs. Harris, the kind that come and go here don't have rights except for a fair trial."

Sienna snorted and turned her attention back to Cort. "I'll get to the bone of the meat. We've worked out a deal that you stay on as foreman of the Circle H. No prison. You'll work your hind end off for my ranch and keep it running like Wade would want for your term. You won't be permitted to leave the ranch boundary except for supplies and cattle drives unless I provide you a written pass."

Her clipped words shot like bullets while his brain stumbled to catch up. This made little sense to him, but riding the range sounded better than being penned up in a filthy cell for the next three years. Besides, nobody would keep him confined to the ranch if he decided to leave. He didn't want to, but his pride reminded him that he knew the mountains too well to get found, should he choose to disappear.

"I expect loyalty, Cort. Wade had a very high opinion of you. Said he'd never met a better cowman. We saw something in you that set you apart."

"I've killed and you know it. Never killed someone who didn't deserve it. Been to prison before. If you're willing to take a chance on me, I'd appreciate takin' the offer. As long as I run things as I see fit."

Sienna moved to stand in front of him, so close that he could see a momentary sadness wash over her eyes. Her skin was pale and her clothes hung on her small frame like she'd been losing a lot of weight. Was she sick?

"Like my husband, I don't trust folks. I can still sit a saddle. As long as you abide by my rules and run decisions by me where money is concerned, I'll give you free rein. Just like before."

"Agreed. I'll give you the three years. I'll sign any paper you need. Is there anything else?"

"You'll need to clean up. You smell like cow dung and your hair and beard are so filthy you could grow a crop of potatoes. I expect my husband to be clean. Especially in my house."

Cort gulped at that revelation. "Say again? Your house? Husband?" He swallowed again and shook his head. What was the infernal woman talking about? *Husband?* He had no such inclination.

"I just told you, I don't trust anyone. Once you sign the lawyer's papers and get cleaned up, we'll get that preacher to follow us back to the ranch. Mostly so Zeke and the others witness the *words.*"

"You can't mean you want *me* to marry you. The answer is no. Hell no."

"I'm not delusional, Cort. I'm twenty years older than you. Damn. You could be my son. I know that. Prideful, brave, and tenacious . . . those things make you a good man deep inside.

Even to shooting that varmint who attacked that saloon gal. Damn the judge and damn that Mark Tenner. Nothing we can do but get you out of this. You won't run from a legal wife. Besides, I'm not taking any chances. The short of this is, you'd be an owner of what I have. You won't give up this chance I'm givin' you unless you're a fool."

"Christ! I don't want a wife. Ever. I don't . . . I can't do what you're askin'. You're Wade's wife, Mrs. Harris. You don't need to be Mrs. Enders."

Her chin tilted up and her boot toe tapped the floor and then stopped. "It won't be a marriage in any real sense. Wade is the only man I'll ever love. Leaving the ranch would be your biggest mistake. For now, I need you to live in my house so my men won't think less of you or me. Or question the arrangement."

Cort turned away from her. The marshal mumbled something about waiting out in his office for a decision, and left. The lawyer had already scurried away. Cort and Sienna were alone. He heard her breathing, this little woman whose demands packed a punch, leaving him without much air in his own lungs.

Finally, he got out one word. "No."

"Then go to prison. I'd be sorry for that." When he didn't answer, she added, "Cort. Only Zeke, and people who need to know, are aware that I have cancer. No cure. Just laudanum. I don't have a lot of time left. No heirs to take over the ranch when I die. I want that ranch to survive. That's where you come in. I need you."

Her words hit him like a blow to his midsection. His knees buckled but he caught himself before hitting the floor. Put like that, he felt boxed in.

She sighed at his silence. "As my legal husband, you know the ranch is yours as well as mine. I don't want the vultures picking over the place after I'm gone. Plain and simple, I'm bequeathing the place to you in a roundabout way. No one will ever question it."

She turned on her heels, her quick steps heading for the doorway and his last chance at freedom. He didn't love her. He didn't want to share her house, not to mention anything else. In a true sense, she'd never be his *wife*. His legs moved independently of his will. He lifted his hat from the bunk and sighed.

The three people in the outer office looked up as he reached the doorway. "To be clear, Sienna, I won't stay because of what you said." He paused, looking toward the marshal and lawyer. *Do they know?* "I'm not one of those vultures and won't dance on your grave. I'm stayin' because that ranch feels like home. If you find you want somebody like Zeke to have the place, I'll step aside. No questions."

She gave him a thin smile. "I appreciate your honesty."

"All right. You win. I'll sign the damned papers. Better order up a bath for me before I say 'I do.' "

Chapter 2
Pretty Prison

Even Sienna figured she'd lost her mind. She stood in her fine parlor beside the man she didn't love, surrounded by the green velvet settee and two plump leather chairs worn with years of sitting. The massive stone fireplace was cold. A polished walnut table with a white marble top sat in a corner where she and Wade played cards. The scrolled wood chairs were set against the wall. On the table, Theresa had set a large crystal bowl brimming with sweet bourbon punch. Nothing permeated the air like that stuff.

She reminded herself that this was a business arrangement. Sienna wanted to make sure that no one, especially Zeke, questioned Cort's place. Once it was done, this ranch would be settled. Truth be told, she liked Cort, though not in the romantic sense. She admired Cort's grit and skills, and the empathy he showed for the plight of women like Sally. Yet he worked hard at hiding his gentle side. His grin was rare and melted just as fast as it appeared. If she had her way, she'd round up a gal and haze her in Cort's direction. That thought took root.

The man beside her stood straight, his face pale and his lips taut. Cort's jaw ticked beneath his hard, clean-shaven face. Standing apart from her with enough distance to punctuate his distaste for this affair, he set his eyes on the preacher while the grumbling, muted voices of the invited cowhands faded. The Bible was opened and she raised her eyes to the ceiling, feeling like a betrayer.

Cort towered over her, radiating hot rage like a badger with his paw in a trap. She empathized with his pain. Still, this scheme was proof she'd do anything to keep the ranch alive. After all, she'd given a deep-down decent man a chance at redemption, free of the bars that would destroy him.

The preacher said, "Do you take this man to be your wedded husband?"

She hesitated for a whisper of a moment. "Sienna?" the preacher coaxed in his deep baritone.

"I do." Damn. Her voice sounded like a rusty hinge, even to her own ears.

More words followed from the fog into which she sank. Bolting would be cowardly. Sienna Harris was no coward. *Sienna Harris Enders.*

Someone cleared his throat behind her. Cort stumbled forward a step as though he'd been prodded.

"I do." He said the two words like he'd swallowed ground glass. At least he wasn't wearing his gun or he might shoot someone. Still, they were now officially married. It was done.

The crowd of gawkers, well-wishers, and curious ranch hands milled around the parlor, speaking in quiet tones. No music filled the room, like the big shindig when she married Wade. Shc was old for a bride by most standards. Tongucs might wag for a long while, but not because she and Cort lived and worked together in this house unmarried.

Theresa set trays of sandwiches out on the dining table. The spiked punch was served and, Lord have mercy, Sienna needed more than a cup. Her loyal friend, Zeke Waterson, had most likely dumped half of their bourbon into the crystal punch bowl.

Sienna circled around the guests so she could look out the front window, where Cort sat on the porch. His booted feet rested on the railing, a bottle of whiskey in his hand. She followed his gaze, staring out across the rolling grassland. The cattle looked like brown rocks rolling through the high waving grass. Twenty thousand acres and five thousand head of cattle. She was counting on her new husband's integrity. Now he had more than enough reason to stay on. Not for her. For this ranch. Pain streaked through her stomach, and she bent and caught her breath. Her time was nearly up.

Many of the hands had already begun to make their way back to their chores. Work didn't wait on a ceremony. Moving to the massive wood-frame doorway, she waved goodbye to the preacher and a couple of neighbors. She clutched the jamb and thought about the talk there'd be around the hearths, campfires, and in every saloon from here to Omaha once they heard about the lonely widow marrying a roving gunslinger. *Let them think what they will.* Her pain was worse these days, and soon the ranch would be in the hands of her only viable choice. What Cort needed was a real wife. Someone to give this place new life. Children.

"You all right, Sienna?"

She recognized the gravelly voice of kindly, steadfast Zeke behind her, and turned to face his piercing blue-eyed gaze. She gave him her best smile, knowing it wouldn't quite reach her eyes. She choked back an urgent need to sob and stood straighter. "Of course I am. Stop wrangling with this. This was my choice."

"Big mistake, lady. Wish we'd have talked it over first."

"Hah. Ezekiel Waterson, you are the best friend I have. I'm warning you to stay out of this. You should already figure why I did this. For Wade. For you and the men working this place."

"Don't kid yourself. You know damned well how I feel about you. Wade won your heart. I'm goin' to keep watch whether you like it or not. I know about the damned cancer and the pain you keep tryin' to hide. Painkiller can mix you up. Don't want the men knowin' you're usin' that stuff. I'm the only one who knows exceptin' Theresa and Nita."

"Thank you for keeping it from the rest." She squeezed his arm. "You're a good man."

"Cort knows, or he's about to know. You just bent over in pain. The others will figure it out soon enough."

"He knows. I told him."

"Shit."

"Doesn't matter. As long as *he* keeps the Circle H alive after I'm gone."

"What makes you sure he'll stay on? He's not a man to stick it out."

"He has to stay on for three years or he'll rot in a prison cell. Besides, if he left, he'd give up ownership of this spread. I have him nailed down. You know he's no fool."

His sharp intake of breath told her she'd hit a raw nerve. If nothing else, Zeke couldn't harm a fly sitting on his nose. "I hope you know what you're doin'. I don't hold with deals that gut a man."

"Zeke . . . you and I both know this ranch needs a firm hand. A man who'll stand up to Indians, thieves, and squatters. Someone with a solid fist and a fast gun. Cortland Enders is that man. Wade knew it and so do you. You and I are too old to take all that on. As much as I'd like to hand this place over to you, the best I can promise you is a home. I won't be around long enough to see how this pans out."

"All right, Sienna. I don't agree with this harebrained scheme, but I'll go along with it 'less I figure he's a no-good sonofabitch, that gunslinger you call a husband. Just one more thing. I know I'm oversteppin' my bounds but you and I go back a long way. What do you plan to do when he wants his husbandly rights?"

She swallowed hard as another pain streaked through her

gut. Then she managed a feeble grin. "Don't go worrying. I'm not the woman he'd touch like that."

Later, pacing the bedroom, she waited for her errant husband to make an appearance. The sun had long since sunk into darkness and a full moon lit the room with milky light. No need for the lamp. Trying to sleep was useless. They had things to talk about. Things to settle between them. Another pain took hold and it lasted longer, squeezing into her chest. She craved a dose of laudanum, but it wouldn't leave her head clear enough to converse sensibly.

Clomping boots shuffled unsteadily from the end of the hallway. The heavy footfalls grew louder and paused outside her door. A knock, then a louder rap. Her courage faltered. She licked her lips. Her derringer was nearby . . . but she wouldn't need it. Biting her lip, she wrapped her dressing gown tighter around her body, making sure the ruffled collar covered her neck. Then she yanked open the door.

Cort stood just outside, his arms crossed. His reddened eyes raked her from her bare toes to her buttoned neckline of ruffles. A man who was twenty years younger than she. A man who should have a young wife in that big bed.

"Just wonderin' where you want me to sleep," he said. "I can go to the bunkhouse if you prefer."

She smelled the whiskey on him. "Are you drunk?"

"I'm mellow. I didn't drink that much. Zeke saw to that. He can be ornery."

She decided it was best not to unsettle his feathers more than they already were. "This is where you sleep for the time being. Come in."

He snorted, then walked into the room. He'd changed into work clothes. His gun belt and holster were riding his lean hips. He kicked the door closed behind him and stalked toward her, backing her toward the moonlit window beside the bed. "This is a mistake, Mrs. Enders. Why would you want me here?"

"Already said I need someone to run this spread. Zeke is too old."

"You shouldn't trust me."

"Wade did. He was a good judge of character. Was he wrong?"

He took one step back and stared, his eyes gleaming in the moonlight. "Maybe."

"I guess we'll find out."

"Sienna, I can run the ranch for three years from the bunkhouse. And after that."

"You have a fast gun and can be hard as nails. Liabilities. Still, I have my failings. One of them is that I won't have my cowhands, friends, and the folks I do business with talking behind my back about a *husband* living in separate quarters. Sleep on the floor if you like."

She gulped down her dread while he studied her, his eyes tracing over her matronly nightgown. Maybe she'd pushed too far. Maybe she *shouldn't* trust him.

"You want me to be your stud?" he asked calmly.

The insult stung. On instinct, she slapped him with as much force as she could muster. His stunned expression and then his hard stare made her wonder if she'd just made a big mistake. Then he grinned. "I deserved that. Touché."

"Yes. You did. Don't ever say such a thing again. There will be no husbandly rights. You can lie on the bed beside me or sleep on the floor tonight. Wade will be the only man who touched me in that way. Do you understand?"

Now it was Cort's turn to be shame-faced. He'd never been intentionally cruel to a woman. He wanted to take back that insult. His face tingled but he wished she had hit him harder. He sure as hell deserved worse. "All right. For now, I'll sleep in your bedroom. Keeping up appearances. Eventually, I'll find another bed in this big house. No sense in either of us gnawing at each other."

She seemed to concede that. Sienna stretched out on one side of the bed, a blanket pulled up to her chin. He removed his gun belt and hung it over a chair. Slowly, he unbuttoned his work shirt and tugged it out of his pants before settling on the edge of the bed and yanking off his dirty boots. Finally, he spread out on his side of the bed atop the blanket, his pants still on and his body uncomfortably tense, his back to hers. This must be what a corpse would feel like if a corpse could ponder.

Her breathing beside him grew steady. He stared at the whitewashed wall where moonlight played and wished he were anywhere but here. Stiffly, he lay awake, waiting for sleep to take him under.

Her whimper cut the air and jerked him awake. She rolled over and he felt her reach out to stroke his upper arm. "Wade." She mumbled the name and her hand fell away. The bed moved when she twisted closer beside him. He'd never believed in ghosts before now.

A pain-filled groan echoed in the room, followed by quiet. The moonlight glinted off a small bottle on the table beside the bed. Clearly, cancer was marching through her frail body. For that, he was immensely sorry and at a loss as to how to help. A bullet was useless against her enemy.

Cort fell into a fitful sleep and woke before dawn, his headache still slugging it out with the whiskey he'd drunk. As quietly as he could, he pulled on his shirt and buttoned it. As he picked up his boots, he spied the little brown bottle again, sparkling in the streak of sunlight. He pulled his boots on, then snatched up the bottle and read the word *laudanum* scrawled on the label. *Damn.*

He put the bottle back down, turned, and crept out of the

room, and made his way to the bunkhouse where there'd be eggs, beans, and coffee. Today, he planned to work his ass off and then some.

One month later, July

The azure clear sky made for a pretty sight over the blowing grassland and low hills. To the far west, Cort searched the mountains peeking above the sunlit horizon. The Blue River cut through the Circle H, forming a swath of deep embankments and muddy paths where cattle made their way to drink. Where the Platte and the Blue came together, a corral had been erected for rounding up strays.

The thought of Lincoln prison, away from this ranch, died. This place was all the freedom he needed. This last month, he and Sienna settled into a quiet, working relationship. She expected him to follow Wade's practices and behind the big desk, he felt like an interloper. Cortland Enders, a hired hand.

One thing they'd settled on were sleeping arrangements. He took to sleeping with a pillow and blanket on the floor of her room some nights, and on others he found a bed down the hall. Her pain had grown worse since the wedding. If Doc Collier didn't do something, he'd find another doctor.

The sound of hoofbeats and telltale dust lifting from beyond a hill told him someone approached at a dead run. He lifted his rifle and clutched it over his lap while his horse tossed its head, yanking at the bit. Zeke's white horse came into view. The buckskin-clad foreman, his white hair flying in the wind beneath his gray Stetson, soon drew up beside him. "Figured you'd be up here."

"This a social call, Zeke? Or just checkin' to find out if I decided to make a run for it?"

"I figure you to be smarter than that. Besides, you got this place in your blood."

The saddle squeaked when Cort shifted his weight. Damned old coot read him too well. He shoved his rifle into the boot and yanked his Stetson lower over his eyes. "Hell. You ought to know I wouldn't think of leavin' the ranch in the lurch. I owe Sienna and Wade too much."

Zeke nodded. "Got you pegged for a decent sort. Just came up to see if you need help."

"Got some new calves we need to round up and get branded. Saw a calf stuck in mud and dragged him to higher ground."

"Yep."

"Since you look like you still got somethin' on your mind, spit it out." Cort watched Zeke's jaw tighten under his scruffy beard. The man looked toward the ranch house.

"She's gettin' worse, Cort. Nita just found her layin' on the floor, writhin' in pain. Ain't the first time."

Cort looked skyward and gritted his teeth. "Jesus Christ. Have one of the hands get the doctor."

"Already did that. She wants to see you. Has somethin' she wants you to do."

"All right. I'll head back. You know what it is she wants?"

"Yep."

"You ain't tellin' me, though."

"Nope."

Chapter 3
Pretty Ribbon

Zeke's cryptic and cantankerous responses irked Cort as he galloped back to the ranch house. When he stepped into Sienna's bedroom, she was sitting up in the massive mahogany bed, looking perkier than she had this morning. Theresa fussed and mumbled while Sienna patted the bed with her bony hand. Cort went over to her and took a seat.

Theresa set a bowl of broth on the table and left them alone. He leaned forward to give it a sniff, wondering if the tetchy woman had laced it with something.

Always forthright, Sienna got to the point. "Cort, I'm askin' a favor of you."

"I'm listening. Even though I got a feelin' I'm not goin' to agree with it."

"There's a Ribbon Cotillion in Ogallala on Saturday. I'm sending you. I've decided I need another woman's help with my personals. Theresa and Nita are busy and neither of them can read to me."

Cort stared into his wife's pleading dark brown eyes. "What is a Ribbon Cotillion, pray tell?"

"It's a gathering, usually at a hotel or other respectable enough place. Women from the East show up looking for husbands among the ranchers and farmers looking for wives. Men come from miles around to stake a claim."

"I don't need a wife. I have one. Or had you forgotten that?"

She gave him a sharp look. "I might be sick but I still have my mind. Of course you're *legally* married. That doesn't mean you can't make an offer for help."

The picture of this *cotillion* started looking ugly inside his head. "How would I convince a woman looking for a husband to traipse out to a ranch with a married man? Besides, I've got work enough to do around here. Do you know today is Wednesday?"

Sienna closed her eyes as if rethinking her harebrained scheme. When she opened them again, she looked more determined. "The truth is the best way to handle this. Just tell her the terms. Cut out a good one for me. Put our best team of horses on the buckboard. Don't dawdle."

Cort couldn't believe his ears. "Dawdle?" He stood, purposefully clomped to the doorway and marched out, slamming the door behind him. The trail of his swear words echoed throughout the house as he made his way to another room for a bath. He couldn't deny the wishes of a dying wife. But he sure could resent them.

Cort bounced along over the rough road toward Ogallala, watching the storm clouds billowing on the horizon. Sometimes a storm like that could come on quick and this old road would bog down the wagon. He hoped. No sense in being in a hurry to make more of a fool of himself. On top of everything, he'd forgotten to bring along his whiskey to ease himself into this fancy dance. If he even remembered how to dance.

But he'd made a promise and dammit, he'd keep it. At twenty-seven, he should be rounding up a wife and having kids. That's what bothered him. He slapped the reins, figuring he could get into town in time to change into some clean pants and a shirt that wasn't sweat stained. Get this thing over with. Now that he ran his own spread, he had pride. The piece missing was what a real wife could give him.

Acrid smoke from the chimneys of Ogallala told him he was just about there. *A woman.* There was a time when he didn't mind flirting with a woman. Now he had no right to be with another woman, even as his manly needs smoldered.

"Lark Marie Garrin."

Hearing her name announced by the buxom, matronly woman in a black dress buttoned to her neck startled Lark back to the present. Lark wore a bonnet to shadow her disfigurement. Still, how would any man look at her? She remembered her mother telling her that her eyes and hair would catch a man's glance. She hoped they would compensate for the scar in attracting a husband. And maybe she was far enough away from the Mississippi to be safe.

"Are you Lark?"

She looked up and saw angry eyes glaring at her. Sweat trickled along Lark's neck. The heat was relentless and her dress hung over her thin frame like a damp sheet. "Yes, ma'am. I'm sorry, I didn't hear you."

"If you got a hearin' problem, you aren't goin' to find a husband who'll want you," the woman warned.

That struck Lark as presumptuous. She glanced toward the boardwalk and noticed a tall cowboy in a sweaty shirt and worn Levi's, listening to the discourse with his arms crossed. His shadowed face beneath his broad-brimmed hat hid his reaction. She wondered how long he'd been standing there. She bit her tongue before replying with like brashness, deciding to set that cowboy's presence aside. "No, ma'am. I was daydreaming. I'll not do that again." That was a lie. Dreams were all she had.

"See that you don't. Now, girls. I'm Mrs. Canaday and I'm here to see you all properly matched with husbands."

Ten women stood circled in front of the hotel where they'd been brought. Six of them had come in on the noon stage. Lark and three others had arrived by train. Mrs. Canaday clapped her hands for their attention.

"Some of you got some age on you. Some look a little young. Others have a mite too much meat. Some need to find a clean dress to wear before the cotillion, which starts promptly at six."

The pompous woman looked each of them over as though inspecting horses for sale. When the woman's eyes settled on Lark again, tremors coursed through her. Pointing her thick finger toward Lark, Mrs. Canaday continued, "Now *there* is an example of someone needin' a bath and new dress. And, Lark? Rid yourself of that unattractive hat and fix your hair. Can't hardly see your face to know if you're ugly or not."

Lark glanced away from her, toward the cowboy. He'd slowly uncrossed his arms and looked about to take a step forward. He wore a gun and holster low on his hips. She wondered more about him even as embarrassment flamed through every inch of her body. Her fingers flexed. She'd never felt so shamed, except for the time on the riverboat when her father had gambled her off. The scar on her jaw was the mark of the Devil. The moment of its making was the only time she'd ever wanted to kill someone, until now. Instead, she smiled. "I'll see that I'm fit for a husband's attentions, ma'am."

Lark glimpsed again at the tall cowboy. Did she detect a frown beneath that scruffy beard?

Mrs. Canaday spoke again. "The hotel is providing a meal and a room for each of you. By tomorrow, some of you will be married. I will be at the event when your ribbon is chosen. Please be certain to bathe."

As Mrs. Canaday stepped away to pick up a satchel on the boardwalk, the other women giggled and chattered amongst themselves. Lark stood alone, mortified. Finally, she removed the straw hat, hoping for a bit of a breeze to dry her damp strands. Mrs. Canaday turned back to the circle of women, satchel in hand, and Lark turned her face aside.

Mrs. Canaday took out a handful of long satin ribbons and proceeded to hand one to each of them. Lark's ribbon was green. "Each of you will wear your ribbon at the cotillion, in your hair or on your dress. The different colors will identify the man's choice."

The women clutched their ribbons and whatever small bags they'd arrived with, and marched into the hotel. Lark was last. A scowl dented Mrs. Canaday's fat jowls as Lark came close to her. "You have a conspicuous scar on your jaw. When you are left without a prospect, you do understand that you will be required to pay your own way back to Omaha?"

"Yes. And if that happens, I'll see to my fare."

Lark watched Mrs. Canaday limp up onto the boardwalk under her heavy weight and make her way into the hotel. When the miserable woman was out of sight, Lark lifted her carpetbag. She searched the busy street where men in buckskins and carrying rifles strolled by. Women in ginghams and bonnets prattled on the other side of the street, most likely about the spectacle they'd just witnessed. Gamblers stood in the shadows of the saloon overhang, casting furtive glances in her direction. Levi-clad cowboys trotted past on horseback, squinting in her direction. One of those men might become her husband, but only if she were lucky. Any would be preferable to the horrid miscreant who had left his mark of ownership on her face. No man would own her. Ever.

Just as she turned to step up onto the boardwalk, the rugged-looking cowboy with the beard walked toward her, tipping his hat and shoving it back on his head. His blue-gray eyes held hers. His full, taut mouth looked disapproving until a boyish grin chased away the hardness and then vanished. "I can take your bag, ma'am."

When he reached for it, she gripped it tightly. His voice was kind. Still, she couldn't trust anyone. "Thank you. But I can see to my things." She found him surprisingly handsome beneath his weathered exterior, despite the dust and sweat stains.

"Suit yourself."

With a swoop of his arm he ushered her a path in front of him. When she didn't move, he shrugged and continued his determined direction toward the saloon, the thud of his hard boot heels melding with the jangle of harness and creaking wagons.

She focused her attention on his broad back. Her eyes wandered down to the gun belt and holster. Heat raced along her cheeks. She wondered how long he'd been listening and if he had overheard all the insults hurled at her. Humiliated, she continued to watch him. After a moment, he turned and caught her gawking. He winked and continued on his way. Her heart pounded. He didn't look like he had come to hunt for a wife. She guessed he'd find what he was looking for in the saloon. What would he want with a scarred wench looking for a husband?

After a swig of whiskey, Cort reluctantly made his way up the back stairs of Gast's Ogallala House down the street where he soaked away the grit of the road and enjoyed puffing a cigar. After pulling on his best cotton pants and tucking in his chambray shirt, he gave some thought to that lady with the green ribbon clutched in her hand. He'd considered kicking the old crow in her considerable backside for insulting that pretty woman, but thought better of it. Sienna wouldn't tolerate him getting tossed in jail again, and all over a woman once more.

His wife. Still, he was a man and he had needs. Top of the list was feeling a woman's touch. The Melody Queen Saloon beckoned. So many willing damsels there to assuage his desires until his marital vows tugged him backward a step.

Today he held the green ribbon woman in his mind a mite too long. *Lark. A pretty gal and pretty name.* If he didn't stop dragging his boots, he'd miss the shindig. It niggled at his conscience, thinking about innocent Lark being carted off with some widowed farmer where she would work herself into old age before her time.

Treating any of those women like horseflesh on the auction block didn't sit well. A bitter thought hit him. He was part of the distasteful event. At the same time, his heart tripped at the thought of the prettiest eyes he'd ever seen. The scar on her jaw nagged at him. Who would have done something like that? Sure as hell wasn't Indians. They'd have used her up and killed her. Prison or not, he'd shoot whatever bastard had marred her if he had the chance. The green ribbon. Maybe he could convince her to come home with him.

Downstairs, at first, he nearly turned around and left the music filled room. Fiddles and a piano pounded out cords of a tune he recognized: "A Starry Night for a Ramble." Turning tail appealed, but his boots felt stuck in mud. A slick-looking dandy had already requested his hat and gun belt, leaving him vulnerable. A shuddering urge to snatch up his belongings and march to the saloon was tempered by the sight of the ladies swirling in the arms of other men in buckskins and dark suits, and farmers in dingy, ragged overalls. He wondered where the green ribbon girl had gotten to.

The scents of flowers and soap wafted around him while neatly dressed women in the arms of every kind of jack, coot, con, and illiterate from who knew where spun in their arms. A few he easily recognized as men on the run from the law. Their eyes kept flicking to the door. Oblivious, the women smiled while their feet were trampled under clomping boots.

There were seasoned widows and some too young and bright to be mixed up in this. Desperation made people do crazy things. That, he understood better than most. Still, he knew some of these women would wind up dying too young. That thought had him squinting in search of the green ribbon.

The gamblers in their black coats would use the women in a different way. They'd end up dead or someplace in Mexico where they'd want to be dead. Deep inside, he knew some of these women were running to something or away from something. A dangerous gamble. What held them in this room were hopes and promises and a single satin ribbon.

The girl with a red ribbon wore hers around her full waist while the one with a blue ribbon had laced it through her long black hair. The yellow ribbon was looped into a bow around a curvy neck, fit for Christmas. Where was the green ribbon? His eyes searched beyond the orange and brown, then settled on a curvaceous blue-eyed wench wearing a pink ribbon in her hair. Still, he sought out the green ribbon.

When his gaze came to rest on the crystal punch bowl near one side of the room, the fiddler and piano player broke into a rousing rendition of "Bright Southern Star." Thumping boots set the bowl of liquid quivering. Ignoring the silly giggles and whirling dancers, he moved closer to the bowl, where he heard tinkling, musical laughter. Turning toward an alcove, he spotted the green ribbon. The girl's light brown hair had been caught into a neat, coiled braid with winsome strands lacing her creamy, delicate skin. He imagined his tongue sliding along her neck. The thought sent his need into a thundering gallop.

She wore a lacy white blouse with tiny buttons, revealing nothing of her skin except anticipation of softness. Her rounded breasts filled out the cotton, while beneath her blue skirt, her toes tapped to the music. A paunchy, dark-suited man talked to her while she searched the dance floor, oblivious to the man's flirtations. Cort caught sight of the distressed frown creasing her rosy lips. Something inside twisted at the thought of that man touching her. His legs carried him toward her as if on instinct. When he finally got close enough to see her pleading eyes, the man tugged her hand with insistence.

Cort stepped up. "I see you've saved this dance for me, Anna."

She looked up in surprise, her eyes locked with his. From behind her unwelcome suitor's shoulder, he winked at her. She nodded almost imperceptibly. "Why, yes. I thought you'd gotten lost. I was just about to tell Mister Jeffery Landon here that I'd already been promised for this dance and the next."

Jeffery cleared his throat, released her hand, and glowered in Cort's direction before stalking toward the pink ribbon girl. Cort held out his hand. When Lark touched his rough skin, a mountain of regret surged through him like a landslide. He'd never wanted a woman more than he wanted this confection. Then he reminded himself he was still Cortland Enders. A man who'd been in a robbery, imprisoned, and killed his share. And now married.

Her soft voice cut through his meandering. "I thank you, Mister . . . ?"

He swept her into a slow dance to "Beautiful Caroline," telling himself to run before restraint was no longer possible. "Cort. My name is Cort Enders."

Her mouth curved into a sunlit smile that could make a man melt into a soppy puddle. "I'm not Anna."

"I know. I wanted to detach you from Mister Jeffery Landon's clutches. Selfish of me, though."

She tilted her head back and her short, musical burst of laughter forced his crusty soul to beg for every song left on earth. "Are you going to tell me your real name?" he asked.

"Lark. Lark Marie Garrin. But I guess you already knew my name. You were listening outside the hotel earlier. Quite civil of you to pretend you hadn't heard."

"A meadow lark, eh? Very pretty name, Lark. Sounds like

you're a bit of an Irish lass with a family name like Garrin. Yes, I overheard. Don't think my pretending has much to do with bein' civil." His eyes took in the nasty scar. He imagined the pain she'd endured and hated whoever had done that. While it meant squat in terms of her loveliness, he wondered how and why she had gotten the mark.

Her smile disappeared. "My pa was from Ireland." The sudden darkness that hovered between them bothered him, and he was sorry he'd pressed her for information. It obviously upset her.

Cort held her against him and his steps became more practiced with the memories of those times long ago when he and his parents, sister, and brother shared a warm farmhouse. They'd danced like this of an evening sometimes. He'd been thirteen when his pa marched off to war. At sixteen, very little music was left. Only sorrow, starvation, and graves to be dug. He had no idea where his older brother or sister had disappeared to.

She studied him while he led her through the strains of the fiddle and piano. Her gold-flecked eyes captured him from his head to his heart. He knew he couldn't allow his feelings for her to go further. If nothing else, he kept his word. His *agreement* with Sienna. As though Lark could read his thoughts, her smile vanished. He pulled her closer against his chest to feel her warmth. The softness of her breasts and the thumping of her heart belonged to him for the moment.

"You were on the boardwalk when Mrs. Canaday rebuked me. I'm embarrassed by that. I hope you'll not hold what she said against me."

He missed a step at that sudden question. "I'd never hold something like that against you. I'm just sorry you were put through something like that. If I thought I'd get away with it, I'd have kicked that *bitch* in her ass as she went into the hotel. I sure felt like it." A moment later, he groaned at his own foolishness. "Sorry. I'm used to bein' around cowhands. Not pretty ladies."

"Do you have a ranch or a farm? I thought you might be a gunfighter when I saw you."

"Ah. The gun. That is as necessary in these parts as air to breathe. In answer to your question, I ranch. I'm on the Circle H."

"So you're looking for someone to live with you on your ranch."

She was partly right. His plan was not to scare her off right out of the gate. He wanted her to come with him tomorrow. He wasn't exactly lying. "I'd like that. Yes. Do you think you could have your things ready to leave here by tomorrow morning? Can't be away from the ranch for too long."

"Even with my scar? You still want me?"

That narrow slice along her jaw made no difference to him. Some of it was still red, which told him it had happened recently and hadn't fully healed. It might even be the reason she was here. To mar such perfection was sickening. Who had dared to hurt her? If Cort ever found out, the sonofabitch would pay for it. "I don't see any scar. I see a sweet, lovely gal in need of a life and home. I'm offering that."

"If you're sure, then I accept." Her fingers clenched his with a kind of desperation, as though she feared he'd change his mind. Those limpid gold eyes held his. Married or not, he planned to dive into them and uncover her secrets.

"I'll let Mrs. Canaday know before I leave. Early tomorrow morning I'll be by with my buckboard. We best get an early start. Have your things ready to go, Lark. It gets a mite chilly at night and we'll be spending one night in camp, so bring something warm along."

"Very well, Mister Enders. We'll have a fine time on that

ranch. I can cook and clean. Just give me time to get used to things, is all I ask."

"No thanks necessary. It'll be a long trip out to the ranch. And it's Cort, not Mister Enders. I'll be by for you. But before I let you go, I'd like another dance, pretty lady." Cort reached for the green ribbon that hung loose from her hair, tugging it free. "I think this is mine. Part of the deal." He grinned at her smile. She made him feel happiness and he soaked it up like rain in a dry desert.

The piano and violin drifted through "Far from Home" as they moved together, dismissing everyone else. The tension in her relaxed and her body fitted with his as they danced, like they belonged together. He could imagine being back in Virginia, dancing like this on a warm summer night. He wished he could offer her more than a fine roof over her head and plenty of food. Finding himself clutching her hand tighter between his fingers, he escorted her to a bench and then hunkered in front of her as she sat down. "Till tomorrow, Lark. I promise you'll find safety where I'm takin' you. You'll not want for anything."

With the ribbon tucked into his pants pocket, he stood and made his way toward dowdy Mrs. Canaday, her arms folded across the black dress and a smirk of pure meanness on her face. Tomorrow he'd leave with the green ribbon. *His green ribbon.*

Chapter 4
Impossible Choice

Thankfully, Mrs. Canaday was nowhere to be seen this early in the morning. The other women had long since either gotten promises or retired to their rooms to await the train leaving town. That set Lark to wondering where she and Cort would wed. Perhaps he would wake the preacher this morning. He'd been adamant about leaving early.

Since she only had one large carpetbag and very few clothes, packing hadn't taken long. While she waited in the lobby, a kindly desk clerk offered her a tin cup of hot coffee and a biscuit. She ate and drank, staring at the dusty floor where dancers had tapped to the music. The dirt clods and mud caught her attention. Mud, horses, and long days of baking and planting crops might be where she was headed, but she'd have the protection of the man who'd chosen her. Thinking about his long, confident stride and the way his gun belt hugged his hips, she suspected he knew how to handle the business end of a revolver.

Running from Will Cardin had ripped apart her life. Her youth had vanished, forgotten under the crush of moving from place to place. Surely, he'd never find her here. At the same time, guilt flushed through her at having dragged Cort Enders into her problem.

"I see you're ready, Miss Garrin."

She jolted at the deep timbre of Cort's voice. Buried in her musings, she hadn't heard him come into the lobby. Their eyes met and held. He took the coffee cup from her hands and moved to the desk, handing off the cup with a nod. Then he turned, snatched up her bag, and moved to the door, where he stood waiting for her to follow.

"This all you got?" he asked as she walked toward him.

She bit her lip. "Yes. I don't have much."

"Hope you've got more usable dresses than the one you've got on. Satins and silks don't hold up well out here. Whatever you need, I'll see you get it the next time I send to town for goods."

"Thank you."

Two large bay horses were hitched to the wagon that stood beside the hotel, their tails swishing, their hind legs slack. Before she knew what was happening, Cort caught her waist with his large hands and lifted her to the wagon seat. She sat waiting as he unclipped the leads on the team and then stepped up, seating himself beside her. He reached behind him, grasped a rifle, and set it beside him, reminding her that there were all sorts of dangers out here. With a slap of the reins and a sudden jolt, the wagon rolled past the buildings toward the rising sun, the wheels thudding into ruts. The church lay ahead. Surely, they would stop.

She gripped the edge of the seat until her fingers ached. The wagon neither slowed nor changed direction. The whitewashed church and steeple grew further from them. Twisting in her seat, she watched the last of the town's rooftops sink beneath the low hillsides.

"Do you need a blanket around your shoulders, Lark? That little jacket is probably a mite light for the early morning."

She clutched her quilted waistcoat tightly around her to ward off the chill of the wind before looking him in the eyes. Their blue-gray hue seemed to change with each shadow. "I'm fine."

Last night she'd trusted him. Today, she wondered if she'd

fallen for a trick. Unease multiplied with each tick of the clock inside her head.

"All right. Still. I'll make sure you get proper clothes for life on the ranch. Just drag that blanket over you if you get colder. You look pale."

"Cort, I hope you won't mind my asking a personal question."

"Depends on what it is. You look scared to death. I won't hurt you." She saw his gaze wander to the scar along her jaw.

"Where will we be married? Is there another church or preacher ahead?"

Cort swallowed. For a moment, she saw anxiety in his eyes that matched her own. He slapped the reins and urged the horses into a faster gait. "I won't be marryin' you, Lark."

"Stop this wagon. Immediately!" she snapped, lifting one foot as though she were about to hop over the side. *Darn fool woman.* He yanked back on the reins, and the horses shook their heads with enough energy to jangle the harness. Lark held the edge of the seat, found her footing, and swung herself to the ground with a thump. Losing her balance, she stumbled backward and fell to the dirt in a heap.

Cort pushed the brake handle, tied off the reins, and hurled himself over the side of the wagon. He came around and offered her a hand up. Her eyes flashed with temper. Her anger had turned her pale face rosy red. "Don't touch me. Take me back to town, you . . . you . . . reprobate. You horse's behind. You . . . do you think I'm a prostitute?"

"Hold on." He reached for her arm, but she slapped his hands away. She stood, brushed off her skirt, and marched to the rear of the wagon to retrieve her satchel. He followed. Somehow, he had to stop her. If she were a man, he might knock some sense into her with a fist. But this was a woman. A gentle, well-bred woman. He couldn't let her go off like this.

"Will you just give me a few words in edgewise?" he shouted. Her eyes glistened with gold and green, her chest heaved in and out, and he could hardly keep from grabbing hold of her to get her attention. "I'm already married, Lark."

She gaped at him, then closed her eyes. When she opened them again, they were filled with sorrow. "You should have said that. Why do you need a woman?"

"It's a long story. I'm not about to explain it all. My wife. The ranch." His tongue was in knots. "Her name is Sienna. She's dying of cancer. We need someone to look after her. The cook and housekeeper are too busy with ranch needs. The pay includes a fine room and good food. You'd be safe and comfortable. No one would dare cross the line, or they'd answer to me."

She just stared, unblinking. Had she heard what he'd said? "I think you're running from something or someone. I know that look. Maybe you could consider this offer as refuge from whatever you're afraid of. I'm thinkin' this might be an answer for you. I'll never let anybody hurt you."

She clutched her bag between two shaking hands. If he had to guess, she was at least giving thought to the proposition. At least he hoped so. Because he didn't want to lose sight of her. She dropped the bag to the ground and turned to look back at the town in the distance. When she looked at him again, he lifted her bag and held it, waiting for her reply.

"If you still want to go back, I'll turn the team around," he offered, though he hoped she wouldn't take it. And he wasn't at all sure he'd be able to do that, even at the risk of becoming a liar as well as a reprobate.

"You won't touch me."

God, she looked so forlorn. So disappointed. And so beautiful. Damn. He wanted to do more than touch her. He had no right to think like that. He had no rights at all. Cortland Neil Enders was as much a prisoner as she would be. Except that she'd be safe from whatever had sent her running here. "No. I won't touch you."

Then she asked a question he hadn't expected. It flummoxed him. "Do you love your wife?"

He sucked in a long breath and looked skyward, hoping for some good answer in the cloud-studded blue. Something that would sound kindly. Something that wouldn't hurt Sienna. The only thing that came to mind was the truth. "No. That's all you need to know."

"You danced with me, Cort. You squeezed my hand, held me against you. You made me like you."

"I hope you still like me, because I like you. Even if I can't marry you. I meant no harm. I just wanted to convince you to come to the ranch. I still want that. More than you can know."

"You are a horse's rear end.

He winced. "Yes, I'm an ass, and a lot worse. Still, don't go callin' me names in front of my cowhands. I don't want to have cross words with you."

"Such as?"

Her unexpected smile wrapped him in pure sunlight. "I'll think of something."

The smile faded. "So long as this is a business arrangement, I'll go along with you. How long before we arrive?"

"Tomorrow late afternoon, if we stop jawing."

"Tonight . . . you will not sleep near me."

"Fine with me. I'll be nearby. We got wolves and coyotes in these parts." He might go completely crazy with her near. If he wasn't already. *Damn you, Sienna. You found a way to torture me.*

That was what it felt like on the way to camp. Neither of them saying much of anything. Both seated beside each other and aware of every bump of their knees and nudge of an arm while the wagon jolted and slammed over ruts.

That night, as he lay in his bedroll beside a fire, he reached into his pocket, uncoiled the ribbon, and held it to his nose. The scent of lilacs clung to it. He gazed into the darkness and saw a sliver of dim lantern light where the most beautiful and cantankerous woman he'd ever encountered lay wrapped in the blankets he'd handed her. They had just crossed onto Harris land. Tomorrow night he'd be on the floor beside his wife, wanting to touch someone far out of his reach.

The next day the wagon rattled along, silence hanging between them. The only sounds were of bellowing cattle dotting the hillsides, jangling harness, and the never-ending plodding of horses' feet. After they'd eaten some jerky and gulped down coffee, Lark climbed aboard the wagon and smacked away his hand as he attempted to help her up. He'd likely be mad himself if he didn't agree with her that he was a mule's hind end.

This was Sienna's fault. Why did she send him for a woman? There was hurt in Lark's eyes and he'd put it there. The woman beside him hadn't deserved being lied to. Even though it wasn't exactly a lie. Just a misinterpretation.

"Is that the ranch house ahead?"

He followed her gaze toward the roof line and the smoke curling from the stone chimney at one end of the big house. "Yep. Welcome to the Circle H, ma'am."

"I'll talk with the owner before deciding to stay on. If I decide to go back, I want someone else to take me back to Ogallala."

She didn't bother to look in his direction but kept her stubborn chin pointed straight ahead. Her eyes were on the house, barn, corrals, and bunkhouses that made up the homestead. "Fine by me, Lark. I don't remember being unkind or indecent toward you."

"You deceived me into thinking you had marriage in mind."

That clenched jaw and pale skin told him all he needed to

know about her stubborn nature. She tucked the blanket around her shoulders. "Maybe a little," he said. "But let me ask you this. You didn't appear to have any offer except from that fancy gambler. He wouldn't have had marriage in mind, either. I saved you from a far worse fate than acting as a companion for a sickly woman. Would you rather I left you to him?"

"I won't thank you."

"All right. Have it your way. You are one stubborn lady." Cort gritted his teeth as he brought the team up beside the long front porch, where a welcoming committee waited. Zeke ambled over from one side and ordered two other ranch hands, Mason and Damon, to take care of the horses and wagon. A third hand, Billy, reached up for Lark and swung her to the ground. Nita, the housekeeper, nearly skipped down the stone stairs to take Lark's hands in welcome. Cort walked to the other side and lifted Lark's carpetbag, squarely ignored amid the cheer. Sienna wasn't there, and he figured his wife was too ill to leave the house.

That thought had scarcely crossed his mind when the massive front door opened, catching everyone's attention. To his surprise, Sienna stood in the doorway, fully dressed and boot-shod.

"Welcome, Miss . . . ?" Sienna called.

Cort stepped forward to stand beside his wife, the carpetbag gripped in his hands. Lark's perusal of Sienna and him together nearly stole his breath. When a smile broke Lark's stern expression, he figured Lark had taken a liking to his wife.

"I'm Lark. Lark Garrin." Lark came up to Sienna, and the two women reached for each other and embraced, then stepped back.

"I'm Sienna Harris Enders. I hope Cort gave you the rundown on the ranch and your responsibilities."

"For the most part, yes."

Wheels creaked and harnesses jingled as two of the ranch hands drove the wagon toward the barn. Billy was still gawking at Lark. Cort saw in her face that the young cowboy's scrutiny made her uncomfortable. He glanced at Billy, his jaw hard. "Billy. You got work to do. Get to it."

Billy's blue eyes settled on Lark's. "Sure, boss. Ma'am. Just call out for Billy if you need anything at all." The young man tipped his hat. His well-worn boots dug into the gravel and his spurs jangled as Billy made his way in the direction of the corral.

Sienna smiled, though Cort saw the pain behind it. "Come with me, Lark. We'll get to know one another. I'll fill you in and let you get settled. You have a beautiful name. I want to hear all about how you came here. Don't think for a minute that you'll be sleeping out in a bunkhouse. We've got a lovely room for you."

Cort handed Lark's satchel to Nita, who followed behind them. Feeling dismissed and ignored, he turned abruptly toward the barn, his stride long and purposeful as it carried him away from the ranch house and the women.

Chapter 5
The Night Brings

Dinner with fine china dishes. Nita and Theresa fluttered around the table while the Indian boy, Adoeete, brought in a pitcher of water. Cort noticed Tangle's apologetic grin and understood the cowhand's discomfiture at being served by the boy. Wade had found the boy a couple of years ago, abandoned by a roving band of Pawnee, apparently because his leg had been mangled and he couldn't keep up. From then on, everyone had adopted him. But the chatter around the table centered on Lark. She was treated like a guest, and Cort watched with pleasure as she smiled more and asked questions about ranch life.

He'd managed to find time to wash up and put on some clean clothes before being summoned to the dinner table. When Sienna sent an order, everyone followed it. Hell, he was her prisoner and he had to follow her orders. His new role as an equal partner hadn't sunk in.

The woman he'd married sat on one side of the table, while Lark took a place to his left. Heat snaked through every inch of his skin, beckoning his hand to touch hers. This might be July, but he was sure the weather wasn't the issue. He reached for the button at his throat, but Sienna gave him a warning look before she returned her attention to Zeke and Lark. For all of Sienna's down-to-earth character, she still carried the schoolteacher she'd once been around with her.

Doctor Collier directed his attention to Cort. "Glad you

made it back when you did. Mace and Damon were shot at. Mace is damned lucky it was just a graze."

"So I heard. I'm hiring on more hands as soon as I can find decent ones. Left ads all over town."

Doc Collier nodded. "Don't think the Pawnee are a problem, but there are some Sioux and Cheyenne that don't agree with the treaty and they can be a blasted nuisance."

"Thanks, I'll keep it in mind. Maybe we should change the subject. Don't want Miss Garrin to be scared away."

The man's face puffed out when he realized his mistake. "Sorry."

Lark glanced their way. "Please, gentlemen. Miss Garrin is too formal. Lark will do fine. As to scaring me. I don't scare easy. I can handle a gun if need be."

"That's wonderful, Lark. Can you also ride a horse?" Sienna asked.

"I used to ride on my grandfather's farm in Ohio. I think I can manage."

Cort was taken aback by his wife's suggestion. "Sienna, she won't have a need for a horse or a gun. That's not why she's here."

Sienna's eyes narrowed and then she turned her attention to Zeke, who'd kept silent through the discussion. "See that you cut out a good mount for Lark. She will have to learn to ride if she's to survive on a ranch."

Zeke cleared his throat, his cheeks flaming red. He gulped some water. "If that's what you want."

Flustered at being challenged, Cort decided to circle around his wife. "I'll find her a decent horse myself. She still isn't goin' to leave the protection of this compound, not without an escort." He thought he'd found somewhat of a compromise.

Sienna nodded before smiling. The drugs made her eyes too bright and her face too drawn. She hid the cancer eating her alive pretty well. She'd barely been able to walk down the stairs, and he wound up carrying her. The doctor had most likely brought her more laudanum, but soon that wouldn't be enough to ward off the pain. And now, Sienna's decision to allow Lark to ride off was just plain reckless.

The rest of the meal was pleasant and quiet. Lark seemed focused on the food and light conversation about the ranch and the cattle. Cort noted her interest in learning all she could. Whenever Wade's name came up, Sienna spoke of her first husband with pride and deep, abiding longing. Zeke recounted stories of rough times when they'd first settled here. Wade was a big part of this land and an even bigger part of the ranch, even in death. Cort's job was to fill in, keeping alive the ranch that Wade had begun. As Sienna's inevitable death drew closer, more of the daily ranch responsibility and decisions fell upon his shoulders.

Glancing at the lovely young woman beside him, he wanted more than anything to tuck her hand between both of his and tell her he'd keep her safe. He wished he could tell her that he was a captive and, once he was free, he'd want to touch her in ways that would make her blush. More than anything, he wanted to know what she was hiding behind those green-gold eyes. A man with his own checkered past recognized the look of secrecy and fear when someone was running. *Did she run from a husband?*

Lark sat on the swing, wrapped in a wool blanket while a glimmer of the full moon passed between the clouds drifting over the rolling dark hills. She wondered if she should stay here at the Circle H, or go. She liked Sienna. The woman made no demands, but clearly, she was dying. Lark saw the pain behind her muted smile, even as she chattered at dinner. Her unhealthy paleness and thin frame revealed the toll the cancer was taking. When she'd shaken Sienna's hand in greeting, the bones beneath the thin skin felt like she'd pressed a bird's wing.

Sienna was quite a bit older than Cort, unless Lark missed her guess. Gray-streaked black hair and lines around her eyes told a little of the years of sacrifice out here on the plains of Nebraska. Sienna must have seen Indians, marauders, drifters, and gunfighters most of her life.

When Sienna had explained the medicines and the pain that came and went without warning, Lark could barely keep from shouting that it wasn't fair. Sienna had loved her buried husband, Wade Harris. That was clear enough. Cort Enders was not Lark's business. Still, she didn't understand why Sienna had married again. Cort was clearly much younger. They lived in the same house, but there was no warmth between them. When Lark first arrived, she hadn't seen them touch each other in welcome. Instead, there was respect and attentiveness. *Friends.* She supposed married folks could be nothing more than friends. And why did she care?

She tucked the blanket around her more snugly and listened to the occasional bellow of cattle and yipping coyotes in the distance. The sound of crickets could easily lull her to sleep. A dim light glowed from a small window in one of the four long bunkhouses. The smell of wood smoke reminded her of the farmhouse where she'd last felt needed. Here, she could hide. Even Will Cardin wouldn't find her . . . and if he did, Cort and the hands would protect her. No. She had no right to put them all at risk.

The squeak of the door opening and the thump of boots along the porch interrupted the quiet night sounds. When she knew it could only be one person, something inside her screamed to run indoors and up the stairs to her room. She was drawn to Cort in a way that had no reason. Instead, she sat with the blanket tangled around her legs while her every nerve quaked. He drew close enough to touch, and Lark looked up into his silvery eyes lit by the moon. When she started to stand, he gripped her shoulder and stayed her.

"Sit." His voice was hoarse.

"Shouldn't you be asleep, Mister Enders? I'm sure you have to be up early."

"I could say the same to you, Lark. Do you think you could start referring to me as Cort?"

"I'll try. It feels wrong since you're my boss."

"I'm not your boss."

He stepped back and leaned against the rail and porch post, one ankle crossing the other. He wore a coat, the collar pulled up around his neck against the cool evening air. She wondered what the reasons were behind his stern detachment around most folks. From what she'd seen since meeting him yesterday, he rarely smiled.

Silence stretched between them while he looked out over the shadowy plains, lit by the moon, brushed by the wind, and serenaded by the on and off music of insects. "Couldn't sleep. Got too much on my mind. Now's my turn to ask you the same. Why aren't you abed?"

A giggle threatened from somewhere inside. An unreasonable reaction to this moment. She tried to hold back a shaky chill that coursed through her skin. "I couldn't sleep, either. Maybe too much to think about."

"You and Sienna seem to be getting along. Hope you'll decide to stay. I never meant to lie. It just seemed to happen."

"I realize that, Cort. Sienna is kind. For the first time in a while, I'm feeling I can be useful. I'm so sorry for her illness and wish I could do more. For you both."

He snorted. "Don't feel sorry for me. I don't deserve your pity. Or anyone's. Sienna, though, is in pain. Doc Collier is doing all he can. It isn't enough."

Sienna's own words haunted Lark. *"Death isn't so bad once*

you lose the man you love. This pain won't be inside me much longer." Lark's eyes welled with tears.

When she sniffled, Cort hunkered in front of her, studying her face, even as the shadows crossed them both. "Now you know why I need you here. She needs someone to help her get through this. I'm not much good at it. Besides the fact I hate seein' her in so much pain, I'm tryin' to keep this place goin' while we're shorthanded."

"The Ribbon Cotillion was your idea?"

"Nope. I never knew anything about it until my wife gave me the order to attend. Thought it was a bad idea until I met you."

He reached up with his rough hand, cupped her scarred jaw, and pressed the pad of his thumb over the wetness. "Don't cry. If you don't want to stay, I'll see you get where you want to go."

"I'd like to stay, Cort." Before he could stand, she wrapped her fingers over his stroking thumb. "Why are you here? Sienna. Wade. You. I don't think I understand."

"You might want to run from me if I told you. The marriage isn't exactly what you'd call a love match. That's all I want to say. Except that I'm glad you'll stay."

"Thanks for that much. I didn't mean to pry. But I can understand how this land holds you. It holds me. The beauty of it. But you could go anywhere. You're so free."

"I'm not free, Lark." He stood and towered over her. His searching eyes sent shivers through her at what little he'd revealed of himself. "I felt the same as you when I first got here. There were times when Wade Harris could chill you to the bone with one formidable glance from atop his Appaloosa. And there were times when he could laugh heartily over a tin cup by the campfire and rib a man into a grin and a shrug. Me, I have no choice but to stay here for a lot of reasons. I'd like you to stay, too."

He held out his hand to help her stand and tucked the blanket around her shoulders. "Better get some sleep, pretty lady." His palm slipped around hers. The impropriety of his touch and words gave her pause. Still, she said nothing. She took a step away from him, but he tugged her back. Oh, God. He was going to kiss her. That would spoil everything.

"You're hiding secrets, Lark. You're running from something or someone. I can't fight your demons till I know what they are."

She yanked her hand from his. He'd gotten too close. If she told him the truth, he might do something to get himself killed. This was her fight and she hoped she hadn't brought trouble to this doorstep. When he'd deceived her, she swore she'd never trust this man or want his touch. Now, she couldn't bear to see him hurt.

She left him standing in the shadows, but wondered what his kiss would feel like. "No. The secrets are mine alone," she whispered to no one.

Much later, as she lay in bed, she heard a door close downstairs and then nothing more. Moonlight danced on the ceiling above her. Something warm heaved inside her heart. The gentle warmth of Cort's hand enfolding hers still lingered. She pressed her palm to her mouth, pretending that he was beside her.

Sienna sat on a plump sofa covered with rich green velvet. Large embroidered feather pillows provided a cheery touch to an otherwise manly ranch house. Morning light streamed in through the window glass, punctuating the massive side table with crystal lamps that produced rainbows across the stone face of the fireplace. The Aubusson rug with ornate red flowers and feather plumes only served to draw the eyes to the polished pine floors. Two heavy mahogany chairs sat on each side of a marble-topped card table.

Lark ran her hand over the striped brown silk pillow while she held a book open to page twenty and read aloud. Sienna had chosen *Far from the Madding Crowd* by Thomas Hardy, a story that dripped with sadness and romantic disappointment. The words filled the room until even Nita and Theresa stopped their chores to listen.

"My goodness, Lark, you have a musical voice that nearly brings me to tears," Sienna said.

"Sienna . . . the story brings you to tears because I think it hurts the heart."

"Maybe. Either way, you must be parched. I'm getting mighty sleepy, what with these drugs that Doc Collier keeps plying me with. I think that's enough reading for today." Sienna turned her head toward Nita. "Please bring us some tea."

"You need something to eat, too. You might get blown away with the first gust of air," Nita warned.

Sienna smiled. "Might do me good to float away. Anyway, it won't stay down. You all know I'm nearing the end."

Nita's eyes narrowed. "Hush that talk."

Lark watched the two women glower at each other. "I'll bring soda crackers anyhow," Nita said.

Lark spoke up to forestall an argument. "Tea is just fine for both of us, I think, Nita."

"I'll be right back." Nita's heavy boots thudded across the floor as she marched out of the room and down the hallway toward the kitchen. Lark couldn't help but see Sienna's face grow even whiter as she grimaced with a pain she rarely complained about.

"Can I do anything for you?" Lark asked.

Sienna shook her head. "It'll pass. It always does."

"I'm sorry for what you have to go through. There's not a person on this ranch who isn't worried about you. Nita's right. You still need to try to eat."

"That's what I like about you, Lark. You're a brave gal. You attend to me and speak up. See that I look passable and understand my needs before I do. And you stayed on even when you found out you weren't goin' to be the bride you expected. Most would have demanded to be taken to the train."

"I almost did. Changed my mind. I'd never stay mad after you and Cort gave me a place to stay until I have to move on. I'm beholden."

Nita came back into the room and set a loaded tray on the side table. "Either of you be needin' somethin' else?"

Sienna caught her eye. "No. Thank you. Except . . . I didn't see Cort this morning. He usually fills me in on the day."

"I looked out that window earlier. A lot of dust stirred up by the horses. Heard from Alonzo that they plan to round up cattle and move them closer in," Nita replied.

"If you see one of the hands, ask them to have Cort come see me before he goes out again."

Nita nodded and moved toward the doorway, her footsteps clipping along the wooden floor. Sienna turned back to Lark. "Now, where were we?"

"I was just saying that I'll have to leave at some point. I'll stay long enough to see you get better."

"Then you'd be waiting a long while, sweet girl. No sense in pussyfooting around."

Lark understood that but wasn't going to be blunt about it. "How about that tea?"

Sienna waved her off. "I don't want it. Pour yourself a cup."

Lark leaned forward, poured herself tea, and sat back to sip the brew. Sienna's dull eyes shifted in her direction, then closed as Sienna leaned her neck against the back of the seat. Silence fell for several seconds, and Lark thought she'd gone to sleep. "I'm awake," Sienna murmured, slurring her words. "Now tell me why you need to leave."

Lark slowly set the cup down. "I'm going to find a job near a large town. Maybe I'll be able to teach until such time as I find a husband."

"Ah. Husband. Did Cort tell you my husband died nine months ago?"

"Yes. I'm so sorry. I hear he was quite the legend around here. Bigger than life, I'd say."

Sienna lifted her head and pinned Lark with her deep brown eyes that looked like countersunk nails. "Wade was the only man I could ever love. I'll soon enough lie beside him on that hill."

Lark choked up at the depth of Sienna's sadness and her uncomplaining attitude. She cleared her throat. "Surely something can be done?"

"I've accepted my end. As everyone does. I'm more worried about you. And Cort. At least he had the good sense to convince you not to turn tail."

"He's your husband."

"That is something best explained at another time. Cort is paying for a wrong. Never did believe that pissant Tenner. And I think you're running from something. Maybe you and Cort need each other."

Confused, Lark tried to make sense of Cort's supposed wrongdoing. The squeak of the door at the end of the hallway barely registered, and she looked up, startled, at the jangle of spurs.

Cort stopped at the archway to the parlor and observed the two women sitting there like they'd become best of friends. Aside from Sienna's pallor, they looked like they belonged in a high society setting. He cleared his throat. "Ladies. Sienna, you should be upstairs in bed. Lark, you look rested."

Sienna nodded a greeting. "Nita tells us you're headin' out to round up cattle."

"Yep. Won't be back for a couple of days. I'm leaving enough hands to keep an eye on things here."

Cort turned his attention from his wife to Lark. Each time he saw her, something dangerous ticked inside him, a jarring desire so powerful that he feared he might make a fool of himself. Damn. He wanted to lift her into his arms and kiss her till she begged for more. The thought of that here, in front of his wife, made him want to run and keep running rather than face the day that he might concede to his unspoken wants. Trouble was, what he wanted was right here.

"Do you think you could see me upstairs? I want Lark to stay here. Maybe you can talk her into stayin' on?" Sienna said.

Cort's head jerked in Lark's direction. She hadn't told him she was leaving. That didn't set well with him. Not when he figured she might be in danger. She was hiding and he'd damned well find out why even if he had to shake it out of her.

He moved toward Sienna and gently lifted her. Her head lolled against his shoulder. Before he left the room with his burden, he turned to face Lark. "Be here when I come back downstairs or I'll track you down."

"I don't like threats."

"Hell, neither do I. But if you plan to leave, I want to know why. Maybe we can come to terms with our situation. I don't have much time. My men are waiting for me."

She stood and picked up the tea tray, then moved toward the hallway with her chin held high.

"Well?" he barked.

She stopped, her back to him. "I'll be here. Take care of your wife."

Chapter 6
Illusions

After Cort settled his wife into bed, he took the back stairs down to the kitchen three at a time. "Theresa."

When the cook tossed down the rolling pin and put her hand to her mouth, he realized she expected bad news. He had no illusions about Sienna's health. He didn't love her, but he respected and admired her grit. Sure as hell, he'd never wish this constant pain on his worst enemy, let alone her.

"She's asleep," he said. "Would you mind keeping watch on her?"

"Course I will. You going to leave?"

"Yep. Be gone two or three days with most of the men."

Theresa looked him up and down, taking in his boots and spurs before settling on the gun at his hip. "That new gal may up and leave. My guess is sooner than you expected."

"Not if I can convince her to stay on."

Theresa sighed. "I know more that goes on than you think. I see the way you look at Miss Lark."

"Christ. It isn't like that." *Shit.* He was a worse liar than he thought.

Theresa set her hands on her hips. "Miss Sienna and I go back a long time. Knew her as a girl back in Virginia. I know what's what."

Cort glared into Theresa's deep brown eyes. "All right. Straight out. Yes, I'm attracted to Lark. That doesn't mean I forgot the vows I took. Those vows don't mean I'm no longer a man, either. Can you go out and tell Zeke to go on without me and I'll catch up to them?"

She nodded. He tugged his hat lower over his eyes. The blasted woman saw too much.

"Go on," Theresa snapped. "I never did think Sienna should've married again."

Ignoring her was easy. Right now, he was damned sick and tired of a bunch of griping women. A thump caught his attention as he marched toward the parlor. Changing direction, he saw Lark in the office, standing on a stool and reaching for a book from Wade's collection. He walked in and closed the door, taking in her slender waist and light brown hair. Sunlight filled it with gold streaks where it trailed over her shoulders. She turned. When her eyes descended to his holster, he saw fear.

He slapped his hat onto a nearby chair, then grasped her by the waist and lifted her from the stool. The feel of her breasts against him as she slid along his length sent fire to his loins. The book in her hands tumbled to the floor. He felt her tremble as he set her on her feet. He didn't release his hold. Her hands flattened against his chest. Without any other thought, he buried himself in her scent while his lips pressed against her neck. Abruptly aware of his foolish, impetuous act, he stepped back, thinking, *A man could drown in those hazel eyes . . .*

"You shouldn't do that. It isn't proper," she admonished.

"I know. I'm sorry for acting on what I feel. I'll try to keep my distance, but that might be impossible."

She cleared her throat. "I hope it's all right to borrow a book."

"Book? Whatever you need. Don't need to ask." She'd shoved what he'd said aside by changing the subject. He bent over and picked up the fallen volume. "*The Adventures of Tom Sawyer.* Good choice. I've read it." He handed it to her and took her other hand in his. The weight of what had just happened between them left him wondering what to say. From the look on her face, she was wondering, too.

Thankfully, she chose to circle around it. "I thought you were heading out to do something with cattle."

Tamping down a grin was impossible. Her innocent question reminded him that she was from a far different world. "I'll catch up to the men. Got something else on my mind."

They still stood close to each other. So close that he could lower his mouth and kiss those rosebud lips. Caress them and make them his. Make *her* his.

He saw her spine stiffen. "This is quite improper, Cort. You promised you'd never touch me."

As she stepped back, he took the book from her hand and tossed it onto the desk beside them. In a strained voice, he said, "We need to talk. I agree, this is improper. The hell of it is, I don't give a damn. I want to get things out in the open."

"Very well." A polite response.

He gripped her hand tighter and led her to the divan on one side of the room. She slipped her hand from his. With a sweep of his arm, he invited her to sit, then picked up a chair and straddled the seat to face her while she regally arranged her simple gingham dress. It outlined her sweet breasts perfectly. Imagining himself undoing each button, leaving her body open to his perusal, sent beads of sweat along his temples. Indeed, he'd make her call out his name.

"Don't leave the Circle H. Please." Begging was all he had in his arsenal at the moment.

She smiled so sweetly that he had to tighten his fists to keep from taking her face between his hands and tasting those lips. "One minute you're angry. The next you're aloof. And then this . . ." She sighed. "We can't. You're a husband. Keep some decency. If you don't, I can't stay."

"Look, I don't mean to scare you. That's never been my intention. I'm doin' everything I can to keep away from you.

That's why I stay out on the range more. You already know my feelings for you are running deep and fast. If you leave, I don't know if I'd keep from goin' crazy. Sienna needs you to see this to the end. *I* need you to see this to the end."

"You're married, Cort."

"I remember that every day I wake up. Wade Harris was my friend and mentor. He died out on the range where I found him. He and Sienna took in a saddle tramp and gunslinger, taught me ranching. I owe them my loyalty. But I don't owe them my life."

She waited, as if sensing he had more to say.

"After the war, I got involved with bank robbers and wound up in prison for three years. Then there was some more trouble in Ogallala. I tangled with a powerful rancher's kid over a woman."

"A woman."

"A prostitute. The sonofabitch beat her up, so I meted out justice."

"A prostitute?" She flinched as though he'd hit her.

"I was defending her. Simple as that. Nobody got killed. But I'm no stranger to trouble. I can handle myself and protect you. I need to know what's scaring you away."

"Your mistakes don't scare me. Why do you insist I need protection?"

He chuckled. "Honey, I recognize someone in trouble from ten miles off. You're scared of more than me. I think you're scared of someone out there. And they're hunting you. Let me help."

He'd never seen anybody turn pale so fast. Her eyes closed and her lips trembled. He reached for her hands and held them. Her skin felt cold. From that moment, he was lost. He'd kill whoever had hurt her. At least he'd begun to dig out the truth.

Her eyes opened, meeting his with hollow defeat. That same

terror haunted him when he remembered at seventeen being locked behind bars for the first time. He'd had no one to call family or friend. *No one to trust.* Was she already married, and running from whoever her husband was? The thought that she belonged to someone else gnawed a hole in Cort's gut.

The question came out before he could grab it back. "Are you married, Lark?"

She drew her hands away from his. "No. I've never been married. Please don't ask me to explain. I won't drag you and Sienna into my problems."

He released the breath he held. "But someone is looking for you?"

"Yes."

"Why?"

Tears swam in her eyes. "If I tell you, you'll know too much. It shames me."

His arm went around her and he pulled her against him. Her head fit against his shoulder and her soft hair touched his neck. He could stay like this forever. "I'll give you the time you need. Sooner or later, I want to know. It's too late now to go back. I'm already involved. You won't be able to get between me and your trouble."

"Why not?"

"I think you know why. Sienna is my wife on paper."

Jolted, she lifted her gaze to meet his. "I don't understand."

He sucked in a breath, then touched her face and traced her mouth with his thumb. "When I get back, maybe you'll be able to tell me more about yourself. Trust me. Believe in me. I lost my family in the war, so afterward I tagged along with a bunch of rowdies. Learned to kill before I learned to be a man. Figure I know something about being scared. I don't want you living like that. One way or the other, I'm not going to let you go without a fight."

He stood, grabbed up his hat, and slapped it on his head. Before leaving the room, he faced her. She was staring at him, one hand to her mouth. "Think about that."

Four long days of thinking made her heart hurt. One moment she wanted to find a horse and run to anywhere. Probably she'd be tracked down for horse stealing. The next minute she'd listen to Sienna's weak voice recount how Wade had first come to Nebraska to work on the railroad. With the money he'd earned and his inheritance from a broken-down Ohio farm, he'd started a ranch and built it into the spread it was today. Gruff, surly, independent, and smart. All the things Lark saw in Cort. *Her* Cort. But he wasn't hers.

"You look far away."

Lark raised her eyes from the sewing in her lap. Sienna looked brighter today. That beautiful graying hair was pulled into a stylish bun at the back of her head. Though nothing could erase the frail look and pale skin. "I always enjoy hearing about your adventurous life with Wade. I feel like I knew him."

"He would have liked you. Just as I do. I'm glad you're here."

"Sienna, for goodness sake. I consider it an honor to be of help. And I love the ranch."

"Then you won't leave, will you?"

Taken by surprise, Lark set the sewing aside and clasped her hands in her lap. "I'll stay as long as you need me."

"That's not what I mean. This place is good for you. I know something is wrong in your past. Cort can be good at solving problems. Long as he thinks before he uses that gun of his."

"Cort is your husband. There is no place for his concern."

"Damnation! I'm plain spoken, and not so old and sick that I don't have good vision. I see how he looks at you. And how you look at him."

"Sienna! I hope you don't think . . ."

The sickly woman found enough strength to wave an arm to silence her. "My time is at hand, Lark. I'm not scared to die. Just scared about leaving this ranch in the wrong hands. Cort is the right person. Wade and I agreed. He's loyal and a deep-down good man. A little taming by the right woman wouldn't hurt. If you think Cort and me are a love match . . . well, get that out of your head. I'm twenty years older and probably the talk of the town for marrying less than a year after losin' my Wade. You might say we have a business arrangement."

Confusion sifted through Lark's brain like water trickling over rocks. She'd never heard anything like this, though, Cort had admitted as much. All she knew for sure was that she missed Cort. Waiting for the sight of him had become a sickness. God help her, she was falling for a married man who held his own secrets. While he'd rocked her heart and turned her world upside down, the indecency of wanting a man out of reach was too unseemly to contemplate. He'd be a widower soon enough. By then, she'd still have to leave. The risk of Will Cardin finding her left no other choice. Cort could easily get killed.

Sienna was looking at her as if expecting some response. Finally, Lark managed one. "I don't know what to say. You've taken my breath away."

"Come closer."

Lark moved like she had chains around her ankles. As she knelt beside Sienna, they took measure of each other. Sienna clasped her hand and held it. Sorrow rose inside Lark, and with her free hand she swiped at the tears forming in her eyes.

"Good. Now I can see into your soul. And that sadness. You and Cort need each other, and I need Cort to fulfill a bargain. You've got gumption and starch. He was lucky to find you. This ranch needs someone like you. That man is splintered and I've seen how he looks at you. Give him the chance he deserves even if you have to wait."

An uproar outside caught their attention. Lark stood and looked out the window. At least fifteen men were riding into the compound with Cort in the lead, all of them unshaven and dust covered, their boots and horses splattered with mud.

"They're back, aren't they?" Sienna asked. The whispered question told Lark the woman was drifting into sleep.

When she turned, Sienna lay with her head back, her eyes closed. Lark left the room, closing the door softly. The winsome smile she thought she'd glimpsed on Sienna's face was surely her imagination.

Cort decided he'd keep to himself. Two women were always on his mind and it was driving him crazy. He needed to feel a woman under him, but he couldn't have the one he wanted. Repairing harness, watering horses, raking muck, and doing extra guard duty was the best prescription for what ailed him.

This Saturday, a bunch of his men were heading to Ogallala for much needed time off. Beer, whiskey, gambling, and women. It scraped his nerves raw at having to carry Sienna's letter of permission with him, or else the damned marshal might be on his ass. Maybe he'd take one of the soiled doves upstairs. No. The thought of rouged lips, strong perfume, and the taste of tobacco on their tongues no longer held any appeal. Maybe it never had. None of those prostitutes would have Lark's pretty lips, silky hair, and smell of spring rain.

When his men rode to Ogallala, he stayed behind. And tried to stay clear of the woman he had a hard time not looking for at every turn. He'd catch her hanging clothes over a rope line out back. Then he'd see her strolling the hillside to pick wild daisies, her hair aglow in the sunlight. Once in a while, he'd walk past the parlor and hear her musical laughter between words as she read to Sienna. One time, he even caught her sitting on the porch in the darkness and he turned around to find a bed upstairs where he lay awake, thinking.

Last night had been torturous at the dinner table, with his wife and Lark chattering about nothing in particular while his eyes kept following Lark's every glance and his ears soaked up her every word. When their gazes met and held, they each searched for another direction to look. That voice of hers was like silk, touching every hardened place in his sorry soul.

Today, he'd eaten breakfast with Juan. He'd already decided to fix the corral fence and then work on a hole in the barn roof, even though it was Sunday. Most of the men were either in town or doing their personal chores. Some were taking extra pay to stick around. The heat of the August Nebraska sun burned through him like fire. He unbuttoned his shirt, yanked it off, and set it over a section of fence he'd already finished. He pulled his gloves back on, ready to set another new post. Every muscle hurt as sweat dripped down his face and made rivers along his bare chest. As he jammed the post hole digger into the dirt, he heard musical laughter for about the fourth time. He glanced up, then picked up his shirt and swiped his sweat-soaked face with it.

Lark's voice reminded him of the bird she was named for. She sat beside Mason Lanning, the two of them talking and laughing. Cort had considered Mace Lanning one of his best hands until Lanning took an interest in Lark. First thing today, he'd been up to the house, helping her with a bucket of wash water. Then he'd returned to help her set the clothesline higher. When Cort finally climbed a ladder to nail roof shingles, he saw her sitting on the front stair chattering with Mace. Jealousy coiled inside him, ready to strike like a rattler. Damned time the man found something else to do besides hanging around Lark.

Cort barely remembered tossing down the hammer and shrugging into his shirt. He barely remembered striding in their direction; it seemed his legs were moving of their own volition.

Suddenly he was standing in front of them, scowling, from one to the other, while his sweat-stained blue shirt stuck to his skin. He hadn't taken the time to button it. That realization hadn't entered his head until his hands were already on his hips and his tongue felt lashed to the roof of his mouth. The words he wanted to say stuck in his throat. Thank God he wasn't wearing a gun, else he might shoot Mace off the steps.

Lark's look of surprise gave him voice. "Miss Garrin. Shouldn't you be checking on Sienna?" The snarl in his tone sounded like it belonged to someone else, but he couldn't curb it.

"This is my day off, Mister Enders. Besides, I did check on Sienna. She's eaten her lunch and is taking a nap."

He looked at Mace and wished he could think straight. "Mason. Find something else to do with your time. I'm not paying you to sit up here entertaining Miss Garrin."

Mason frowned. "Thought I was owed time off."

"Not when you take pay for Sunday. I'm paying you as of now. Go finish that corral fence and then ride out and check the cattle. If that isn't enough, I'll find something else for you to do."

"Yessir. If that's what you want."

Cort felt almost disappointed that Mace didn't give him more of an argument. The ranch hand stood, slapped his hat on his head, and turned to a red-faced Lark, ignoring Cort. "I'll see you on the porch after dinner. Promises to be a nice night for a walk."

"Thank you, Mason. I'll be waiting right here."

She smiled, and Mason winked. Cort's fists were balled at his sides. Mace was about her age and must have been in a few fights before, because his nose was bent. The man was a good drover and kept to himself. Mostly. Cort saw him as maybe handsome by women's standards. Short and stocky, he looked like he could handle himself in a fight. And right now, Cort was flexing his fingers and brewing for one. A strong need to make his knuckles meet the man's nose and move it the other direction set his reason over a cliff. "Miss Garrin is otherwise engaged this evening."

Mason stopped mid-stride. "Now that ain't fair. She already accepted my invitation."

"I'm cancelling it," Cort snapped.

Lark threw him a sharp look. "Cortland Enders. You don't have any right to interfere in who I see and talk with."

Well. At least she'd called him by his full name. He wasn't a *Harris.* Which everyone seemed to be forgetting. He was an Enders. And he wanted more than anything for Lark to have his name. He looked away from Mason long enough to pierce her with a hard glare. His anger roiled inside like a prairie fire and with no rain in sight. "Don't I? You work for me."

"That's not what you said before."

"I changed my mind."

Mason came up behind Cort and wrenched him around with a vice-like grip. Cort shoved the stocky man backward and followed him to the ground. Fist raised, he was about to let loose, but even in his black fury he heard Lark's voice. Her plea stopped him. Instead, he got up and did the only thing left to ease his jealous outrage. "Collect your pay by morning."

Mason stumbled to his feet. He looked ready to slam into Cort again. "Fine. I'll just do that. You got no call to boss the lady around like that."

Cort advanced on him until they stood face to face. "Maybe you need a different kind of lesson."

"Cort. Please." Lark touched the back of his shoulder. Then she stepped around him. Looking straight at Cort's face, she said, "I'm sorry I caused this, Mason." Her eyes locked with Cort's when she spoke.

"Don't worry about me. Maybe another time or place." Mace gave one last, longing look in her direction and marched off.

They watched his long angry strides as he made his way toward the bunkhouse, his boots crunching the gravel. "How could you do such a thing?" Lark said.

"How could you sit here flirting the afternoon away with someone you don't know?" Cort's teeth clenched. He took a long breath, but it didn't calm him. His next words were spewed like acid. "Stay away from my cowhands."

"No. I'll speak to whom I please. And another thing, that man you just fired didn't deserve that. You must be half mad. Will you fire me, too?" Her face flaming with embarrassment, she turned and rushed up the porch steps.

He followed after and grabbed her arm, spinning her around to face him before she reached the door. He dug his fingers into her flesh when she tried to yank free. "No, you don't. Let's settle this, Miss Garrin." He stalked off the porch and headed toward the barn, nearly dragging her along until he heard her sob. He slowed to a walk with her still in his grasp. When they reached the other side of the barn, he gripped both her arms and pressed her back against the wall. Her angry, tear-filled eyes caught him off guard. Her chin lifted in defiance, but he'd gone too far to stop now.

"For *your* information, any of my hands who defy me will be fired. I'm the boss and if I choose to fire you, I will. That isn't goin' to happen. As to your other question, *How dare I?* I'll tell you how I could do such a thing."

He leaned downward, his mouth finding hers in a demanding kiss. When she turned her face up to his, he felt the world collapse under his feet. Freeing her arms from his hold, she pressed her hands along the sides of his neck. The kiss softened but was as pure and wanting as anything he'd ever known. Once he left her mouth, he released her from his hold and moved away from her. "You've gotten into my blood."

CHAPTER 7
COLD, PAIN, AND SORROW

The next day was a quiet Monday. The wranglers had already made their way out of the corral, the cook's dog barked for leftovers, and Sienna looked chipper as Lark sat in a chair beside her bed with a book on her lap.

"Are you sure you don't want to go along with us?" Lark could hardly keep the pleading from her voice. The last thing she wanted was to travel to Ogallala with Cort. The memory of that kiss burned through her like wildfire. The man's wife sat here serenely, while it was all Lark could do to keep from relieving her guilt by confessing.

"For goodness sakes, no. I never did like doing that chore. Theresa and you will do a fine job with the list. Don't forget to buy some sturdy goods to sew up suitable ranch clothes for yourself. Make sure you get plenty of canned peaches if they got 'em. Seems like the only thing that stays down."

Lark put the book down and knelt on the floor in front of Sienna. "But we'll be gone for at least five days. Will you be all right?"

"Of course I'll be all right. I'm sending a note to the doctor for more medicine. Pains are gettin' a bit ornery and it's harder to sleep. He'll know what to send."

Lark patted the woman's hand, then stood. The gray gingham dress and waistcoat would do her well, but she'd set about making some new clothes to see her through the winter. She hoped confinement in this house wouldn't cause problems with Cort.

"I'm sending along my wool coat in case the night air chills you," Sienna said. "Cort will make sure you're safe and tucked in. You and Theresa ride in the wagon and don't forget to ask for a nice hotel room when you get there. Paid for by the ranch."

Why did he have to be one of the men escorting them? "I'm sure Cort has better things to do with his time. Zeke, Billy, and Tangle could go along so Cort can stay with you."

Sienna lifted her head abruptly. Blood trickled from her nose before she had time to dab it with her handkerchief. "You and Cort were mighty quiet at breakfast. I hope you're both getting along. He told me he got you to change your mind about stayin'."

"There's nothing for you to worry about. I'll make sure Doc Collier sends medicines. Cort has moods. Guess you know that better than me."

"That man bottles more inside than an overfilled vinegar jar. And just as sour. Now you best get along. Burning daylight, and Cort likes to get to Ogallala in no more than two days."

Lark picked up the carpetbag by her feet. The bag hung from her hand and somehow, a premonition struck her that she'd never see this woman again. Would Sienna be alive when she got back? She thought of staying behind, but everyone was waiting downstairs.

The sharpness of Sienna's voice surprised her. Had the woman read Lark's mind? "Glad you're staying. Cort's a hard man to know. Deep down, he's a good man."

All Lark could do was to nod and bite her lip before going downstairs to the waiting wagon. Tangle took hold of her bag, while Lark tried not to look at the stoic man beside the wagon, mounted on his bay horse.

Nothing could have prepared her for the coldness that gaped between herself and Cort. Thankfully, Theresa kept up constant prattle, apparently trying to fill the obvious rift that yawned. Cane drove the buckboard while Billy came up alongside, tipped his hat, and politely asked the women to let him know should they need to stop. Tangle flanked the other side of the wagon, occasionally riding forward to speak with Cort, who kept a distance, his rifle across his lap.

That evening, Tangle set up a campfire along with a pot of soaked pinto beans and dried frizzled beef. Theresa and Lark worked together, heating coffee and baking biscuits in a pan near the fire. Just as the women set out plates, Billy's harmonica filled the air with a soft, mournful tune.

Theresa chattered about how quiet it was without more cowhands along to stir up dust and trouble. Lark watched Cort staking out tie lines, assuring the horses didn't wander along the river. Cane and Tangle took first watch. The music stopped as Billy walked into the darkness.

She and Theresa had begun nibbling on biscuits, beans, and some meat by the time Cort ambled over to a log, picked up his plate, and forked his grub. Lark stood and used her skirt to lift the coffee pot so she could pour the brew into his tin cup.

"You don't need to wait on me. I can get my own," he growled.

She poured and handed him the cup. "Not a problem. Just trying to be helpful."

Theresa's voice broke the silence that followed. "Where's Billy?"

"He'll be along. Seein' to his personals. He and I take the second watch while you gals get some sleep up in the wagon. Goin' to be cool. Blankets in the back."

Lark stood and started for the river with her plate in hand.

"Where you headin', Miss Garrin?" Cort asked.

"Thought I'd wash up my plate and fork before we all turn in."

Theresa stood and grabbed up an empty potato sack. "I'll take them all down to wash up once Billy and the others get done eating. Maybe you'd like to take care of your personal business before those stars blink out behind the clouds, Lark."

"That all right with you, Cort?" Lark asked.

He gulped his coffee and his unfathomable eyes locked with hers. The chill in them baffled her. What had she done? "Suit yourself. Remember we got snakes around here."

"I'll remember."

The sound of the rushing water, the distant sound of nickering horses, and Theresa's chattering all reminded Lark that she was safe as she walked to the river. The night was so dark out here. She squinted and made out a rocky outline along the bank. Stooping beside it, she scooped water between her hands and washed her face, drying it with the edge of her skirt. More voices drifted to her from camp. In fact, there was a fair amount of laughter and the harmonica tune filled the blackness again. Billy, Tangle, and Cane must all be finishing their supper.

She crouched down, settled her derriere on the flat top of a boulder, and stared into the rushing water. A few moments later the clouds cleared and the moonlight made the water sparkle. Behind her, someone cleared a throat. Startled, she turned and saw the outline of a large man leaning against one of the trees, his ankles crossed.

"Cort?"

"Yep." He watched her a moment and then strode closer, his boots crunching against the pebbles.

"Did you need to follow me?"

"I assure you, I wasn't invading your privacy. Just thought I'd make sure you found your way. Looks like you were far away in thought."

"I heard the men's voices. Guess everyone is in camp."

"Uh-huh. You ready to head back?"

When she stood, her foot caught between two jagged rocks. She pitched forward, and he grabbed hold of her arm to steady her. Just as quickly, he released her.

"Thanks."

His eyes fastened on hers. "I'm sorry, Lark. I had no right to do what I did the other day."

"I'm just as guilty. If you remember, I kissed you back. I can hardly face Sienna."

"I remember every minute of you. There's a woman I'm supposed to be married to. I wasn't raised to spit on an oath."

"Both of us were wrong. That doesn't mean we can't still be friends and go on from here."

His teeth clenched. "No. I can't be your friend. We've gone beyond that and you know it. I want more than friendship and it's eating me alive. Being near you and wondering what happened in your past has me twisted in knots. You say you weren't married. You won't give me the chance to understand your fears. You've gotten inside a part of me where you shouldn't be. And you won't let me see what's inside you. I can't help you and it kills me."

"I can't open that part of me."

Cort sighed. "I'm serving a sentence for shooting a rancher's son in the arm, paralyzing the bastard after he beat a local whore. Whenever I leave the ranch, I have to have a pass from my keeper . . . Sienna. By marryin' me, she gave the ranch ownership over to me. But I'm still just a hired hand. And I love every inch of the place, so I won't walk away. Unless I have to."

Wide eyed, Lark ran her hand over her forehead. "How could Sienna concoct such a warped plan?"

"I don't know the answer to that. And a lot of other things. Like, who is after you?"

"Why did you tell me all this?"

"So you'd know where I stand. Most of all, you should know

I already spent three years in a Texas prison. Like I told you before, I was a wild kid from Virginia and got sucked into a gang of robbers. I know what it's like to be on the run. You can't keep running. Besides, if I'm honest with you . . . why can't you be straight with me?"

"I don't believe you're as bad as you want me to think. But know this. If I could admit everything, you'd be in danger."

She could just see his scowl in the moonlight. "Once we get into Ogallala, I'll be blind to whoever is tearing you apart. If you don't explain things, I won't be able to help you."

"I can't. If you care about me, let it go."

"That is no reason at all." He sighed. "Come on. I'll walk you back so I can get some shut-eye before my watch."

"I'm not forgetting that kiss."

"I'm not forgetting, either. When the time is right. I'll want another."

They rode into Ogallala with rain pelting them while jagged lightning streaked across an angry black sky. The two women pulled their coats on and held blankets over their heads while Cort escorted them to Gast's Ogallala House. Tangle and Billy helped with their satchels before taking charge of the horses and wagon.

"Want us to take your horse along, Cort?"

He shook his head. "I'll leave Lincoln tied here until I get the women settled. Meet you both at the saloon shortly."

He watched the women step back near the doorway, waiting under the overhang while water gushed over the edge, splashing mud up onto the boardwalk. He hefted his rifle and saddlebags from his horse and opened the door to allow the women to enter the dim interior. His spurs clanged on the pine floor as he led the way to the concierge desk.

"Five rooms. Mrs. Amilio and Miss Garrin each need a room.

I'll need two more for my men as long as they got extra beds. One room for me. Cort Enders."

The hotel clerk nodded. "Just sign in, Mister Enders, and I'll see the ladies get fine rooms toward the back. You'll be in Room Ten at the front. The usual. Paid for by the Circle H?"

"Yep."

Once the signatures were settled, he took up Lark's carpetbag while a hotel boy hefted Theresa's. The four of them went up the stairs to their rooms. After he made sure the women were landed for the night, he returned to his horse and led the animal to the stable. The rain had become a near torrent, rivulets of water running along the street and leaving deep ruts filled with muddy water that splattered his oilcloth jacket and boots. By the time he plodded back to the saloon, he was thoroughly soaked.

He went in and ordered whiskey at the bar. While he sipped, he kept his eyes peeled and ears open for prospective cowhands. If Mason Lanning showed up, he planned to hire him back with an apology. Lark had driven him crazy, or he'd never have fired the man. Between the Indians, the weather, and branding, he was pretty desperate for help. What would Wade do? *Wade would have made sure enough hands were hired on by now.*

Tangle and Cane were set up at a poker table in the corner. Billy must have gone off to fill his gut at the McLaughlin Boarding House where a pretty gal worked. He'd brought her name up often enough to make Cort wonder if they'd get married. He looked around the saloon. In the mirror behind the bar, he saw a finely dressed man wearing a gun, with a bottle and glass in front of him. Looked like a gambler by the cut of his clothes. Interesting that the fellow sat alone. Then again, Cort liked being by himself. He didn't recognize the three other men at the table with Cane and Tangle. The clothes and guns they wore didn't fit working men. He'd bet they were trouble.

Cort sipped his whiskey again, watching the loner. A scarred face. Some kind of pox, he guessed. Must be why he kept to himself with his hat pulled low to shadow his eyes.

The bartender leaned toward Cort. "I can see you watchin' that loner. Best stay away from him," the man mumbled under his breath. "Got a mean streak."

Cort shrugged. "Didn't think he'd make good cowhand material. Looks like his hands are soft. A dandy isn't what I need."

"Those three at the poker table are with him. They're up to no good."

"Yeah? What's his name? The one with the scars."

"Will Cardin."

Cort jerked his head up and gave the fellow another gander. He knew the name. He'd run across mean sonofabitches in his day, but Cardin stood a cut above them. While they'd never crossed paths, Cort had heard he was a fast gun and killed for the fun of it. As he debated talking to the varmint, Cardin grabbed his bottle and headed upstairs, tugging a reluctant saloon gal behind him.

"So you heard of him," the bartender said.

"Yep. Nothin' good. Pretty sure he's done a fair share of banks. Heard tell he goes after trains these days. Can't understand why there's no wanted poster on him. The marshal ought to know."

"I done told Marshal Varnum. He said he can't arrest somebody just cause of his reputation. He said he'd send some telegrams to find out if there's a poster."

"As long as Cardin moves on. Can't help but wonder why he and his friends are here." Cort figured there was plenty behind it. It rankled that the outlaw was in Ogallala, though he'd bet the marshal was letting the man alone to avoid any confrontation that could easily get bloody.

The bartender shrugged. "If they plan to rob the bank, I

can't understand why they haven't done it by now. Been here about five or six days. Looks like he's been in some rough knife fights."

"Makes me nervous, since I've got two women with me," Cort admitted.

"Sienna made it to town?"

"No. She's sick, Ben. I'm pickin' up more medicine from Doc Collier before we leave. Just came to get some supplies. Got Theresa and our new help along. Miss Garrin."

"Well, now. Don't recall seein' Theresa in a long while. Don't know the other one."

"Yep. You hear of anyone lookin' for work, Ben, I'd appreciate it if you'd send 'em out to the Circle H."

"I surely will. Don't think anyone in here fits what you want, though. Except Tangle and Cane."

Cort tossed two bits on the bar and picked up the whiskey bottle, then gave his men a long stare. He hoped they'd get the hint. He didn't want them to get so drunk they either messed with these hombres or got thrown in jail. Worse, unless he was stone dead in his head, he'd bet there were more of Cardin's men somewhere, and that could land him square in the middle of a fight.

He stopped in his room and tugged out of his damp coat. Shrugging into a clean shirt, he figured he'd best check on the women. He'd stalled long enough. Looking into Lark's eyes might wind up pulling him into her room. And he couldn't do that to Sienna.

He went down the hall to her door and tapped lightly on it. "It's me. Cort."

The door swung open. His breath caught in his throat when he saw the pretty blue dress Lark wore. There was just enough décolletage to put a man's eyes where they shouldn't be. While he stared, she stepped back to grant him entrance.

"Did you need something?" she asked.

Yes, pretty lady. You. So much it kills me. "Maybe you and Theresa would like me to escort you to the mercantile before we have supper. Best I stay with you both."

"Is something wrong?"

Nothing wrong but Will Cardin . . . here in town. "No. I'm a mite hungry, so if we could get going?"

"Theresa already went to the doctor's office. She'll meet us at the dry goods."

He swallowed as her gold-green eyes studied his. "Something *is* wrong. You get that hard look when something's bothering you."

"Just wasn't expecting a pretty dress like that. Better put on your jacket to keep dry. Rain's mostly stopped, but not entirely."

"All right." She turned and he slipped the wool coat around her shoulders . . . the same one he recollected Sienna wearing.

Once out on the boardwalk, they walked side by side. Lark had a difficult time keeping up with his long strides. Jaw taut, he slowed at the sight of four horses outside the saloon. She sensed his hesitation and when he touched his revolver grip, she looked toward the saloon. Something was very wrong. When they continued on, they didn't make small talk like usual. Taciturn and grim, he searched the street with somber eyes, as if looking for someone.

They reached the store and went inside. Her gaze fell on the older man behind the counter, who offered them a brief smile. A table was piled high with bolts of ribbon and cloth. Gingham, cotton, lace, satin, taffeta, wool, muslin, and linen drew her like a fly to honey. She ran her hand over the shimmery taffeta. So many colors. What she needed was practical, though. Not fancy.

She'd nearly forgotten Cort was with her. His broad smile was the first she'd seen from him today. "Go on. Pick some things out. You'll need something to wear besides the few things you brought." He winked at her.

A soft voice interrupted them. "My. You're a pretty one." A silver-haired woman, with skin so delicate it reminded Lark of bone china, came up beside her. The woman's blue eyes twinkled with merriment. "We just got all these in a few days ago. And once you decide on fabrics, we can choose some patterns and lovely buttons."

Lark turned and saw Cort still grinning. "I can't buy much but a few buttons and a little lace," she said.

"Lark, this is Glory Sanderson and that old man behind the counter is Macon. You pick out whatever you need and the Circle H pays for it."

"I don't know how long before I can pay you back."

"Consider it part of your earnings for hiring on. Sienna would agree. Besides, I'm the authority on what we spend here. Take heed. I expect to carry back enough cloth so you can make at least five dresses and whatever else. No worryin'."

With that, he turned to follow Macon to a side room where there were guns and ammunition on the shelves.

Glory gestured toward a bolt of cloth. "My dear, this brown taffeta would be so good with your hazel eyes and light hair."

Lark ran her hand over the taffeta but settled on wool and muslin. Glory convinced her a little lace would help fix up the plainness. Before long, Theresa waddled in and joined them. "That's mighty fine-lookin' cloth," she said. "You'll look lovely in most anything."

Lark glanced toward Theresa and smiled. "Cort told me to pick out what I needed. I plan to buy practical things."

Cort came out of the back room and slapped boxes of cartridges on the counter. "I'm taking these fine ladies to supper at the hotel. Fill this order." He removed a piece of paper from his pocket and handed it to Macon while Glory applied her shears to cutting the cloth.

Theresa said, "I'm havin' supper with Laura over to the boarding house. I'm betting that's where Billy will be, what with Ginny setting out a fine meal."

Lark felt a jolt of indecision. She couldn't take supper with a married man in plain sight of the townsfolk. It wouldn't be proper. *Cort, please don't do this to me.*

"Sounds fine. Keep one eye on Billy. Miss Garrin and I plan to eat and then I'll see her back to her hotel room. Early day tomorrow. Have some things I need to attend to but the next morning, we'll head out."

Was he thinking straight? They'd be the center of gossip. Once the two of them left the store, her heart raced. They entered the small hotel lobby, and Cort gripped her arm with one hand and his hat in the other. He wore his gun, the holster lashed to his leg. Was the town dangerous? They started for the dining room just as a dark-coated man with black hair and a scarred face came out of it, his eyes on the door leading to the street. His boots were shined, his hair wavy and well groomed. She froze. Cort stopped beside her. *Cardin. Oh, my God.*

He'd never given her a glance. She thanked God and the stars in a silent prayer. A wave of nausea surged, and she searched for a place to hide. Beads of sweat formed on her hot face. Had Cardin seen her and was just waiting to pounce? After all, she wore his brand. Cort tugged at her arm. She couldn't find words to tell him what ailed her. Spots formed before her eyes. The room spun. The walls looked vague. She couldn't faint. She *couldn't.*

"Cort. I can't . . ." Fear paralyzed her. What if Cardin came back and faced Cort?

"What is it? What's wrong? You look like a ghost. Lark?"

His muffled voice faded as he repeated her name. She clutched at air, and things went away.

After a while, the gray fog opened like a curtain. Cort held her gently against his side. Her head rested against his chest as his gentle fingers stroked her hair. "Cort?"

"I ordered some food brought up. You must have needed it. Next time, tell us when you're hungry."

She winced as she sat up. His arms curved around her. He leaned over and brought a glass of water to her lips. She sank into his tenderness and sipped. "I'm sorry. Did I hit the floor in front of everyone?"

"I caught you and carried you upstairs. Doc Collier wasn't at his office. Theresa checked on you."

"Oh, Cort! What will people be saying?"

"I don't give a damn. After you've eaten, you're goin' to explain what's going on. Everything. Something got you in a panic. Tell me. Or by God, I'll find out another way."

Chapter 8
Facing the Devil

Theresa bustled around the room, pacing one moment and watching out the window the next. The woman kept busy, mumbling and complaining under her breath. Lark followed with her eyes while nibbling on bread, bacon, and eggs. Even though Lark was under orders to stay in bed, she worried about all the attention.

"Theresa. Stop. I get the gist of what you're asking but I can't understand you when you get into your Italian."

Theresa turned and steepled her hands over her mouth. "Mister Enders is furious. Something happened to make you faint. He's downstairs with Tangle and Billy, giving them orders to get the wagon loaded. Never saw him so mad and upset all at the same time."

"I don't want him getting into trouble. Please take the tray so I can go talk with him."

"Don't you dare. He's fuming." Theresa lifted the tray and carried it to the door. She opened it to reveal a furious Cort stomping toward the women's hotel room, his spurs jangling. He gave Theresa a dismissive nod, stepped into the room, and slammed the door closed. His eyes were riveted on Lark.

"Good morning. I see you ate some. Can you be ready to leave by noon?"

Why was he so upset? And curt? "Of course. I'm sorry to cause a fuss. I don't know why I fainted. I'm not usually the fainting kind."

He crossed the room in three long strides, crouched beside the bed, and rested his hand over hers. Willpower fought with desire inside her. She needed his strength. But not at the cost of having him face down Will Cardin. If she had the funds, she'd be on the next train to somewhere away from this man she loved, and the man she hated.

"You were pale as snow when I carried you up here. You didn't want to talk last night. So I did some recollecting. The only thing I could come up with was Will Cardin. He walked through the lobby and you froze like a deer about to be shot. You going to tell me why he upset you? I'm convinced he did, so no more beating around the bush. Why?"

"You're wrong. I don't know anything about any Will Cardin."

He looked skeptical, then sighed. "All right. For now. Tangle, Billy, and Cane will be loading the wagon and getting the horses ready to set out by noon."

That meant they were leaving a day early. "Cort. Don't do anything. Please."

"You needn't worry about hiding. Cardin's gone. If he were still in town, I'd be taking him apart, limb by limb."

"If you're determined to confront him, then I'll be forced to leave."

"Damn. You are the most stubborn woman I've ever encountered. So it *is* about him."

"You are impossible."

He stood, then sat beside her on the edge of the bed. "*Impossible?* When you're hurting, I hurt. Letting you run off somewhere out of pure hellish fear is not going to happen." His lips brushed her forehead. Then he trailed soft kisses along her neck before taking her mouth in a gentle, possessive caress. Time slowed and then sped, and then he was gone. The door closed between them and Lark was left alone. Tears filled her eyes. Oh, God. What had she done? What had *they* done?

Clouds threatened. Cort worried as he led his entourage out of Ogallala, the wagon loaded with supplies. Once they crossed onto Circle H land, he'd be able to get the women to a line shack that was still under repair, by his orders. Winter snows and stranded cattle made the shacks a necessity for his men. Now it would be handy as a way station.

Glancing behind, he saw the two women bundled in jackets against a cool wind. Billy had taken on driving while Tangle and Cane rode on his right flank, chattering from time to time. Cane tugged at the lead line of the packhorse while the new cowhand trailed behind them. Seemed to be a loner, but right now, Cort needed everyone he could hire on. And the man had sounded like he knew cattle.

The day wore on and the rutted, muddy trail gradually gave way to Indian and switchgrass. He watched for signs that Indians had crossed this way. Raiding parties weren't uncommon, especially where the Sioux and Cheyenne were concerned. They were out to pick a fight after Custer's blunder. Ranchers had lost at least a hundred head of cows to thievery over the last couple of years. Cort looked over his shoulder again toward Lark. She was holding onto the seat as the wagon bumped and shook from side to side.

Lark . . . the name suited her. Pretty as a delicate bird. The more he knew her, the more he became lost in her. With every fiber of his being, he wished he were free to make her his. He loved her. And that, of all things, scared him. A married man in love with a woman who'd make him the kind of wife he'd dreamed of. Keeping away from her was getting harder. Sienna had forced him to bring Lark into his life. He'd bet his saddle that Sienna had planned this scheme, hoping for a match. Still, his sense of decency wouldn't give in to Sienna's approaching death. He wanted his wife to live, even if he also wanted another woman who'd captured his heart. He refused to be like a vulture, picking at entrails. And he'd give his right arm to keep Sienna from suffering.

The sound of hooves pounding closer brought him out of his reverie. Tangle rode up alongside him and they settled their mounts into a walk.

"What do you think of the new hand?" Tangle asked.

"He'll do. Seems like he's had experience on ranches."

"He got a name?"

"Clay Brant." Cort cupped a gloved hand over his eyes and looked toward the horizon. "You see those clouds ahead?"

"That's why I came over. We might be in for a storm, boss."

"Yep. Got to make it to the first shelter for the night. Don't want the gals out in the rain."

"That's another thing. I just rode up beside the wagon. Miss Garrin wants to ride Billy's horse. He said he'd bring it up for her."

"What the hell for?" Cort whipped his head around in time to see Billy giving Lark a hand up into the saddle. "Christ's sake." Cort glared at Tangle, even though he knew it wasn't the ranch hand's fault. "Sonofabitch. That woman has a mind of her own. What will she do next?"

Instead of answering, Tangle pulled his hat lower against a gust of wind and turned his horse toward the ridge ahead. Cort sat waiting for Lark to ride in his direction. Before long, she pulled up beside him, her hair whipped into a stormy sea of gold. Sexy as hell. His fingers itched to stroke the loose braid.

"Cort."

"Lark. Next time you decide to go riding, I expect you to check it out with me first."

"Since I haven't had the pleasure of your company since we

left Ogallala, I had little time to ask. Besides, Billy assured me his mount is well behaved."

"Why are you doing this?" he snapped.

"Doing what? Riding a horse?"

"Dammit, woman. I gotta keep watch on that wagon that's almost over the ridge. Can't sit here jawing."

"Why are you being so disagreeable? Can't we be civil like before?"

"Before? Before I kissed you? Christ, Lark. You are driving me crazy. I don't even know if you can handle that horse and I don't want to scrape you up from the ground."

"I can ride as well as any of your cowhands. Learned from my grandfather and cousin back on our Ohio farm. I could be of help."

"A storm is comin'. Catch up to the wagon and tell Billy to tie off the horse."

Her pouting, kissable lips left him speechless as she kicked her mount into a ground-eating run while her skirt lifted to her knees. He shook his head and followed after her, bringing his own bay close enough to reach out and grab her. He chirruped to Billy's horse, and the animal slowed in response. Cort leaned toward Lark, lifted her from the saddle, and ignored her sputtering protest as he seated her in front of him. He urged his horse toward Billy's, latching hold of the reins, and led the animal to the wagon. Every movement of his thighs against Lark's derriere brought him near to gasping. He might drown himself in a bottle of whiskey if he had one handy.

Billy jumped down from the wagon and took hold of his horse's reins. "Sorry, boss. Thought it'd be all right."

"Another time, Billy. Maybe you'll find me a fine mount so I can ride on my day off," Lark said.

Cort said nothing. Instead, he dismounted and lifted her

down. Then he slipped back into his saddle and rode off like he was leading a regiment into battle.

The rain poured down as they finally made their way to the first line shack on Circle H land. Dry wood was stacked just inside the door, and Theresa filled and lit the potbellied stove. Tangle and Cane set sacks of food next to the woodpile, along with some damp blankets. The women worked cooperatively to get some beans and bacon heated up, then threw the blankets over the three stained cots. Coffee and bacon smells filled the one-room shack, eclipsing pungent boot dung, leather, and tobacco.

From the one dusty window, Lark made out the men leading horses to a lean-to on the right side of the shack. Cort stood on the wagon bed and unrolled a tarp, forming a kind of tent. Water ran over his hat and soaked into his coat in dark patterns. As though sensing her watching him, he looked in her direction. Their eyes met and held just before he jumped down from the wagon and headed toward the horses.

Theresa broke into her contemplation. "Those men. They will be sick if they don't get dry."

"Looks like they'll be in for grub any minute. We better see to the food."

Theresa clutched Lark's shoulder. "I see things. Cort is handsome. You are beautiful. I feel pain for you both. But he is married. My heart hurts for all of you."

Lark touched the woman's hand but chose not to admit the truth of her own feelings. Leaving here as soon as she could was her only plan. If she stayed, the next time she wouldn't be so lucky as to avoid Will Cardin's notice. And Cardin killed with no hesitation. She drew in a soft breath and set plates and tin cups on the rough table.

"Where will they sleep? We could make room in here on the floor, don't you think?" Lark asked.

"Oh, Dios! That would not be proper. They will sleep under the tarp while two are on watch."

"It might be a cold night. There's room here."

Theresa cupped Lark's cheeks between her hands. "No. You must learn that life here is hard. They are used to this. Men don't like being bossed by a woman."

All Lark could do was nod her acceptance and begin the task of dishing out the food as each of the men crossed the threshold, tossing their coats and hats into a wet heap near the stove to dry. Cort settled himself on the floor against one wall, silent and contemplative. His wet hair and scruffy beard made him look like the gunslinger and drifter he'd described himself as. Without looking her way, he forked his food and gave only short responses to questions.

The new cowhand, Clay Brant, was the last to clomp inside, where he picked up a plate and leaned against a wall to eat. Cort introduced him, but didn't spare Lark a word. The distance between her and Cort was like the path between stars. He wanted what she couldn't give . . . the truth about Will Cardin. The sooner she accepted that, the sooner she could leave without crying.

The next day, breaks of sunlight were followed by dark clouds in the distance. Cort saw signs of unshod horses, so vague that he had no idea if they were moving away or circling behind them. Once he'd warned his men to be watchful and have their guns ready, he moved his horse to flank the wagon. When they were within twenty miles of the homestead, he saw a faint line of horses in single file on a far ridge. He rode to the back of the wagon and gave Billy the order to pull up, then yanked a sack of potatoes and flour from the wagon bed. "Billy, you and the others keep moving toward the homestead. I'll catch up."

"Where are you going with the food, Cort?" Lark asked.

He avoided looking at her. The woman didn't understand that he wasn't used to being questioned about how he conducted ranch business. "See that line of riders over there?"

She followed the direction of his pointing finger. "Yes."

"A family of Indians. Can't tell if they're Cheyenne or Pawnee from here. Sure enough, they got some hungry kids along. Can't abide a little one goin' without something to eat. No matter what color their skin."

Unexpectedly, she smiled. "That's exactly what I'd expect of you. Be careful."

"Take the beans too, Cort. We got plenty at the house," Theresa added.

He reached for the bean sack and tugged his hat low over his eyes. "Ladies."

Billy slapped the reins and sent the wagon jolting ahead while Tangle and Cane rode beside them. Clay Brant stayed to the rear. Once they neared the homestead, the cowhands waved their hats and everyone dropped what they were doing to welcome them all home with hoots and hollers. Nita ran down the porch steps and walked beside the wagon.

Dressed in a split skirt, simple blue blouse, and worn leather boots, Sienna stood on the porch, her hand cupped over her eyes, taking in the wagon's arrival. Clouds drifted overhead, blocking the sunlight and sending eerie shadows over the porch.

As Theresa stepped down, her husband, Alonzo, ran over from inside the livery, his leather apron flapping against his legs. He lifted her against him and pressed a kiss to his wife's mouth. The men joked and patted each other on the back in welcome. Lark stepped down with Billy's help and turned to face Sienna. Cort's wife looked stronger. She was still pale, but her brown eyes looked clear instead of glazed. They studied each other for a moment before a smile curved Sienna's mouth.

"Good to have you back. Nita is good company. But I missed you."

"Thank you. It's good to be back."

"Where's Cort?"

"He rode off to attend to something." Lark had no idea whether it was wise to tell a tale she had no business divulging.

Billy, unloading the goods with Tangle, winked in Sienna's direction. "You know how Cort is. We're a little short on some provisions . . . a few potatoes and beans."

Sienna laughed and Lark thought she'd never heard a heartier sound. "Oh. Cort is one to help all the Indian families he comes across. Tonight they'll circle back and take a steer with them to have with the potatoes."

She took Lark's hands. "I trust Cort was attentive, and made sure you got everything you need."

The truth of his attentions was best left secret. Something she'd carry with her when she had to run. "Yes. He was helpful."

"We better get tucked inside. We've had a lot of rain and now it looks like more comin' over there from the west. Got to send out men to check on the cattle. They can wind up dying in the river when they try swimming across. Those animals have no sense."

Chapter 9
Drowning

Sunday should have been a serene day. Work never ended on the ranch. Horses needed to be shod, repairs made, cattle checked, and food cooked. There were twenty-five hands, including the new man, Clay. Today was different.

Lark looked out the parlor window. The wind gusted so hard that the corral fence leaned over precariously. Rain pelted against the windows and roof, while a door on the barn rattled and slammed.

"Almighty! I've never seen an August like this. I'm worried about the cattle. Even more worried about the men out there," Sienna said from behind her.

Theresa wrung her hands and paced, stopping long enough to look out the window toward one of the two barns where her husband worked. Today, Alonzo had been called upon to go out with the others. Lark hadn't lived here long enough to understand the seriousness of the storm. But she sensed something was very wrong.

"Surely they take cover in one of the line shacks?"

Sienna's long stare didn't leave the window, where wind was blowing the tall grass into swirls and then laying it flat like a man's hair part. Lark saw what Sienna saw. Except for what she was in the dark about. So much could go wrong on a ranch and she was still learning about this violent, intriguing land.

Not taking her eyes from the dismal sight outside, Sienna's voice cut across the sound of the wind that moaned as if the plains were screaming in pain. "The water, Lark. It's the water. The Platte will be swollen and it fills the Blue River, where our cattle tend to range. We'll lose hundreds if they spook and decide to cross. They don't have sense enough not to."

"And the men? What are they doing?"

"We got twenty men out there trying to work the cows away from the river. It won't be enough. Cort went out with Zeke and Jude. The others are who knows where out there."

Theresa headed for the kitchen. "Alonzo will be hungry. All of them will be hungry. Juan and I will have something hot when they get back in."

Lark touched the woman's arm. When Theresa shook her head, Lark saw her lips tremble and knew no words were necessary. Keeping busy would keep them all from worrying.

Lark and Sienna sat beside each other, the rain splattering the windows and the wind howling like the devil. Cracks of thunder echoed through the house, shaking it to the foundation. Suddenly, Sienna rose from her perch near the window and nearly toppled. Lark caught her, holding her steady. Their eyes met. In Sienna's, Lark saw panic that matched her own.

"This ranch is everything. But not enough to lose my men," Sienna said. "I'm goin' out and call them in. Somehow. Otherwise they'll stay out till they're killed by a stampede of cattle or the swollen river. I won't have them dyin' for my ranch."

Once Sienna had made up her mind, there was little chance of changing it. Still, Lark tried. "No, Sienna. You're too weak. You'll die out there. What good would that do?"

"I'd feel like I'm doing something. Cort, Zeke . . . all those men are wasting their time. This storm is different. The cattle will have to drown. Some might have more sense than others. I won't risk my men."

Physical pain from the cancer would never let Sienna ride more than a few feet, especially in this hard rain. Lark watched helplessly as Sienna shrugged into a long coat. Theresa must have heard the commotion—she marched into the parlor, her eyes flashing. Nita rushed in behind her, both of them ready to do battle with their stubborn boss.

"You will not be leaving here while I can sit on you," Nita snapped.

"We can stop you. Three of us against one," Theresa added. Lark moved to join them, and all three women stood side by side, arms crossed.

No one had the chance to argue further. A horse splashed through mud and pulled up in front of the porch. A man slid from his saddle, soaked, filthy, and bedraggled. Lark tried to make out who it was under the caked mud. She hurried to the door and yanked it open. The ranch hand who entered had a mud-streaked face, and his shoulders slumped under the weight of his sodden duster.

"Ma'am." He tipped his wet hat. Water ran over the brim, splashing in front of her. Sienna moved Lark aside with a brush of her hand while Nita and Theresa crowded behind them.

"Sorry 'bout that. Mrs. Harris. Pardon . . . Mrs. Enders." He nodded and swallowed. His Adam's apple rode up and down in his long throat while his gaze moved from one woman to the other.

"Spit it out, Damon," Sienna ordered.

"Cort told me to call in as many men as I found. He'd do the same. Ain't no use in everybody gettin' killed. Except one other problem. Zeke is missin'. Cort said he won't be back in till he finds him. Don't wait on him."

Sienna gasped. "Lord Almighty! Does the Blue look as bad as I think it does?"

"Surely does, ma'am. Never seen it this bad. Afraid a lot of your cattle tried to get to the other side in pretty deep water."

"Thanks for telling us. You go dry off and get some chow.

Juan's most likely got a stew in the pot, and coffee to warm you up. Soon as you take care of your horse."

"Alonzo? Damon, have you seen him?" Theresa broke in.

"No, ma'am. I saw some fellas off in the distance. Don't think I'd recognize my own mother in this mess. I waved 'em in. I'm sure they'll be comin' along."

Theresa turned away, sad eyed. "Nita and I will get food ready to help out."

Damon watched her leave. Then he turned his attention to Sienna. "Ma'am, I don't think Cort will find Zeke. Zeke's horse is dead." She stared at him, wordless, as he quietly walked out of the room, closing the door quietly behind him.

"If anyone is goin' out there, I am." Lark didn't know where that had come from, but it felt right. Someone had to pitch in besides those worn-out men. Zeke had to be found. The man was a pillar of this ranch and kindly, to boot. She was an excellent rider. This was something she could do.

"Do you even imagine what it's like out there? What trouble you can run into?"

"I may not know much about cattle ranching, but I ride well. My brother and grandfather taught me back at our home in Ohio. If I can't chase some cows away from a river, my brother would be ashamed of me. Zeke's more important, though. I'll do my best to find him."

"What if I try to stop you?"

Lark and Sienna glowered at each other. "I'm going," Lark said. "That's my decision to make. And, like you, I can be one stubborn lady."

A thin smile flickered across Sienna's pale face. "You got gumption, Miss Garrin. And I sense an Irish temper. We don't have time to argue. Least I can do is offer my horse and some boy's clothes that might fit you. They belonged to a young cowhand used to work here. And you'll take my rifle and revolver. You see a cow in trouble, shoot it. You get into trouble, fire three shots into the air. You're not good at takin' orders, but I hope you listened to that one. And one important thing. Don't cross the river."

Wearing boy's clothes and boots beneath a long canvas coat, a wool scarf tied down the broad-brimmed hat as she headed out the door. Sienna's parting words played over in her head. "Mind you stay out of the river. The Blue will swallow you. One other thing. Cort is a good man." Sienna's frail voice sounded like a whisper of a ghost.

In the barn, she found Juan inside the stall with the buckskin horse saddled and ready. A rifle poked from the boot. He took her saddlebag and tied it down behind the cantle. With help from Juan, he lifted her and settled her onto the saddle while the horse chomped the bit. Juan adjusted the stirrups and gave her a last warning. "You look out, ma'am. I got orders to let you go and I plan to do that. But that may be the biggest mistake I ever made."

Rain hit her with a gust of wind as she and the horse headed away from the barn. She tucked her chin and pulled her collar up around her neck. As she turned the horse toward the north, she hoped the wind wouldn't knock her from the saddle. Hunched over, her head down against the rain, she kept going while cold water drizzled over her coat and turned the buckskin dark brown. Red and black mud splattered her coat, boots, and saddle. A stupid thought struck her. What if she found Zeke and couldn't help him? What if it was too late?

Lark's bones ached. She hadn't found a trace of another rider. Only vague hoofprints filled with water, some deeper than others. For the last hour she'd ridden toward what she thought might be the direction of the river. Maybe Zeke was holed up someplace. He surely knew where a line shack would be. Knowing him, he'd probably decided to see what cattle he could chase, even on foot. Right now, she wasn't sure she could find her way back to the ranch house. By this time, she had hoped to see some of the other cowhands, or else she might wind up being the center of a search. She imagined Cort's fury if that happened.

The noise of rushing water ahead drew her closer toward the river. Sienna's warning words niggled. Still, just maybe she could chase cattle away from the bank. The cottonwoods bowed their wet branches. She thought of Zeke and bit her lip against what might turn out to be an awful sight if she found him floating in the river. What would she do? She nudged her horse through the trees, then reined up.

Rainwater plopped against her slicker and rolled over her hat, running over her face so she had to blink to see. The Blue River was raging. Memories of the Mississippi when it overflowed didn't compare to this wild image. Roiling, muddy water swirled, catching limbs and tossing them against the rocks. She'd seen this creek when it looked blue as the sky and clear as ice. Hardly a river at all.

Loud bellowing caught her attention. She urged her horse toward the bank, but the animal balked and backed up. "Easy, Butter." Turning the horse to plod along the bank, she followed the desperate sound of a cow in trouble. The rain eased but the sky was leaden gray. And her teeth chattered with cold.

Three cows lined the bank. One stood ahead of the others with one hoof ready to plunge in. Then she saw the reason, if cows reasoned at all. This was a mother watching her calf flounder in the middle of the swirling, splashing water. Its small hooves slapped the surface while its head peeked out and then sank, over and over again while the water carried the animal further along. When she saw the calf's long pink tongue and heard the pitiful bawling, she gave in to her softer instincts.

She didn't think the river was that terribly deep. She didn't think at all, just kicked her horse forward, sliding downward and into the water, then headed the buckskin toward the drowning calf. Water rolled over the saddle while the horse lifted his mighty head to stay above the surface. She managed to reach for the frightened calf, but the animal's ears slipped from her hands. The buckskin was fighting to find footing in the sand and rock, and with each lurch, sent Lark precariously close to following the calf into the river. Reaching again, she grasped the calf behind the neck only to have it yank away hard, pulling her from the saddle and into the swirling water.

Still near her, the buckskin kicked, nearly catching her in the arm. The flailing calf bawled and sank before her eyes as she slapped the water to keep her head above the surface, while the tumbling water swept her along. Her body hit submerged rocks, sending pain through her arm. A last look toward her wild-eyed horse showed the buckskin stumbling to the far bank. Lark tried to stand but the current kept dragging her away. The river was too deep, and her boots and slicker dragged her down ever deeper and further.

Abruptly, she plunged beneath a deeper part of the river. A futile glimpse at the bank made her slap at the water that wanted to kill her. Water filled her mouth and she spit it out. What was it like to drown? Maybe if she just closed her eyes and let the river take her body. She'd lose this fight because her arms were too tired to lift her any longer. Just as she slid beneath the angry water, a powerful hand gripped her arm painfully and dragged her through the blackness. Muscular yanks of a horse beside her nearly sent her beneath again while the hand held on, dragging her somewhere. She gasped for air each time whoever it was tried to lift her free of the river.

When she surfaced, her eyes met her rescuer's in a brief,

intense connection. *Cort.*

"Sonofabitch. I don't know if I can hold on." His voice was choked.

She felt a jolt and his tight fist wrapped around her coat but slipped away.

"Cort!"

Had she screamed his name or just thought she'd screamed? Where was he? Then there was nothing.

Chapter 10
Desperate

Cort's boots and coat kept dragging him downward. Reaching her was all he could think. Her coat floated on the surface and from what he could see of her face, it was a white mask of death. Her hair lay around her face like gold grass, twisted around her neck. He slapped through the water until his feet finally found purchase in hard gravel and he was able to yank her from the river. He lifted her into his arms. His unsteady legs splashed through the water, and he finally struggled up the bank and set her beside a fallen tree. He crouched beside her and turned her head. Water ran from her slack mouth while he punched her back through the soggy wool of her coat.

"Come on, honey. Breathe for me. Breathe."

He slipped out from under the weight of his own coat and rolled her onto her side, then pressed her back with more force. On his knees, he settled his mouth against hers and puffed. Water trickled from her lips. He tried again. It wasn't enough. He leaned back, trembling through every wet inch of his body. "Dammit, Lark! Come back to me." He leaned down and puffed against her cold mouth.

She coughed. Water shot from between her lips and she gave a rattling cough followed by another. Her eyes opened and she stared vacantly before turning her head. She traced his features, first with her eyes and then her cold fingers. "Cort. You're here."

Something of exaltation erupted from the deep reaches of his soul. A deep, loud bark of laughter shot from his throat as he lifted her into his arms, holding her tightly while his entire body shook. She felt so cold and limp. He hooked one of her arms around his neck and stood with her enfolded in his embrace, then slowly walked her toward higher ground. "I'm here, honey. You scared the tar out of me."

"Sorry. Tried to help. So cold."

"I'm going to set you down and put my coat around you. It's wet, but the best I can do till I find my horse. I've got a bedroll and with any luck, the matches are dry."

He left her just long enough to pick up his wet coat. He wrung some water from the sopping oilcloth and then tucked it around her while her lips trembled with cold, knowing he had to get them both warmed or they'd die. Their best chance was to find his horse so he could set out for a line shack about four miles from here, from his recollection. He wouldn't be able to carry her all that distance.

"Scared. You were in the water," she stammered as her lips quivered.

"Yes. And I'd do it again. Just don't make me ever have to. Once we get warmed up, I'm goin' to want to know why you're even out here."

Her head lolled against his chest. He rubbed her arms, hoping to warm her skin. His own chattering teeth told him he was in danger of succumbing to the cold if he didn't figure something out quick.

"Hang on," he said, and released her so he could stand.

She clutched at his shirt. "Don't leave me, Cort. If I'm going to die, I want to be with you."

"Hey. No talking like that. I don't plan to die and I'm not lettin' you die, either. Just close your ears for a minute."

He got to his knees. Aching from hitting rocks and feeling weak, he wondered if he'd be able to stand. He drew in a breath and shoved himself to his feet, balanced on unsteady legs. Two fingers between his lips and he was able to whistle for his horse. He whistled twice more. Nothing. Maybe his horse was too far away. Maybe the animal drowned.

"Dammit. Where are you, Lincoln? If you broke your leg . . ."

He sat back down beside Lark, took her in his arms, and set his chin on her wet hair, holding her against his pounding heart. Think. He could try carrying her over four miles of rocky terrain. Odds were against them. Suddenly he heard a muffled snort and whicker. He turned his head and saw his bay horse standing just beyond the cottonwoods, head down and covered in mud. He could barely tell the animal belonged to him. He gave a short whistle, and Lincoln lifted his head and trotted to him. The horse bent its neck and nuzzled him.

Cort patted Lincoln's nose. "About time you showed up, partner."

He made quick work of getting his bedroll unfastened and snugged it around Lark. He slipped into his wet coat, set her in the saddle, and swung up behind her. When he wrapped his arms around her, he felt her shivering. There wasn't enough time to circle around looking for Butter, Sienna's horse. The sooner he could get Lark warmed up, the better her chances and his. He set his horse into a lope, with a glimpse toward the raging river, the last place he'd seen Sienna's buckskin. His heart had tripped and then stopped at the vision of Lark plunging headlong into the depths of this roiling river.

At least the rain had quit. The sky was still dark gray. Early September weather was unpredictable, and today was no exception. A cold wind blew large flakes of snow toward them as they made their way upward along a long ridge of rock boulders and red cedar. Wind and snow blew the bunchgrass within a long valley below them that terminated at the glittering North Platte. At a slow walk, he guided his horse around a sharp abutment that sheltered a smattering of cedar and scrub pines. The shack he aimed to find sat before them like a reclusive old man. With any luck, the meager biscuits, jerky, and beans inside his saddlebag were still edible. More importantly, he hoped the matches were still dry in the tinderbox. If not, there'd most likely be some inside the shack. He worried about Lark. She'd dozed and then woken with a vacant stare.

He reined his horse beside the shack just as a streak of sunlight burst from the clouds, a hopeful sign that the rain and snow had come to an end. Maybe in a day or two, they'd make their way back across the Blue or the Platte and head for the Circle H. He dismounted, lifted a sleeping Lark down, carried her to the shack, and kicked open the wooden door. Squinting, he took in the dim room. Thin shafts of sunlight pierced the small dirty window. Two cots had clearly been home to mice, the mattress feathers strewn across the floor along with pine needles and seeds. He set Lark gently down on the bunk, then went out to his horse and unstrapped the saddlebags with his goods and cartridges. He carried them and his rifle inside and settled them on the crude wooden table beside a cracked lantern just inside the door.

Looking around, he whispered, "Lordy. What am I goin' to do? Don't look down on me like that. I can hear your boomin' voice lecturing about vices and vows and oaths. And damned propriety. I expect Wade to give me some advice on stayin' alive. If not, then I'll leave it to God."

Cort sat on the floor and leaned back against the bunk where Lark slept. She felt a mite warm to the touch, but he'd bundled her with his bedroll. He'd spread his damp horse blanket and coat over the mouse-eaten mattress. The potbellied stove gave off a pleasant heat, filling the room with the scent of dry redwood and sycamore that he'd found stacked against the wall. The coffee pot was hot and he'd stirred a pan of beans with crumbled biscuits that made for a passable meal. All he needed now was for this lady to wake up so he could get some food into her.

His saddlebags sat beside him and his rifle leaned against the wall. Whether his Colt would fire, he didn't know. It had been with him in that water. Tomorrow he'd take it apart. For now, he just prayed no trouble came to their doorstep. He leaned back and closed his eyes. Thoughts of how he'd lost hold of Lark when his horse bucked made him swallow hard. He set his tin cup on the floor beside him, flipped open the leather flap of his saddlebag, reached inside, and withdrew the green ribbon. He ran it through his fingers and pressed it to his nose.

The satin softness of it was the same. There was only a vague scent of lilies, the fragrance he remembered after dancing with her in Ogallala. After long days with cattle and men, and sometimes at particularly lonely moments, he'd pulled the ribbon from his saddlebag and held it against his face and smelled her scent. He had no other rights. In fact, he shouldn't be thinking about another woman. Lark Garrin tempted him to forget his promise.

"Cort." Her whisper behind him caught him by surprise. He leaned over and jammed the ribbon back inside the bag before she saw what he held.

Lark watched as Cort swiveled onto his knees to face her. "How are you feelin'?"

She smiled at him. "Got a headache. At least I feel warm. I have clothes and food on my horse."

"Don't know where your horse got to. I'll look tomorrow. In the meantime, I put together a little food . . . such that it is. And hot coffee. Think you can sit up?"

She shoved herself to a sitting position and looked around the room. A single lantern burned low. The glow of flames in the stove and the fry pan on top all looked like they could be in their own paltry home. Their home. Silly dream. He belonged to another woman. And she'd have to leave before long. She'd spend a long time forgetting him. If she ever did.

"Sit right there. I'll dish out the grub and get you some hot brew. No sugar for the coffee."

"It all smells good. I'm hungry enough to eat a raw chicken, feathers and all."

He got up and moved toward the stove. "I won't consign you to that, pretty lady. My poor cookin' might push you toward those feathers scattered around the floor, though. Mice."

Looking around the room, she winced at the thought of varmints skittering across the floor and cots. "They're gone?"

"Probably. I promise to shoot them if they come back."

She laughed at his humor. They had nearly lost their lives and here they were, nearly out of food, maybe sick from the cold water, and he was making light little jokes. The blanket around her fell away. Startled, she realized her clothes were missing. A cotton shirt covered her upper body. Beneath the blankets, she still wore her underthings. Embarrassment shot through her. She bristled at the thought that Cort must have removed her clothing.

Before he approached with her meal, she tucked the blanket around her again. *How dare he?* She took the proffered pan and fork. Then he handed her a tin cup filled with strong-smelling coffee. She ate a few bites, chewing slowly, and looked up to see him staring at her, his arms crossed.

"Where are my clothes?" she asked, hating the sound of her own smugness.

"You were soaked. Your clothes were soaked. I did what I had to do to keep you from getting sick. I had one spare shirt that was reasonably dry. Your horse is missing so I had no way to figure out if you even brought spare clothes. And I doubt they'd be dry. Your clothes are over on a chair near the stove."

She still felt mortified, but his explanation was acceptable. Her priggish attitude wasn't like her. "The food is good. Thank you. For everything. I'm sorry I snapped at you. I'm not used to having a man undress me."

He turned enough to drag up a chair and straddled it while she sipped the hot coffee. "I surely am glad you aren't used to a man undressing you."

"I'm sure you did what you had to do. Thank you."

"As long as you're lookin' better, this might be a good time for an explanation."

"Explanation?"

"Why were you out there? And in the middle of a river trying to fish out a calf."

"Oh, that."

"Yes, *that.*"

She set her cup on the floor. The plate still lay in her lap. His blue-gray eyes were steady, unwavering. "Damon came riding in during the storm. The wind and rain rattled the windows and we thought the house would shake apart. We were so worried about the men. Damon told us Zeke was missing and that you were staying out searching for him. Damon said about ten others had gotten the word to get back to the homestead and the rest were probably holed up. He'd found Zeke's horse dead but no sign of Zeke."

Cort crossed his arms and sighed. "All right. I still don't see why you were out there."

"At first, Sienna wanted to come looking for you and Zeke. She's so sick, Cort."

"I know. And I don't know what to do about that. Except give her more medicine and have you three women lookin' in on her."

She nodded. "I wouldn't let her leave. Nita, Theresa, and I all agreed to sit on her if need be. Still, I wanted to help find Zeke."

"Jesus Christ. What did you think any of you could do? Even if you found Zeke?"

She shrugged, knowing he was right. "I guess I didn't think it through. But I am a good rider. I figured I could at least try to find Zeke and maybe bring him back on my horse. And chase some cows away from the river."

Cort threw his head back and pinched his nose, then looked in her direction again. "You took a helluva big risk, lady. Look where it got you. And me. I'll give you credit for guts."

"I'm sorry for the trouble I caused."

"If I hadn't come along and seen you . . . I don't think I would ever have gotten over that."

Clutching the blanket around her, she stood, her legs trembling with the exertion. "Give me the damned plate," he said. "You stay on that cot. You need to rest up."

Shakily, she walked to the table and set her plate and cup down before turning to face him. "I needed to see if I can walk." She paused, then breathed, "I'm indebted."

His face hardened under his scruffy beard. His straight back told her he was about to lecture. His eyes searched hers. What else did he want from her?

"I need to know something. Straight out. Explain how you got the knife mark."

She ran her fingers over the place that had bled, crusted, and healed as best it would. She figured the salve had done all it could. The memory of the night on the riverboat still haunted her. Sometimes she woke in chills, soaked in her own sweat, feeling the pain of the blade. And the shame that went even deeper.

She sat on the nearest chair and stared at her outstretched hands against the scarred wood table. "My ma died. She was well educated and taught me. My pa was an incorrigible gambler. He lost more than he ever won. Spent the money Ma inherited from her parents in Ohio. After that, he took on work with a riverboat on the Mississippi and the Missouri Rivers. As long as Ma was there, it wasn't so bad. Then she took sick with pneumonia and died. Pa stayed on, gambling down to his last dollar. I worked in the riverboat kitchen, making enough money to feed us and cover his losses. One night, Pa lost big. To an outlaw."

She swiped tears from her cheek. He moved near enough to place his hands on her shoulders, and with a squeeze, encouraged her to go on.

"He lost and had nothing to pay up with. Except me." She choked the admission from her taut throat.

Suddenly his hands left her and he hunkered down beside her, waiting. Fathomless eyes locked with hers. What could she tell that gaze but the truth? "He lost to a notorious gambler and thief. Will Cardin."

Still he said nothing. There was a glint in his eyes. They looked more gray than blue and his hands clenched and unclenched beside him. "Cardin and three others burst through our unlocked door. He was wearing a gun on his hip. I tried to run. He caught me. Told me I belonged to him and he was going to take his due. In time. He warned me to get off when the *Memphis Queen* docked in Memphis in three days. He said that if I wasn't there, he'd hunt me until he found me. When he held a knife in front of my face, I tried to scream. They held me down. Stuffed handkerchiefs into my mouth while I struggled. The pain was so vile, so brutal. I woke with blood on my face and over my neck."

She broke down for a moment then, unable to hold back a sob. Cort stood abruptly, his hands braced flat on the table, head bent, shoulders hunched. Lark got hold of herself and continued. "I kept thinking, where is Pa? Why did he sell me?

Why isn't he here helping me? No one came. The steel of the blade glittered in the light from the lamps on the wall. Ever so slowly, it touched my skin. I held still like he told me. The pain of it. I wanted to retch. I wanted to draw breath.

"After they left, I lay there for a time. I felt my own blood running down my neck. I knew I had to get up and stop the bleeding or I'd die. I didn't want to die. I just wanted to stop the bleeding and run. And hide."

Cort's hoarse voice cut through her sobs. "Cardin didn't come back. And you got off the boat before Memphis. He's looking for you. That's why you fainted in Ogallala. He was there. You saw him."

She nodded. He lifted her from the chair. Holding her close, he lowered her to the bunk and followed, taking her quaking frame against his. He held her face and pressed his mouth against her trembling lips. "Shh. He won't touch you. Because he just ran into a faster gun. And I promise you, I'll kill him for this."

"Don't go after him. Leave it be. If something happened to you because of me, I wouldn't live with that. I don't want you to get into trouble."

"Let me do the worryin'."

Cort touched her scar gently. Then he kissed the scar, over and over again. She should tell him to stop. Instead, her arms wrapped around his neck.

Chapter 11
Impossible Promise

His mouth feathered the ridge of her jaw, touching the narrow brand with his tongue. His warm breath moved higher, over her cheek. When his mouth left her, his eyes looked into hers with desperate pleading. Tick. Tick. Tick. The beating of time and the distance between the stars arced between them, sending them closer. His heart pounded against her, sending warning of the edge of a nameless place. He slanted his lips over hers. The touch was soft and warm. His tongue lined her mouth until she opened to his entreaty.

Against her mouth, she heard a low growl. His tongue explored while hers danced to the silent music that lovers knew. The newness of this intimacy felt pure yet dangerous. The fear she held within a dark place remained locked away. Instead, she gave him leave to be her teacher, exploring with his gentle search, enticing her to want more. Mindless, she lifted one hand and twisted his hair between her fingers. His hands pushed the blanket further from her shoulders and his fingers released the shirt buttons far enough to reveal the curves of her breast.

An unsettling moan came from deep within his throat. Abruptly, he set her back from him, his hungry eyes tracing her mouth where moments before his lips had been. He held her arms in a strong grip, seeming undecided. Fighting some inner contradiction. She saw desperation in his eyes. He gulped and swallowed. When his arms dropped to his sides, he stood and took a step back from her.

"Cort?" she whispered. "What is it? Me?"

"Not you. Not ever, sweetheart. What I felt just now is something very rare. I don't know how to handle what's between us. And if I even have a right."

"You're a married man. Guess that means I'm about as low as a common—"

His finger touched her mouth. "Don't say it. Don't ever say that." His voice was hoarse and his lips formed a thin line. He dropped his hand away from her face.

"I'm sorry. We better get some sleep. I promise that we'll figure this out." He sighed. Those blue-gray eyes studied her. "This was not your fault. We both know we've been fighting this thing between us. I'm married and I've given my sacred oath to live up to the *deal.* I don't know what will happen. I do know I can't let you go. Some way I'll make this right."

"How can marriage be a deal, Cort? Isn't there supposed to be love?"

He snorted. "Love is for folks who don't have a lot to answer for. I'm paying for mistakes I've made. And I hope to God I can one day show you what I feel for you. Protecting you from Will Cardin . . . that's something I can do. For now."

She stood and went to pick up her dry clothes. "I won't let you. I'll leave the ranch before I'll let you get into trouble over me."

In one step, he yanked her around. The cold in his eyes and the hard lines of his face told her he was determined to have it his way. "You'll do no such thing. Even if I have to set one of my men watching you every minute to keep you safe. As to my marriage, Sienna is a good woman who needed a good foreman. That's what she got. A *foreman.* She's very sick. If I could find a doctor to keep her alive, I'd move heaven and Earth to do it. But there is no doctor alive who'll save her or make me think of her as a wife. If you ever left, I'd break into thousands of pieces. I want you. No one else. But I can't have you. Not now. Give me a chance."

She touched his face with two fingers and nodded. "Best we both get some sleep. I'll stay on for Sienna's sake. For now."

His eyes narrowed but he said nothing else. They both sank into wordless quiet with only the hiss of burning wood as they settled into an uneasy night. He left to check the horses and his personals. Then he waited at the door while she took care of her private business. She lay down, set her boots beside the bed, and pulled the blanket over her. The boy's pants and shirt she'd worn were damp but not soaked. Lying on her side, she watched through the dark as lantern light played over Cort's handsome features while he worked at the table.

Like a surgeon, his skilled hands unbolted parts of his Colt while he used a cloth to wipe it down. Clanking, clinking, and the distinct clicking of the gun hammer reminded her of both his skill and his burden. Once in a while, he glanced in her direction. She knew when he paused that he watched her. Still, he said nothing. Instead, he kept his eyes and hands busy. Her gaze took in the pleasure of him until she fell into a restless sleep.

Cort was glad the two guns seemed in fair shape after being in a river. After he got them dismantled and cleaned, he'd feel a lot better about depending on them. If he didn't have them, he and Lark would be in trouble come morning when he needed to find some game. That river wasn't about to recede for a few days. Tomorrow he'd ride out and see if he could locate a safe crossing. His men would be out looking for them. He could only hope they'd also found Zeke alive.

If he didn't get Lark back to the ranch soon, he'd go crazy. He'd already crossed the line. Things might get a whole lot worse if he was near her much longer. Damned if he'd allow her to leave without a helluva fight. If Cardin found her outside of Cort's protection, he'd take a particularly slow time killing her. He most likely figured she'd double-crossed him, which is why he was in Ogallala in the first place.

Cort lay on what was left of the second feather mattress, his duster serving as his bedding. A sliver of light gleamed through the window on the other side of the room. Dark clouds crossed the moon and the light faded. The storm was passing. The crackle of the embers and Lark's soft breathing were the only sounds. Except for his thumping heart in his ears.

He didn't know how much time had passed when he heard a whimper. He lifted his head and saw Lark thrashing beneath the horse blanket. Her arms reached upward and she screamed. "No! No!"

Cort tossed his coat aside, got up, and crossed to her in three long strides. He took her in his arms and held her shaking form against him, dismissing niggling warnings. To hell with propriety. Smoothing her tousled hair, he crooned, "Shh. Lark. You're having a bad dream. You're safe."

Her eyes stared into his with a blankness that alarmed him. The gold in them sparkled in the dim light, revealing unshed tears, while her face looked pale with fear. A fear he didn't know how to fight for her. At this moment, she was a child while her body was every bit woman. God help him. He wanted this woman all to himself.

What she had revealed about what Cardin had done left him shattered. But the hardened part of him filled with bloodlust. No matter how long it took, he'd seek revenge. Some men needed killing. And the killing of Will Cardin consumed him. Followed second by her gambler father who'd sold his own daughter to pay a gambling debt.

"You're safe. I won't hurt you. No one will hurt you," he muttered as she clutched his shirt.

Her head rested against his chest while he fitted her across his lap, running his hand over her silky hair. A soft sob and hiccup punctured his heart. After a time, she lifted her head and their breaths mingled.

She groaned and closed her eyes. "I'm sorry. I woke you up. The knife. His hands held me down. I couldn't breathe. I fought. I screamed."

The hell she kept living through. The nightmares of his time in prison didn't come close to what she'd suffered at Will Cardin's hands. Cortland Enders would be coming for that monster. "I know you did. But it's over."

Her fingers traced the curves of his face, reminding him that his scruff must make him look like the outlaw inside the man he was now. If she knew all that he'd been and done, she'd run from him. She deserved to know.

"I have a pretty good idea of what I look like," he said. "Sorry."

"You're a very handsome man, with or without your beard."

"If you had any sense, you'd slap me for touching you. For holding you. For wanting you."

He made out her soft smile. "I'm not running. Besides, there's no place to go."

"I won't take advantage of you, pretty lady."

"That's part of why I care so much for you. I see beyond the man you want everyone else to see."

"Yeah? What do you think you see?"

"A man who suffered. A lonely man who hides behind a toughness that suits him. But he keeps everyone at a distance. Skilled with that gun but honorable. A deep kindness lives inside. You are a man with a deep capacity to care."

He leaned back and let his hands drop away from her. *Love.* She'd carefully avoided that word. Fool that he was, he wanted to hear her say it. Because he loved her.

"I promise you my heart. No matter what happens," he breathed.

Her head tilted and she lifted her hand to touch his face. He grabbed it and held it away. "Best we keep some distance. If you think you're all right now, I best go back to my bunk."

"Cort. You admitted you want me. I've lived in fear for so long, I never knew how lonely that made me until now. For the first time, I don't feel alone. I'm a jealous woman, though."

He snorted. His finger ran over her pursed lips before he could call it back. "Jealous of?"

Tick. Tick. Tick. Time froze like shards of ice suspended between them. The sun would rise tomorrow and they'd still have this chasm that neither could cross.

"Sienna. She's your wife. I like her very much. I hate the pain she endures. Still, I'm filled with jealousy that she can have you beside her at night."

He heaved in a long breath. Men didn't talk about bed partners. Men didn't disclose intimacy. But they were both starved for honesty and trapped by circumstance within a glimmer of hope.

"Been an outlaw, in prison, and involved in things you wouldn't want to know. Got drunk and rowdy plenty of times. Prison was humiliating. That changed me. Maybe not for the good. Except that I don't ever want to go back. I've wound up in bed with a sour smelling whore many a time. I'm no preacher, Lark. I just want you to know what kind of man I was. I hope I've changed."

Those small hands of hers covered her ears. He grasped her wrists. "Sienna is my wife on paper. *Paper.* I must have said the words to love, honor, and obey in a room with witnesses. The words meant nothing. Gave my promise I had no choice but to make, else I'd be in prison serving three years. Sienna's persuasive. She wields power and usually gets what she wants.

She somehow got the judge to be lenient enough to let me serve my time working the ranch.

"The marriage, as she said, is an insurance that I would stay on even after she passes. As her husband, I now control the ranch. Never figured she'd want to give up control. Every inch of the place is mine, but I'd walk away if Sienna got well. Since she wouldn't have me run a ranch from the bunkhouse, and she minds gossips, well . . . I had to move into the house for appearances."

He stopped. Her shaking hands covered her eyes, her head tilted downward. He'd said too much. He'd hurt her. But maybe now she'd be more willing to reveal more of herself.

"Tell me why you were about to be sent back to prison. What did you do?"

"Another time. Another place. I might tell you."

He felt her watching him as he padded across the room toward his bunk. Boots and socks draped beside the warm stove where her own jacket and boots lay drying. He stretched out and the room grew silent except for a pop of the burning wood. She held his gaze even in the shadows as he watched her from across the room. Indecision washed over her face. He could guess her thoughts. If she crossed the room, she would be a fallen woman. Betraying a dying woman's trust. But she wanted just this one moment. Just a sliver of happiness.

Like a wraith, she stood and moved toward him, one careful step after another. He swung his legs over the edge of the bunk. His hands clutched the edge and he looked up into her eyes as she knelt before him, her hands running over his legs.

"Damn it, woman. You make it hard to be honorable." His voice was raw. Sometimes right versus wrong no longer mattered.

"I've never been with a man. Instead, I've just survived. Loneliness is a sorry way to live. I have no right to ask. God forgive me. Give me something to take to my grave."

"Jesus Christ. I've fought this thing for too long. If what we do here is wrong, then I'll pay for it. Not you. No talk of graves. You will live. And so will I."

She unbuttoned her damp blue shirt. He watched every motion of her fingers with a kind of hunger. "Are you sure? Be damned sure, Lark. Because I might not be able to stop."

"I'm sure."

Cort felt fire burn from his head to his heels. Mercy wasn't going to call him back to sanity. Leaning forward, he tugged the rest of her buttons free. Then he stood and held her in his arms as his mouth settled over hers in a soft whisper, followed with forceful demand. Shudders rippled through her under his hands. Slanting his mouth, he implored and taught. When she opened her lips, his tongue made hot forays. Sweat rolled down the center of his back. His manhood prodded, and where he touched, he felt her uncertainty.

When his mouth returned to her jaw, he planted tender kisses over the place that would forever be a reminder of her torment. And the tormenter. His mouth foraged along her throat while his hands folded the shirt off her shoulders. Her soft skin reminded him of the silk ribbon he carried with him. Finally, he released her, sinking downward to run his mouth over her soft mounds. A camisole did little to hide the dark nipples beneath the lacy confection. Dragging the lace ever downward, his mouth followed, feathering the hard buds, so moist and sweet that he could take them all night.

Lark's mewling burst through his raging hot senses, almost destroying his last bit of consciousness. He lifted his head, and her hazy green-brown eyes stared into his soul, searching. He read more than her hesitation. He viewed the tapestry of all of her innocence. He'd taken her to a place where she'd never been, reminding himself that for now, he couldn't keep her there. Still, he faltered.

He took her areolas into his mouth, suckling each with urgency. Her fingers twined in his hair as he bent to take more. His hardness pressed, now dangerously close to erupting. On the verge of taking her, one last shred of decency still lurked inside. He latched onto it, grasping her arms and setting her back from him while his heart thundered.

"Cort? What's wrong?" she cried.

"Me. I'm wrong, sweetheart." He dragged air into his lungs. Gently, he tugged her camisole downward to cover her heaving chest. Her breathing slowed. Her denim pants pooled around her bare feet where he'd dragged them. "Get dressed," he ordered.

He hadn't meant to sound harsh. At this moment, he was angry with himself for letting this happen. Twice in one night. She leaned downward to grasp her pants while he walked to the other side of the room, his back to her. The last thing he needed to do was scare her with the sight of him. "I'll be outside a few minutes. Checking the horse."

He picked up his coat and paused at the doorway. "This was wrong. No matter how we might want this, I'm still married. Until I'm not, I have no right to make this thing between us tawdry. Both of us would have to live the rest of our lives with that. I'm not willing to have either of us do that. You know I'm right."

Behind him, he heard the rustle of cloth. When he closed the door, he sucked in long drafts of cold night air. As badly as he wanted her, the last thread of integrity in his sorry conscience still left an unfilled hole in his heart. He loved her. There was nothing else to say.

CHAPTER 12
DISTANT STARS

Leaning back against the side of the building, he stared up at the glimmering stars. The distance between those orbs seemed so close, but they were so far apart. Much like he and Lark. *Stars.* The storm had passed. The sky was clear. Come morning, he'd hunt around for her horse and check the river crossing.

The door opened, and he heard her footfalls along the broken porch. They paused, and he imagined she peered into the darkness looking for him. He'd bet she had no idea why he needed the cold air. The woman was pure as new snow.

"Cort?"

He closed his eyes and decided he'd best face her now as later. Stiffly, he walked around the corner and found her staring into the night sky. Without looking toward him, her voice cut through the silence. "The storm is over."

Ordinary comment. The storm between them wouldn't leave as easily. "I'll look for your horse and check the river come first light. We might not get back across till the following day. I can sleep outside."

Her head turned. Anger flared in her fiery eyes and tilted chin. Taking the steps to be near her, he thought better of it and paused. "I don't know what to say. We've gone too far, Lark. I'll take full blame and promise it won't happen again."

"I'm ashamed that I . . . Sienna. She's your wife. I have to keep that in my head. And leave as soon as it can be arranged."

"Lark. For Christ's sake. If you leave the ranch, I can't keep you safe from Will Cardin. I'd never know if he found you. I'd die inside. You can't leave. Be reasonable."

"What do you propose? Stop loving each other?"

Cort swallowed a growl. *Love.* She'd said it. The word that hung between them. Forgetting the warning bells in his head, he moved closer and wrapped her in his arms, warming her against the chill of the night. His trembling fingers combed through her love-tousled hair.

"If I stopped loving you . . . I might as well give up living. You make me feel worthy. Eventually, things will be different. Once I serve my time. Sienna deserves my loyalty until the end. I owe her. I hope she lives. And if she does, I'll ask her for a divorce. None of this will be easy on any of us. I think she'd want you and I to marry as soon as the end comes. As unfair as all of this is, we have to stay away from each other. Come spring, I'll be away most of the time on roundup. And by then . . ." He found himself unable to say anything about Sienna's inevitable death.

She drew in a shuddering breath against his chest and nodded. When she leaned away from him, her mouth juddered with a half-hearted smile. "Will you get upset if one of the cowhands talks with me? They're just trying to be helpful and polite. I have no interest in any man but one."

"Hell, yes, I'll be upset. If one of them so much as tries to sneak a kiss, I'd—"

"Fire him," she finished.

She had him there. He'd already fired Mason, a perfectly good drover. And he could use him back again. "I'll set the men straight. And most of my men are upright. One or two don't know the meaning of polite. But you're off limits. Besides, I don't want you giving them the wrong impression. That can cause more trouble."

"I'm not a flirt, Cort. And I have an outlaw after me. I don't want anyone caught in the middle of that."

He loosed his hold on her and marched to the doorway. Suddenly he slammed his fist into the damp wood.

"Cort! Oh, my God! Let me look at your hand."

"It's fine," he growled between clenched teeth. "Go on in. Once you're settled on your bunk, I'll come in and stay in my own. From now on, I'll keep my distance."

He listened as she moved about inside the shack and he ran his fingers over his scruffy face. The day he helped that whore and shot a hole in Mark Tenner's arm, his life caved in. The only saving graces were that the kid had lived and Sienna had influence with the judge. Otherwise, he might have been hung. Of all people to have tangled with, he'd shot the son of a prominent Nebraska legislator, Calvin Tenner. No one understood that he easily could have killed Mark, but he'd pulled his shot, wounding him instead.

Once he was back on his bunk, his stare fell again on the woman at the other side of the room. Luck was not in their favor. Once he found Will Cardin, he'd kill him. At least she'd be free of that threat until he could make her his wife.

Sienna sat beside her dearest friend and watched him scowl at the bowl of soup. "Do you need help with that spoon, Zeke?"

"Rather have some beef. Ain't never gonna get outta this bed if all I eat is soup."

Crotchety, cantankerous old fool. Zeke had nearly been killed out there, dazed and wandering around for days before Tangle and Adoeete found him. "Doc says you can have meat in a couple more days. In the meantime, I'll sit here and badger you."

Zeke lifted a spoonful of liquid to his mouth and swallowed with a grimace. "You win. Now, when you goin' to tell me what they found out about Cort and Miss Garrin."

"They couldn't pick up much of a trail. Rain washed everything away. Lark went out lookin' for you and must've decided to cross the Blue River. Never heard of it getting so bad. My horse's prints were found near a cottonwood grove by the damned river. No sign of the horse. I told her not to go into that river."

Zeke dropped his spoon and it clattered on the tray. "You tellin' me you knew she was out there?"

"Stopped me from goin' out there. Those three women threatened to sit on me if I tried. So, I gave in to her insistence. Much as I hate to admit it. Should never have let any of us go out there. Lark feels she has a lot to prove. Figured she'd be back in a short time once she figured it was no use lookin' in the storm. She is stubborn."

"Like you. Wade and you were a pair, that's for sure."

Wade's name always brought pain to her heart. And the damned pain in her stomach was getting worse. Zeke reached across the blanket and grasped her hand in his work-roughened leathery palm. "I'm glad you didn't go out there. Never saw so much rain and that river was roaring. Thought I was in one of those eastern hurricanes."

"None of you should've been out there. Didn't know it would blow like it did, else I'd have stopped you."

"Sienna. We've known each other since Wade and me first came out here together with practically nothin'. You don't need to look out for me. I'm tough as old boots."

"I thought they'd ride in with your body tied over a horse. I couldn't bear that."

"Don't worry about an old man like me. You got more important things to think about."

"Sorry about your horse. Tangle found him with a broken leg. You shot him." *Zeke. Dear Zeke. I loved you but Wade held my heart. Choosing was so hard.*

"Best horse I ever had. When he came down on my leg, I didn't know if I'd be able to yank free. Holed up as long as I could between some rocks. Then I decided to try bracing my leg with a crooked branch I found. Walkin' was like having the devil's pitchfork in my leg."

"At least you're alive. Now we got all the men out lookin' for Cort and Lark."

"Knew you'd get around to them. You don't fool me, Sienna. There ain't a drop of love between you and Cort. Course, I figure you know what you're doin'."

"You're too nosy for your own good, Zeke. I'm worried about Cort and Lark like I'd be worried about you or anyone else works for me."

"That Lark is young and a looker. I got eyes. Think you do, too."

She slid her hand from his and stood. When she looked out the window at the barn and corral, she noticed a few horses were tied to a rail. Smoke drifted from the chimney in the cookhouse. She sighed, keeping her back straight. His eyes were on her and she knew he waited for something more than her silence.

"I'm old enough to be his mother. You know damned well I married him to keep him here. And he'll take over when I'm gone. You and I know I won't be here for his three-year term. This ranch needs a firm hand and an iron fist. And younger blood. The law says the place belongs to him as my husband. I hope they don't bother him when I'm gone."

"He's also a fast gun, and that got him into more trouble than you bargained for. You or Wade. What makes you think he'll change? God, Sienna. He's unpredictable."

"Thought you liked him."

"Oh, I like him. One of the smartest men I've ever met. Knows how to keep the finances goin'. Man knows horses and cattle. Best of all, everybody respects him. Still, he manages to get into trouble. Already fired Mason for no good reason. We need all the hands we can get."

"What you're thinking is, he'll hightail it before I'm cold in the grave."

"Didn't say that. I said he's smart. Why would he walk away from the Circle H? He's got Lark on his mind. And you damned well know it. And we don't know what's goin' on in her pretty head. I'm worried that she's spooked, and he might follow her and get himself into more trouble."

"Zeke. I'm in pain and takin' drugs. But I have my eyes and ears. He calls her name in his sleep."

"Jesus. Don't want to hear about what goes on in your bedroom."

"Nothing goes on. How would it look for my husband to live in the bunkhouse? I won't have folks talking about me and him after I die. Now that's between you and me. He keeps to the floor. More often now he sleeps in a room down the hallway."

"You know me better. I ain't no gossipy old biddy."

"Yes, I do know you. Just so you know, that lawyer drew up papers to transfer the deed to Cort at my death. Cort is more a son to Wade and me than anything else. You have a place here and land to build on, too. I made sure of that. And a steady income."

"Come here, lady." Sienna scooted closer to the bed. That fatherly tone usually meant a lecture. "Thanks for that. I want to live out my days here. Tell me the truth. How long does the doc say you got left?"

"He gives me a month at most. I'm ready. The pain is worse every day."

"I see it in your eyes and face. And you're too damned skinny."

"Nothin' left to do about that." Drawing in a shuddering

breath, she stood and lifted the tray. "Guess I better see if I can round up a horse and go out lookin'. It doesn't feel right sittin' around here."

"Don't you dare. Don't want to come lookin' for you on this bum leg."

"Zeke. Would you sit around waitin' to die or would you get on a horse whenever you could while there was still time?"

A hint of a smile beneath his scruffy beard reminded her of all the years they'd teased each other. "You already know the answer to that, Mrs. Harris. Wade was a damned lucky man."

Dull light on her face forced her sleepy eyes open. Dawn. She had lain awake half the night, staring at the restless form on the other side of the room. How she wished she could have curled beside him and felt his arms wrapped around her. Betrayal tasted bitter this morning. The memory of his hands and mouth on her skin sent tremors through her. Thinking about his manhood pressed against her shook her. And her guilt swamped her, making her feel more like a harlot.

Soft breathing from his bunk told her he was sound asleep. Deciding she'd get the stove going to set on the coffee, she swung her legs to the floor. Just as she bent over the woodpile, she heard the nickers of several horses outside. Glancing in Cort's direction, she noticed his revolver lying on the floor near his hand. His rifle leaned against the wall. Quietly, she padded to the dust-covered window. Using her elbow, she rubbed away some of the grit. What she saw startled her, and a cry lodged in her throat.

Eight men on painted horses. Two wore buffalo robes while the others wore buckskin pants. Bare chested and bedecked with amulets, they were handsome dark-skinned Indians. Their scalp locks were curved backward from their heads, decorated with colorful feathers and beads. Lark had never been so close to Indians. They stared in her direction. Would they attack? Then she spied Sienna's horse and saddle, the reins held by an older man who sat in front of the others. Mesmerized, she didn't know whether to stand still or scream.

"What is it?" Cort's voice cut through the air.

"Indians." She squeaked the word as she stepped back from the window.

Cort picked up his gun and took her place, squinting into the dull morning light. "Pawnee. We might be in luck. They're the ones I helped out on the way back from Ogallala. Gave them leave to cut out a couple cows from our herd. Stay here. Don't want them to get the idea that I'd trade you for that buckskin."

After he opened the door and went outside, she lifted his rifle and held it so tightly, she thought it would snap between her hands. Her feet planted to the floor like they'd grown roots. Their voices carried through the window glass. Cort apparently knew what the Indians were saying because he replied in some kind of gibberish language. There was friendly laughter. Horses moved around and nickered. Just what was Cort talking about? Trading?

Finally, she peeked from the window again and saw Cort holding the reins of her horse. One of the younger warriors, his face painted, handed down a burlap bag. Cort stepped back and nodded. The Indians turned their mounts and left as silently as they had come, vanishing into the trees like wind through grass. Cort led the buckskin to the shed before he ambled back to the door.

When he stepped inside, he held up the sack in one hand. He set it on the table and then he took the rifle from her grip. "They're gone. You won't need this."

"What did they want?"

"Well, nothin'. They recognized me and gave me back your horse they'd found wandering around. They saw the buckskin as fair trade for the beef. Couldn't argue with that reasoning. Now that we have your horse, we can eat the bread and dried meat they gave me before we get outta here. Appreciate it if you'd make some coffee while I check on the horses and have a look around. Make sure the Pawnee left."

"They gave us food?"

"Nothing is for nothing with most of the Indians. They wanted to trade the horse for you, until I reminded them of the cows they took. Then they wanted to trade food for you. After some negotiating, I was able to come to terms."

Cort grinned at her stunned expression. She touched her chest and her face flushed. "I told them to take another cow in exchange for the food," he said. "Not a good deal. But I'd have to be starving to trade you for a sack of victuals."

When his joking finally sank in, she looked around the room. Before she could throw her boot at him, he'd already ducked out of the door, laughing.

They set out toward the river late that afternoon. He hoped he'd be able to get them across because another night sleeping near her would exhaust his willpower. They had enough food to see them through another night, since he'd been able to bargain for the damp edibles that Lark had brought along with her. With the Indians nearby, he had no plans to leave her alone to fend for herself while he hunted. A rangy bunch, the Pawnee looked to be heading somewhere to escape the Army's push toward Oklahoma. If he had to guess, they'd probably head north into Sioux country.

After a few hours of riding along the river, he found a possible cut that might allow them safe traversing. "Stay here while I check this out. Do not follow me. That's an order."

He didn't wait to hear her reply. Instead, he nudged Lincoln into the fast-running water. Lincoln found his footing and easily emerged on the far side, climbing the steep bank with little problem. When Cort turned to face Lark, he waved his hat. "Start across. If I see you in trouble, I'll be out there. Just take it slow and hang on tight."

Her mouth drew taut and she surveyed the water while she hesitated. Cort saw her fear. "Stay there. I'll come get you and lead Butter behind."

"No. I can do it," she shouted.

Before he had time to give a second thought to her response, she kicked her horse. The animal hesitated, trying to back away. There was only one thing to do. He kicked Lincoln into a plunge and urged the animal across, his boots and pants soaked through in the high water. Once he met her, he sidled up beside her and reached for her, seating her in the fork of his saddle while he slid back to accommodate her.

He took up the reins of the scared buckskin and tugged the animal forward, all the while gripping his own horse's reins with one hand. Cradling Lark between his arms, her bottom pressed against him, reminding him that he had better return her to the ranch pretty quick. Otherwise, he might as well rip his agreement with Sienna in half and finish his term in prison. Because he wouldn't keep away from Lark. As it was, he planned to be out on the range a lot.

By the time they'd dismounted and nibbled a few pieces of jerky, they heard pounding hooves approaching. He lifted his rifle and waited. Lark took her own rifle from the boot of the buckskin's saddle and stood beside him, squaring the sight, not knowing it wouldn't fire. Cort hadn't taken time to clean and dry her weapon. From this distance, the approaching riders might be his own ranch hands, or they might not. Cort Enders took no chances.

Chapter 13
Discovered

The riders got close enough so Cort and Lark recognized the drawn faces of the men, along with Sienna, and lowered their guns. Sienna caught the quick look of despair and relief that passed between Lark and Cort. The trademark signs of guilt were written on Lark's face. Clearly, they weren't just friends. A little niggle of jealousy circled around in Sienna's head until it dawned on her that Lark was the key to keeping Cort on the Circle H. Love was more powerful than the threat of the law. And those two loved each other, whether they'd figured it out yet or not. And she had no intention of standing in their way.

"Well, well. So you found our wayward Miss Garrin. Glad to see you both found each other. Not one of us got much sleep."

Sienna waited. Cort reached for Lark's rifle, still clutched in her hands.

"Cort? Perhaps you can tell us what happened?" Sienna pressed.

"She ran into a little trouble with the river. Mind tellin' me if you found Zeke? I didn't find him on the other side of the river."

"Tangle, Cane, and Billy found him in a draw near the east side. He'd been thrown and broke a leg. He's at the ranch healin' and grouchy enough that I'd like to strap him on a horse and send him lookin' for cattle. Except he'd be lookin' for you two. Both of you worried us sick."

From the looks of Lark's disheveled clothes and filthy boots, she had certainly been in the river. Exactly where she shouldn't have been. Lark lifted her chin and stepped forward, her pants and shirt streaked with mud and her hair in wild tangles, but looking all the while like a poised, well-bred woman beneath that grime. "This wasn't Cort's fault. I was looking for Zeke when I drew up near the edge of the river. I heard bellowing and splashing. I saw a calf struggling in the middle, her mama bawling at the riverbank. I decided to try to drag the poor thing to safety. I had hold of that slippery neck but the calf kicked and my horse reared and when I grabbed—"

"You went into the river," Sienna finished.

Cort stepped forward. In the tick of his jaw, Sienna read his protectiveness. He would defend Lark to his death. Darned if she didn't admire him for that.

"When I heard the commotion, thanks to her screaming and the cow bawling, I saw her pitch forward into the river. She nearly drowned. I went in and was able to drag her up to my saddle. The current was so strong that my horse balked. There was no way in hell I'd watch her die in that river."

Sienna noted her husband's defiant chin and pursed lips. She turned her attention to the bedraggled woman beside him. "I'm sorry I caused all this trouble," Lark said. "I meant to help out. Guess I have a lot to learn. I'll understand if you feel you need to let me go."

Sienna hadn't expected that kind of apology but it came at the right moment. Lark was trying to please everyone. After all, Sienna had come to this ranch and made her share of mistakes. Luckily, Wade was understanding. And in love.

"Like hell you're goin' anywhere. I have a say in this," Cort growled between his clenched teeth.

"From where I'm sitting up here on my horse, you both look like you could use a cleanup and some food. Zeke will be up and around in a month or two on his crutches. No one died, except maybe the calf. And Zeke's horse. That's all that's important. Mount up so we can get back to the ranch house before more of our men come lookin' for us."

The ride back was fairly quiet. Cort rode beside his wife as she clutched her saddle horn, leaning forward with pain. A pain that had to be agonizing. When he twisted in the saddle to look for Lark, he found her riding beside Tangle, her eyes unreadable.

He guessed Sienna had figured out the feelings between him and Lark. Cheating on a wife was something he'd never consider. He'd been brought up decent. From now on, he'd stay in the saddle and work himself hard enough to keep Lark out of his mind. Staying away from her was going to be hard but he'd reach inside what was left of his tattered honor and do what was right.

Cort glanced at his wife's pain-filled face while they rode slowly beside each other, the creaking of saddles the only sound. "I'm sorry, Sienna."

She looked toward him. "Sorry for what? Saving a woman's life is what I'd hope a respectable man would do. It's what Wade would do."

He nodded and tugged his hat brim. "You know what I mean. About lettin' my feelings out. I'll abide by our vows. Nothin' happened that you have to worry about." Her reference to Wade niggled. He was not Wade.

They pulled up their horses and Cort waved the others to move on without them. Lincoln shook his head at stopping. Once the troupe had passed beyond earshot, Cort sighed. "Maybe we ought to put our cards on the table."

"Simple from my standpoint. I've seen how you look at her. We both know this isn't an ordinary marriage, Cort. I never expected you to stop thinking about other women, but you know how I feel about propriety. If the men think you're using me or sleeping with her, not only will you lose their respect . . . well . . . let's just say that I'd be disappointed."

"Don't you think I've already given that some thought? And just for the record, nothin' got out of hand last night between Lark and me. Not that I didn't want to have her. I just can't go against what I know is right. Still, this agreement between us is eating me."

"You're a damned sight better off here than in prison. Besides, you and I both know I'm not long for the world. Once I'm gone, you and Lark can carry on. Build a life right here. I'm betting the two of you will turn this ranch into a place to envy. In the meantime, you need to cool down and bide your time."

"Fair enough. I respect you, Sienna. I don't wish you to die. If I could figure out a cure or find the right doctor, I'd do it. I hope you know that."

"I know. That's why I respect you."

"We better catch up with the others. Anything else happen while I was gone?"

"That new fellow you hired on. Clay Brant. I talked with him. Seems a bit slick for my liking. But he's working hard. Billy said he'd seen him at the saloon in Ogallala hanging with Mason Lanning."

"Interesting. I fired Lanning."

"Thought you liked Mason. What happened?"

"Guess I was mad at him."

"I guess he must've shown interest in Lark. At least that's what Zeke says."

"Zeke needs to mind his own business," Cort snapped.

"Maybe you'll be able to hire Mason back if you eat crow?"

"I'm not partial to crow." Cort grinned and caught Sienna's smile.

"No. I guess you're not. Well, I suppose you can figure out how this Brant fellow works out. In the meantime, I expect you to see what we can do about our lost cattle. And find more ranch hands."

"Yep. Boss lady."

They laughed as they nudged their horses into a faster pace. Cort winced at how hard Sienna clung to the saddle while she held a hand to her side. She wasn't the kind of woman who'd give up easy. For certain, this was her last ride.

The next morning, Lark found herself sitting alone in the dining room. Theresa had set out a serving of biscuits and gravy alongside the pot of coffee on the sideboard. Sun streamed in through the window. She'd decided to wait out the usual breakfast held with Cort and Sienna until everyone had gone their own way. Facing the husband and wife this morning would have been unbearable.

Lark had seen Sienna sitting behind her desk, scratching notes on paper. Theresa had warned her that Sienna had spent a miserable, pain-filled night.

One thud and then more in succession had Lark looking toward the doorway. Zeke stood there, staring at her, his new crutches supporting his weight.

"Mind if I join you?" he asked congenially. His sunny grin surprised her.

"Not at all. I was just getting ready to knock on Sienna's door to see if she needed me for anything."

"Maybe give her a little time. She was a bit groggy when I saw her earlier this morning. Those damned drugs."

Zeke thudded awkwardly toward the table. When she started to stand to help him, he gave her a stare. "Gotta do this myself." He nudged the chair back with one crutch before he plopped down with a grumble. "Damn leg gives me some pain. Doc said

I'll be good as new in a few months. Too long."

"I'm sure the doctor is right and I'm glad that leg is all that happened. Could have been worse."

"True. But I lost a damned good horse. Fred and I go back. Had a lot of talks."

Lark laughed at Zeke's humor.

"Heard all about how you nearly drowned in the Blue," he went on. "That's one crazy river. Can be peaceful one minute and the next minute, it wants to kill you. Guess that's true about some people."

"Agreed. I'll never make that same mistake again. I learn from my lessons, Zeke. I shouldn't have been so overconfident in my riding abilities. Tried to prove to everyone that I could be useful. Instead, I caused more problems."

"Young lady, you're useful, all right. Just don't try doin' things till you learn how. And don't go into the river unless you got company."

"Everyone seems to be avoiding me, except you. Cort must have left early."

"Yep. Ate quick and was on a fresh horse at dawn. Billy, Cane, Tangle, and the new wrangler left as well, and probably won't be back in till late. Expect them to be brandin' calves and waitin' out the winter once they get a count."

"A new wrangler?"

"Brant. Clay Brant."

"The one who came back with us from Ogallala." She tried to hide her frown, too late.

"You look a might irked about Clay. You know him?"

"I don't know. Something felt familiar about him."

"If you got somethin' to hide, you best get it out before too long. I'm a good listener. And I know when somebody is scared. And when something's botherin' you, it's written on your face."

She shook her head and stood. Before she left the room, she

paused at Zeke's chair and squeezed his shoulder. "Thanks for the offer, Zeke. Sometimes, there's nothing anyone can do. So no use in hashing through it. I best go see Sienna."

Lark knocked on the big oak door that led into the ranch office. She waited. A few moments later she heard a weak voice.

"Come in."

Lark opened the door. Sienna was looking in her direction, her face the color of chalk. The woman pointed at the leather chair in front of the massive mahogany desk. "Sit down, Lark."

Lark sat and twisted her fingers in her lap. Even through the pain, there was a stern, reasoning question in Sienna's eyes.

"Don't look like a frightened rabbit, Lark. I'm not planning to shoot you or give you a lecture. I think we both know what's been goin' on and I'm not surprised. Cort is quite a handsome man and we're both women with eyes. But there's only one man for me and he's buried up on the hill."

"I've made up my mind, Sienna. Gave it a lot of thought. I'm leaving as soon as you can find someone else."

"Why?" Sienna dropped her nib pen and their gazes locked.

"I don't want you to think badly of me. Or of Cort. What I feel for Cort, I have no right to. My ma taught me right from wrong."

"I know you would never betray me. Intentionally. But if you leave here, so will Cort. And I need him here. For more reasons than I can count. Reasons that have nothin' to do with my illness."

"Even if I explain it to him?"

"You're no fool. So don't say foolish things. He'd go after you and I wouldn't be able to stop him. And I'd lose this ranch to the vultures that thrive on stealing. Stay. I'm asking you to stay."

Lark stood and leaned over the desk, her hands flat on the

polished wood. Sienna was the strongest woman she'd ever met. "You were right. I'm running from someone. If he gets too close, you, Cort, and this ranch will be in danger."

"My men can take care of themselves. Cort is one of the fastest guns anywhere. You don't need to run unless there's another reason. Is this man your husband?"

"No. He isn't a marrying type. He owns. He possesses. To him, I'm a possession, won in a card game."

Shock crossed Sienna's face. "Oh, my God. What kind of man does that?"

"The lowest, most vile animal who ever lived. He has no feelings for anyone."

Sienna struggled to stand. "We take care of our own. Don't leave," she pleaded.

Lark felt a bitter laugh bubble up in her throat and choked it down. When she left the room a short while later, the sound of shattering glass brought her up short. But Lark kept walking away, imagining the proper woman in the office behind her hurling a glass against the wall.

Chapter 14
The Enemy at the Door

Dog-tired after seven days of campfires, bedrolls, and long days in the saddle, Cort rode into the ranch compound. He pulled up and dismounted near three of his weary men standing beside the corral. He unlatched his chaps and handed them off to Juan. All Cort wanted was a hot bath, food, and a soft bed. Bones and muscles ached and the horses were worn. While his men had worked hard, he'd never been one to sit on his ass and ask others to do what he could do himself. He expected the same from his men. Still, the thought of his wife and Lark waiting for him gave him pause. He shoved open the back kitchen door to face whatever emotions he tried to keep buried.

Hard work had only been a temporary solution to his pent-up frustration. The only salve had been his whiskey. And he hadn't drunk any while working the cattle for fear he'd appear to be a weak sniveler. From some of his men's remarks, they'd assumed what his wife assumed. That he had been unfaithful seemed to be the undertone. He didn't bother to defend himself, though he'd sorely wanted to punch a few in the mouth. That would only lend credence to their notions.

Theresa was standing over a fry pan where she stirred a white-looking sauce. Water bubbled on the cookstove, where Lark was dropping potatoes and carrots into the pot. After a sidelong glance and a nod from Theresa, he turned his attention to Lark. She kept her eyes focused on the wooden spoon handle as though she feared looking toward him.

"Ladies." He offered a sweeping grin at both women.

Theresa turned away from the stove. She scrutinized him from his head to his dirty boots. "You know how Miss Sienna wants boots off at the door. You look like you've been riding for a month."

Without comment, Cort backed toward the bench and sat down to apply the boot jack. When a shadow crossed over his bent head, he looked up into Lark's beautiful hazel eyes, sending his heart into a gallop. How he wanted to kiss her hello.

"See you're none the worse for wear, Miss Garrin. You look rested."

She made no response to his compliment. Instead, she said, "I'll set your platter on the dining table if you'll tell me when you expect to eat."

"I'll take a platter right now and clean myself up afterwards. I'm hungry enough to eat a bear. How's Sienna doin'?"

"She's been in considerable pain. Doctor Collier came by yesterday and left more medicine. I think you'd best talk to her about taking it, though. She might listen to you. Theresa and I tried to coax her. You should know she isn't eating much, either."

"I'll see to her after I shovel some food into my gut. My stomach is gnawing a hole in itself. Thanks for taking care of her, Lark."

"No thanks needed. Even if you didn't pay us wages, we'd look in on her."

Cort glanced toward Theresa. The woman's expression was closed but her eyes were filled with sorrow. It felt like the pall of death had stepped into the house while he was gone.

Theresa interrupted his thoughts. "I'm takin' her food up now. You go ahead and eat. Maybe Lark will keep you company."

"That so? Will you join me? Maybe eat somethin'?"

Theresa walked out of the room with a platter and a cup of coffee. Lark moved away to shrug out of a ruffled yellow apron.

"No. I think I've already done enough damage to your reputation and mine. I'm going out for a walk. Alone. Your food is still warm. If you'll excuse me?"

Cort shot up from the bench and followed her as she strode down the hallway as if trying to escape his pursuit. "Wait, Lark. We need to talk."

"Only about business."

"All right. Have it your way. Sooner or later, we need to talk. I haven't forgotten your threat about leavin'."

She stopped suddenly and he nearly slammed into her back. She spun around and glared up into his face. "There is nothing either of us can say. You are married. For now. And I have to leave. Soon."

He reached for her arm but she yanked herself from his grip. "I stayed away for more than a week," he said. "All I could think about was you. I worry about Sienna's health and I plan to live up to my obligations. That doesn't change what is going on between us. There will be a time when we can have a life together."

"You don't know what trouble I can bring. I already have."

The thought of her leaving triggered gut-wrenching pain. With his heart pounding inside of his chest, he felt like he was reaching for a lifeline. Without thinking, he grabbed her and clenched her against him. When his mouth settled over her pouting lips, all the fires in hell wouldn't stop him. Her mouth softened and settled with the sweetness of heaven. When he stepped back, her eyes glittered up at him.

He clenched his jaw. "Don't you get what's going on? I can't breathe thinking that you might leave me here. That isn't going to happen."

She looked away from him, twisting her fingers nervously. "I never meant to be trouble. I only meant to find a place. Wherever I go, there won't be peace."

She whirled and marched out the front screen door. From inside, he watched her walking toward the distant pasture, her boots sending puffs of dust into the air around her skirt. Going after her would only make matters worse. And cause a scene. Protecting her reputation and Sienna's was keeping him busy. If she left him, he'd go after her. Damn the law and the contract.

A sharp rap interrupted Cort's figures as he checked the ledgers for errors. The household knew he hated to be bothered when he was working in the office. Sure as grass grew, he hated being pinned down in an office, but this was his job now.

"Come in," he grumbled.

Clay Brant stood in the doorway, holding his Stetson between his hands. So far, the man had been good help, but even Zeke didn't seem to take to this stranger. The fellow's blue eyes were like cold glass. That wasn't the only thing about him that bothered Cort. But he couldn't peg what sent warnings through him that seemed out of reason. So far, the man had done his job.

"I just came in from breakfast," Clay said. "Billy said you wanted to see me. Hope I didn't do somethin' wrong, Mister Enders."

"Take a seat. Just have somethin' I want you to do for me."

"What's that?"

Cort leaned back in his chair and took in the man. While he hadn't heard any complaints about Clay, the fellow didn't mingle or talk much. Nor did he like to eat with anyone. More, Cort had heard from both Tangle and Dan that Clay was often seen riding out somewhere in his off time. Billy admitted seeing the man drinking with a bunch of rowdies in Ogallala one time. Then again, maybe Cort was imagining something that wasn't there.

"Miss Garrin and Theresa are going to Ogallala with the

buckboard. Jude, Adoeete, and Damon are goin' along as escort. That means I need you to fill in riding in the higher pastures for strays. Got no others to spare. Take enough gear and food to camp. I'm needed here or I'd join you. Even with Nita helping out, my hands are full."

"Sure. No problem. Sorry about your wife. Heard about that."

"Well. That's not somethin' I want to talk about. You do know that I expect the women to be treated with respect as long as you work for me. Any hint of trouble, and you'll be through." Cort didn't know why he felt obliged to warn him. There was something about the man that rubbed him the wrong way.

"Wouldn't do anything less, Mister Enders."

"Cort. Don't need to be formal around me."

"Heard you were once in trouble with the law. Even robbed a bank down in Texas."

Cort's hackles rose and he clenched his teeth at the audacity of his hired man mentioning his personal history. How had Clay heard about it? Cort's men weren't old women gossips. "Are you asking a question or just nosy?"

"Maybe a little of both. Sorry if I offended."

"See that you do your job and stay out of my business and we'll get along."

When Cort stood, his gun belt and revolver in full view, Clay must have taken that as dismissal. Cort watched him leave. The last he heard of him was the man's heavy boot heels against the wood floor. After he'd gone, Cort stepped over to the window and surveyed the pastures while giving thought to going along to Ogallala. But he trusted Damon and Jude. Cort had a signed paper that said he belonged to the woman upstairs. Just like the cattle and the buildings. But there was one woman on his mind constantly. She kept him awake at night. If he went along, he'd break his vow. Best to stay here for both their sakes. Besides, Sienna's health hung by a thread. Even so, something felt wrong about Clay. Keeping him busy here on the ranch might be the best way to relieve some worry.

All Clay could think of was how lucky he'd been. After he'd spent days trying to figure out how to get Miss Garrin away from the ranch, an opportunity had fallen right into his lap. To find the woman Will had been looking for was a real pleasure. Once he'd seen that scar along her jaw, he knew she was Will Cardin's property. Cardin was nothing to mess with. Him and the boys had robbed, killed, gambled, and whored their way from here to Texas. Cardin never gave up his rights to the women he marked. And this one had gotten away before he'd been able to claim her in a far more pleasurable way. No one got away from Will Cardin and lived to talk about it.

A lucky break that they'd taken on that Mason Lanning fellow. Out of work, he'd been fired from the Circle H by Cortland Enders. Once he'd mentioned the name of the pretty woman he'd been fired over, Will had made a special project out of getting her away from the ranch. Even sent him to keep an eye out and wait for an opportunity. That day had arrived.

Yes, indeed. He'd get a fine reward for this. But if Cort Enders got wind of what he was up to, Clay had no doubt he'd be dead. He heard the man had a wicked temper and a fast draw. Even Will Cardin might be no match for him. Clay had to handle this easy. Circle back and intercept them. That other woman, Theresa, might be a problem. He'd shut her up. And shoot the others out of their saddles if they got in his way.

Theresa and Lark sat side by side on the wagon seat while Damon held the reins and spit tobacco over the side every once in a while. Damon twisted around to look behind them for the hundredth time since they left the ranch this morning.

"Are you expecting trouble, Damon?" Lark asked.

"Nah. Doin' just fine. We'll stop by that line shack for you ladies tonight afore we make a go into town tomorrow. Got nothin' to worry your pretty heads about while we're here."

"Are you watching for someone? You keep looking behind us."

"Thought I saw that Clay feller a while back. Maybe he was heading somewhere. Haven't seen hide nor hair of him since we crossed the halfway."

"I don't like that man. He's a sneaky one," Theresa muttered.

Lark looked toward her. "I've only seen him either from a distance or in the shadows of his hat. His name seems familiar. His eyes remind me of someone."

Theresa snorted. "Good you stay away. His eyes are devil's eyes."

"Well, ladies. Looks like the devil found us. I see him ridin' over the ridge."

Clay loped toward the wagon while Damon pulled up the horses. "What the hell are you doin' here?" Damon asked, as he leaned over and spit tobacco juice over the side.

Usually Lark would be appalled at tobacco spitting, but the sight of those cold blue eyes of Clay distracted her. And chilled her. Those same eyes had been there when she'd been cut. Or was she imagining that? Lots of men had blue eyes. *No.* He'd stood to the side, watching her writhe in pain and never lifted a hand to help her.

Terror grabbed hold of her, and for a moment, she couldn't breathe. She wrestled the fear down lest she give herself away. She had to think. *Why was he here?* Will Cardin must be close. She had to lead Cardin away from the ranch before Cort did something to get sent to prison. Worse, Will might bring his men down on the ranch. Blood spilled would be on her hands.

Clay Brant was talking to Damon. "Had to take care of a busted saddle cinch. Went back and got another saddle when

Cort stopped and asked me to follow you. Make sure you had an extra gun along. Glad to see you ladies are safe and sound. These boys are fine escorts."

"Huh. That so? Ain't like Cort to up and change plans. Never said nothin' about you coming."

"Cort has a lot on his mind what with his wife to tend. Just followin' orders. Hope you aren't calling me a liar."

His sappy grin hid his menace. When he looked into her eyes, he must have seen her recognition. She looked behind her, wondering how far they'd come. Tonight, they'd stay at the halfway line shack. Did Clay intend to carry out something there? What if Will Cardin attacked them? These men and Theresa would be killed. If she warned them, Brant would shoot them and be done with any interference. Maybe he hadn't realized she recognized him. Maybe she could just pretend she had never seen him before.

"I ain't calling you a liar. Just questioning the change." Damon slapped the reins, and the wagon jolted forward. Theresa clasped Lark's arm and shot her a questioning look. All Lark could do was nod and swallow against what Clay Brant's presence had stirred. Run. She had to find a way to run. Lead Clay and that outlaw on a chase. Someplace where Will Cardin would never find her. There was one chance. When she got into Ogallala, she could get help from Glory Sanderson. Glory and her husband, Macon, might loan her enough money to get away on the train. *The train.* Her mind spun. One direction and then another, confusing them all. Her stomach tightened and she watched as Clay rode up beside Jude. Adoeete was so young. Too young to die. She nearly retched.

She thought she had found safe haven. With a broken heart, she had no choice but to leave in order to keep the Circle H safe from the terror of Will Cardin. And maybe outrun him. The woman who'd been kind to her and the man she loved could face the wrath of one of the most dangerous, vindictive outlaws of the West. Unless she led him away.

Chapter 15
Hunting a Rabbit

Theresa heated the biscuits and gravy in a fry pan on the big potbellied stove. Lark lifted the three-gallon pot of water and beans to one side. The glow from the flame beneath the grate was the only source of heat on a chilly night. Her heart was cold with fear. Jude and Damon took first watch. Adoeete didn't have a revolver like the others. He carried a rifle on his saddle. If he lifted his Winchester in Clay's direction, she had no doubt Clay would kill the boy without blinking.

She looked out the dirty window of the line shack and saw Clay seated at the fire beside Adoeete. They appeared to be in agreeable conversation.

"What has you so nervous, Lark? You look like a scared little rabbit. You keep lookin' from that window," Theresa said.

Lark jumped at the suddenness of the woman's voice. "Nothing. Just wondering about Indians."

"Indians, my foot! You won't get away with lies round this woman. Ever since that Clay Brant looked your way, you've looked like you're steppin' over raw eggs. Best get it out so we can tell Jude what's botherin' you."

Lark turned to face Theresa. "Don't say anything to the men. It has nothing to do with you or them. I'll take care of this once I get to Ogallala."

"Don't you know by now that Cort, Sienna, and me all figure you're runnin' away from somebody? A husband? Lover? The law? Don't matter. Cort will defend you and so will Sienna."

"That's the trouble. I don't want them getting in the middle. There's a man after me. He's unspeakably dangerous and he won't quit until he finds me. I can only bring trouble to the ranch and to Cort. Just leave it be, Theresa. I have to handle this alone."

Theresa slapped the spoon down on the table and moved the pan from the heat. Then she turned and sat at the table. "Is it Clay Brant who's after you? I never did like that man. Gives me the shakes just lookin' at him."

"Clay works for him, I'm pretty sure. I'm not saying anything else. Do not step between us if it comes down to it. Otherwise, some fine cowhands could lose their lives. Please."

"Baby, you gotta whole lotta things to explain. But I'm not the one you should be tellin.' You should've told Cortland Enders. He's got a mean streak himself and he won't let some no-account hurt the woman he loves. Nobody outguns that man. Course, that's why Sienna wanted him to run her ranch."

"Maybe nothing will happen. Maybe it's just coincidence that Clay came upon the ranch and found me there. And just maybe he isn't with the man I'm evading anymore."

"And maybe elephants can fly and rabbits can't run."

"I'm about to find out. Adoeete just bedded down, and Brant got up and is walking this way."

When the rap on the door came, Lark quivered all the way to her toes like she'd been dunked in ice water. Theresa came out of her chair and gripped the iron pan before stepping back. "Stay here," Lark snapped. "I'll talk with him. Maybe it's nothing."

She shrugged into her coat and stepped out into the cool night air, one hand fingering the meat knife she'd tucked into the pocket.

One corner of Clay's mouth turned up. "Well, ma'am. Thought you might like to take a short walk. Seems we have something in common." At that moment, she'd like nothing better than to carve that smirk off his face. She'd been a fool not to recall him. Now that he was closer, she remembered. On the riverboat, he'd been clean-shaven. Now he fit in with the cowhands.

"We have nothing in common, Mister Brant. Maybe you should make clear what you're here about."

He took her arm in an iron grip and they walked side by side toward the slack-legged horses. He let go of her as they faced each other, and he lowered his arm to his side. "Thought you must've recognized me. You write a lot of what you think on your face, Lark. The minute I rode up to the wagon, I saw it in your eyes."

"What do you want?"

"You belong to Will. He's been looking a while for you. In between robbin' trains and such, I'm planning to help him find you."

"And if I tell the law?"

"That won't stop him. That scar on your face is interestin'. He only carves his special women. You being more special than most, I wouldn't advise tryin' to outrun him. Will won't take kindly to that. He's already mad as a bull without his horns."

"What will you do? About me?"

"I don't think I'll share my plans, honey. Just stay close or I might get real mad."

"If I tell the cowhands?"

"That'd be a real shame. I'd have to kill that young boy first. Then the others would feel a bullet in the back. And I won't mind shootin' that big mouth woman."

"Don't hurt anyone. I'll cooperate if you leave them all out of this."

Lark's body shook and she gritted her teeth. Clay cupped her cheeks between his palms, the moon lighting his eyes into blue flames. When his hands left her face, she released her breath, but then his hands slid over her jacket where he traced the curve of her breasts beneath the wool. She wanted to slap him but knew how like Will he was. A scream would bring Adoeete running and mean the boy's certain death. She'd made a deal with the Devil.

She slipped one hand into her pocket and touched the knife. If only she could plunge it through his heart before he took it from her. For her trouble, she'd only be slapped or worse. Like Will, he was cruel. She was helpless and consigned to his abuse until she got to Ogallala. Once there, she would find a way to run somewhere far from Cort. She hoped Clay would try to follow her. Leading him away would bring Will Cardin after them. But they'd be far away from the Circle H. She didn't plan to be found.

Theresa pried, cajoled, and surprised Lark with the use of "*sonofabitch*" during her morning tirade. Even so, she hadn't gotten Lark to admit what Clay Brant had talked about. Instead, Lark made every attempt to convince her that Clay was just a man interested in pleasantries. They packed their things and the group resumed their journey toward Ogallala under a cloud-covered sky.

Once underway, Clay stayed ahead beside Jude, seeming to make light conversation. None of these ranch hands were used to men like Clay and Will. Clay would kill these cowhands without compunction. Lark's mind raced with what she would do in town. There would be no time to explain her decision to Theresa. And she couldn't take the chance.

They rolled on, the horses snorting and the clouds darkening in the distance over the long slopes of grass. The wind lifted dirt and sent it against the horses while she pulled a scarf over her nose. After half a day's progress, the tops of tents and buildings appeared. Construction was happening everywhere she looked. A new hotel, another saloon, a few smaller stores, and some houses were springing up along one of the new streets. Each time she saw this place, she felt at home. A place for possible dreams. Too bad she was locked in a nightmare.

They pulled up beside Gast's Ogallala House, and Damon helped the women down. Jude and Adoeete lifted their carpetbags from the rear of the wagon and set them inside the open hotel doorway.

"Ma'am?" Jude interrupted her thoughts. "You and Theresa get settled in and we'll take the wagon and horses to the livery for the night. They have mighty fine food here. Cort said to put everything on his account."

"Where is that man, Clay Brant?" Theresa asked.

"He went right off to the telegraph office. Said he had to wire his family to let them know he was in Nebraska."

"I'll just bet he did. Be careful around him. I don't trust him."

"Yes, Miss Theresa. I already figured he's not quite everything he wants us to believe." Jude winked and tipped his hat before he left the ladies to tend to their personal business.

"Well. Come in before it starts to rain and we get soaked, Theresa," Lark coaxed. She hoped the woman didn't say anything more to Jude or the rest that would alert them. Or the marshal. Lark could guess who Clay was wiring, and the thought froze her blood. "Stop worrying. If I thought something was wrong, I'd tell the marshal."

"I may walk over to talk with Marshal Varnum. Maybe he can send that man on his way."

God, no. Please keep Theresa from doing anything that could get the place shot up. Maybe Brant had some of the Cardin gang nearby. They'd overrun the town and kill until no one was left. She knew the kind of men these were. "No! Please don't talk to the marshal. Please, Theresa." To emphasize her plea, Lark grasped the woman's arm. "I'm begging you."

Theresa's determined look softened. "Since you seem all fired up, I'll keep quiet. But when I get back to the ranch, Cort will hear from me."

All Lark could do was nod and accept that small concession. At least it would give her time to make her escape, with Clay behind her.

Once settled in, Theresa promptly fell asleep in her room. That left Lark time to make her own plans. She went downstairs to the lobby and started toward the hotel desk, intending to inquire about writing paper, but pulled up short. Clay leaned back on two legs of a chair near a window, a newspaper resting on his lap and his hat setting on a table beside him. Regarding her dead on, he offered her an almost imperceptible nod. Chills trailed along her spine. The message couldn't be clearer. She was trapped.

She hurried back up the stairway and returned to her room. Biting her lip, she observed the street from her window. And prayed she'd see Clay leave the hotel. Twenty minutes dragged by. Then she spotted him, making his way to the saloon just down the street. She'd heard he was a gambler. Maybe that would buy her time. She went back down to the lobby and hurriedly looked around. Thank the stars, the clerk was nowhere to be seen. She spied what must be the door to the kitchen and darted through it and out the back, then marched along the alley toward Sanderson's Mercantile. Once there, she hesitated, then tapped at the rear door.

It opened with a suddenness that startled her. Glory Sanderson's scowl melted as the woman recognized her. A broad smile lit the woman's face and Lark found herself hugged against the store owner's ample bosom.

Lark leaned into the hug, then stepped back. "I've come to

ask for something. I'm not usually so bold, Glory. But I have no one else to ask, and you've been my friend."

The woman pulled her inside and locked the door. And listened. Afterward, they both sat down over a cup of tea and wept together. "I just need to borrow enough money to take me as far as I can go east by train," Lark said.

"Macon wouldn't like you taking off like this. He'd want to talk to the law."

Lark shook her head. "These are vicious scoundrels who'd tear apart the town just because someone here helped me. If I leave on my own, I'll find a way to get help. Please don't tell Cort where I've gone."

"That wouldn't be a lie. I don't know where you're goin', honey."

"Good. Then you won't get in the middle of this."

Glory stood and walked to a cookie jar. She reached in, lifted out a wad of greenbacks, brought them back, and set them in front of Lark. "Hope you know what you're doin'. I don't want to be the one to tell Cort I let you go and even gave you the money to do it. There's about seventy-five dollars there. It should see you through and get you settled."

"I'll pay the money back as soon as I can. That, I promise. But I have one more thing to ask. Do you have writing paper? I need to write out two letters. One for Cort. The other for Sienna. If you would, could you leave them at the hotel desk tomorrow morning, after the train leaves?"

"Surely I will. I just hope you know what leavin' here means."

Head bent over the paper, Lark scrawled her apologies and asked forgiveness for her sudden departure. Glory left her alone. Once finished, she waved the letters, drying the ink, and then folded the missives. Glory came back into the room, and they hugged each other and pulled apart. Glory squeezed Lark's shoulders. "I'll keep your secret for now. And pray for you. You are brave to do this."

Lark swiped tears from her cheeks. "I'm no braver than I've had to be. Thanks. I don't know what to say."

She stepped out onto the street and hurried to the depot, where she hoped to buy a ticket before Clay found out where she'd gone. Then it wouldn't hurt to stop at the McLaughlin Boarding House to see if Ginny would sell her a revolver. She didn't want to buy it off of Glory's husband, Macon, else he might try to stop her.

The man behind the window at the depot listened to her request, looked at her in disbelief, and then turned downright contrary. "Miss. I can't rightly sell you a ticket there."

"Why not?"

"Because you're a woman. No decent woman goes there. I just wouldn't feel right about selling you a ticket. Maybe you could just stay in Omaha and not go on."

"Mister?" she prodded.

"Kirby Smith."

"Mister Smith. I have the cash and I aim to be on that train. I'd appreciate if you'd hand over the ticket and let me be on my way. And please don't tell anyone you've seen me here. If someone asks, you tell them I'm in Omaha. Safe and sound."

He puffed out a long breath. "Guess it ain't my lookout. Train robberies been goin' on. Best hide your money."

"Thank you. I'll do that."

At the evening meal, she sat across from a harried Theresa and Jude. The others had thankfully decided to take their leave and head for the saloon. Jude, at least, had not developed the nasty habit of chewing tobacco like Damon.

"Where were you?" Theresa asked, jolting her out of her thoughts.

"I rested and then went to see Glory. Talked about the things we'll be needing. Then I went by the boarding house to visit Ginny and find out how her sickly brother is doing." *You've become an accomplished liar, Lark.* There was a considerable pile of lies beneath her.

"Seems like it took a long time. I knocked on your door at four o'clock. You didn't answer."

The two women glowered at each other. Jude cleared his throat. "The food here is good. Why don't we dig in? Long day of getting supplies together afore we leave day after tomorrow. The rain should let up by then."

Bless Jude's heart. He'd stepped in at the right moment. Theresa shrugged and scooped potatoes onto her fork. Jude sipped his coffee. Lark felt so nervous, she didn't know if anything she ate would stay down. She was about to leave good people behind for a dangerous place. Will Cardin would expect her to go someplace safe, and he'd look there first. Ripples of cold ran through her. The urge to tug her hair out had her grip her fingers together. She had to be steady or they'd suspect something.

"Where's Mister Brant?" she asked. There was no way to keep the nervous twitch from her lips. "I saw him a little while ago seated in the lobby."

"He came over to the saloon a while back and set himself down to a card game. He looked perky and even smiled at me. The way he was drinkin', I'm bettin' he'll be tied up with a long-legged gal upstairs tonight. Pardon."

She would've found Jude's red-faced embarrassment amusing if not for the seriousness of the situation. A liar didn't deserve respect, but if she didn't lie, they were doomed. Her misery was her own and she planned to keep it that way.

"That man is out for somethin'. Be careful around him, Jude," Theresa warned.

"Yep. Well, if you ladies are ready, I'll see you both to your rooms. Then I might go have myself a beer at the saloon."

"Thanks for your kindness, Jude," Lark said. He hesitated as he stood. His mouth curved downward and his frown deepened into the weathered crevices of his face. "Ma'am. You seem a mite nervous. Somethin' botherin' you?"

Theresa directed a long stare at her and waited for her answer. "No," she said. "I'm just tired. But I have a favor to ask."

"Name it. Me and the boys will be glad to do whatever you need."

Tell Cort and Sienna I'm sorry for running out on them. Tell them I'll be eternally grateful for the glimpse of happiness. "Never mind. Just thank you and take care of yourself."

Theresa and Jude watched her without moving. There hadn't even been a blink as they stared dumbfounded. If they knew that she'd be on a train tomorrow morning, Theresa would knock her out flat and have Jude and Damon tie her to the wagon. Tomorrow she would be on her way to a place that even Cort wouldn't figure on.

CHAPTER 16
THE LONG GRIEF

The ragged carpetbag was hefted by a rotund conductor when Lark stepped aboard the Union Pacific Railroad passenger car. She'd eluded Clay Brant easily enough, making her way out early through the kitchen and avoiding the main street. He'd most likely spent the morning sleeping off his drunk, but Lark had taken no chances.

At first, she dared not look toward the folks boarding for fear of being recognized. There were several cowboys and three uniformed soldiers with rifles sitting across the aisle from her. A woman and child walked past to take a seat beside a handsome, well-dressed man.

A pang of jealousy slashed through her at the thought that she might never have a child or husband. A rangy looking man with a scruffy beard and long, dark hair took the seat across from her. His buckskin clothes were stained and dusty. He wore a holster and gun at his hip. His dark eyes pierced hers with a kindly stare, as though she reminded him of someone, and he smiled at her with surprisingly straight white teeth. Thankfully, he said nothing. Clearly, he was some kind of mountain man or maybe a hunter, judging from the size of the knife in that beaded sheath at his belt.

The train whistle blew twice. A short time later, the train jolted and the engine moved them forward, slowly leaving the town buildings behind. For a moment, Lark thought she caught sight of Damon out in front of the mercantile. Ogallala was quickly falling away from her vision but not her memory. Her breathing began to relax but a sense of loss filled her, along with the uneasy feeling that Clay could easily have figured where she was going. She swiped away an unbidden tear at the corner of one eye.

The mountain man across from her leaned forward. "Ma'am. You seem jittery. If you got any notion that I'd hurt you, think again. I got me a feelin' you're in trouble. If anyone bothers you, I'll step in. No one messes with Gus Quaid."

She managed a shaky smile. "Thank you. Appreciate your concern, Mister Quaid."

"Nobody calls me that. Gus will do fine." He winked. "You goin' to Omaha, I expect?"

"Yes. Omaha. I've some family there." Omaha was only the beginning. *Please don't ask more. I don't want to keep making up lies.*

"That's a right respectable place. Somethin' tells me you got a bushel of trouble, and if I was a bettin' man, I'd say you'll do right well there. I know Omaha pretty well. Where'd you say your kin lives?"

"I can't remember the street. I expect they'll be there to meet me." Darned if he wasn't too astute. "And where are you going, Gus?"

"Wichita. Not any place for a lady. Do you have a gun in your fancy bag?"

"Yes."

"I'd keep it handy if you go anywhere besides Omaha."

"Thank you for your advice. Don't think I'll be needing it."

They settled into quiet. He leaned his head back and dozed. She wondered if he slept soundly as the train rocked from side to side while the landscape skimmed by. She watched the rolling hills dotted with tall grass and cattle pass outside the window. Occasionally, a cowboy waved his hat in the air from the seat of his saddle, reminding her of Cortland Enders. By now, Theresa would have rounded up the men to look for her. They'd most likely head back to the ranch with all due speed to inform Cort that she'd vanished.

By the time they reached the ranch house, two or three days would have gone by and they would have no way to trace her. She imagined Clay Brant's fury when he discovered her missing. Worse, she could only imagine the depth of anger erupting when Cort and Sienna found out she'd disappeared. She'd left letters for each of them with Glory Sanderson, to deliver to the hotel. Hopefully, they would one day forgive her for her deception. No. Cort would never forgive her for this. Above all else, he expected her to trust him. But this wasn't about trust.

"What do you mean, you don't know where Lark is? Goddammit! I send you to Ogallala and you come back without her. I should've gone myself."

Theresa hopped after Cort, his strides too long for her short legs. She'd never seen him so desperate. His stormy blue-gray eyes were ringed in black, and he moved with such recoiling fury that she'd swear he would bust open. He barreled inside the ranch house, his boots clomping against the floor. He went into his office, yanked a rifle from the wall, and checked the chamber. When he looked up to see Theresa standing in the doorway, he set his rifle across the desk and leaned against the edge, his arms outstretched and his hands flat against the wood. She expected him to explode like dry tinder. His jaw clenched.

"Get some food ready. I'm goin' to Ogallala and find out where she went if I have to tear apart every building to do it." His voice was dangerously calm.

Damon and Jude came up behind her. The three of them blocked his only way out. His holster and gun were seated low on his hip and Theresa figured he wouldn't hesitate to shoot them.

She summoned up her courage anyway. "That would be a fool thing. Damon, Jude, and Adoeete already looked around and asked questions. Besides, she left of her own accord. You got no right to stop her. Or are you forgettin' you gotta a wife upstairs."

Cort let out a long breath and glanced upward at the ceiling. He swallowed before he looked at them again. She might as well have waved a red blanket in front of a bull with blazing eyes.

"Another thing, Cort. Why'd you send that Clay Brant along? He gave us the willies."

He squinted at each of them in turn. "Jesus. Are you telling me Clay was with you? I never sent him. He's supposed to be out looking for strays."

Jude stepped around Theresa and faced his boss. "Interestin'. He sure was there. And he disappeared, too. He helped us look for her and then took off like his ass was on fire. Never said nothin' to us. Just left. After Theresa here talked to the desk clerk, we got a picture of what happened. Miss Garrin left a letter for you."

"Where is it?" he barked. "Took you long enough to come out with that."

Theresa tugged two envelopes out of her coat pocket, stepped forward, and handed them to him. "We'll do whatever you want after you read them. One's for Sienna."

Cort nodded. "Can you go up and see to her? She's been pretty bad. Nita sits with her. She's been asking for Lark."

"We'll help Adoeete with the horses and supplies," Damon said hoarsely.

Cort nodded again, smoothing his fingers over the envelopes in his hands.

"We'll leave you to the letters," Theresa murmured.

No words. A cold, dark silence. As the three of them left, they heard the crash of splintering glass hitting a wall. Then there was a thud. No one saw Cort until the next morning.

When some of the ranch hands came up to the house the next day, the cheeriness Lark had brought to the place had been swallowed into mournful stillness, as though death had rooted itself in every room. Cort set the letter addressed to Sienna on the corner of his desk. His hands shook when he reached for the bottle of whiskey and lifted it to his mouth. He gulped the dark liquid and winced at the sting. Whiskey might kill the crushing pain in his heart. She hadn't trusted him enough to protect her. He couldn't keep his eyes from the blur of his name on the envelope.

His rough fingers twitched when he ripped open the envelope. He slipped the carefully folded paper from inside and holding it against his nose, he breathed in her scent of lilies. Her words were neatly scrawled, powerful enough to send him to his knees, and frightening enough to make him want to retch. Fevered words. And he was damned if he could do much about it.

Cort,

By now you know that I've left for good. The decision to leave has been in my mind since the river. We are a hopeless pair. You with your demons and me with my fear. Turns out you and Sienna were right all along. I'm running from the ranch and I hope you'll understand. I'm hunted and I have to run. Don't try to find me. Let me do this for you and what you have there. Stay away from me. Don't try to follow me. You won't find me. I've lied to you and Sienna. I don't deserve your trust or forgiveness. I can only imagine your hurt and disappointment in me. Please stay near

Sienna and help her through her last days. I expect Wade waits for her. God be with you, Cort. Take care of the ranch. It gives you strength and happiness. It's as much a part of you as blue is part of the sky. Always, Lark

Cort dropped the letter on the desk. He leaned on his elbows, his head between his hands. The trembling grew inside him like a mountain slide. Emptiness left him with little air to breathe, and fear shot through him like streaks of lightning. After a moment, he sobbed. To the empty room he asked the questions that would haunt him for a long time. "Where did you go? My God, Lark. Where are you? I need you. I will find you."

Theresa and Nita sat beside Sienna. Her fever and paleness frightened them. When her eyes opened, she gave them no more than a vacant stare. Her legs moved beneath the blanket as though she were trying to stand. The doctor had been by again this morning, shaken his head, squeezed her hand, and left another bottle of the medicine. An opiate that now made her heave convulsively sat on the table. Neither of the women had the heart to give her more of that. After two days of grief-stricken drinking, Cort finally staggered to her bedside.

"Are you hungry, Mister Enders?" Nita asked.

"Coffee. Maybe a couple eggs and a biscuit. Sorry I haven't been myself. I'm here now."

"I'll bring a tray up for you."

Nita scurried from the room. The door closed and Theresa sat across from the haggard man. His eyes were bloodshot, his hair disheveled, and his scruffy beard reflected the dangerous gunslinger who used to ride alone. His words were somewhat slurred. He sighed. "I'm sorry. I should have been sitting here. Not you."

"You have two women to worry about."

"Apparently, one doesn't want me to worry."

"I think you'll worry anyway."

He nodded. "How's Sienna doin'?"

"Doc left stronger medicine. It makes her sick. When she wakes, maybe you can get her to drink water. That bottle of liquid poison ain't doin' her no good."

"I'll try. Just so you know, I've stayed near her while you were away in Ogallala. I haven't forgotten that she's my wife."

"She's always belonged to one man. He's calling her. I always knew that. Crazy idea she had, gettin' married to you."

"Wade was the better husband. In fact, her only husband."

Theresa smiled. She liked him a bit more than she had yesterday.

Sienna spoke, her words garbled. "I hear you two talkin' about me. Not dead just yet."

Cort looked at Theresa. "Can you leave us alone for a bit?"

"I'll be downstairs if you need somethin'."

The door closed behind her with a click.

Cort mustered a faint smile against the pain of loss that still burned inside. He'd found that no amount of whiskey killed what he felt. He leaned forward. Sienna's eyes were open a sliver. He wondered how clearly she could see him. He already knew he looked like hell.

"You look terrible," she mumbled. "You've been drinking."

"I wouldn't try to lie to you, honey. Got drunk last night."

"Wade did his share when he got down."

"What Theresa said . . ."

"Don't go around the same corral. Leaving soon. First, tell me what's goin' on."

"I've got a letter here for you. From Lark."

"Letter? She here?"

"She's gone. Left. Went to Ogallala and didn't come back with Theresa and the hands I sent along to keep them safe."

"Didn't go with her?"

"I have a wife. Right here. You need me. I'm not pretending I didn't want to go. I almost did. But not at the price of dishonoring my wife. I took the vow . . . same as you. Heard most of the words."

"Foolish promises, Cort. Imperfect promises. Good intentions," she slurred. He watched her grimace with a wave of pain.

"You saved me from a prison in Lincoln. I don't think I'd have lived through that again."

"You're tough. You woulda made it. Been a waste of a good man. God must've sent Lark for a reason. Damned woman. Too brave for her own good. Thought she'd have more sense than to run off. Where'd she go?"

Cort shrugged. "Damned if I know. I'm not leaving your side to find out. Her letter says most of what I need to know."

"You say there's a letter for me. My eyes . . . blurry. Head hurts. Read it. To me."

Cort tore open the envelope and scooted his chair closer to the morning light streaming from the window. His throat tight with emotion, he read the missive.

Dear Sienna,

By now, I expect you are reading this letter. All I can offer is my profound sadness at leaving you when you most need a hand to hold. I wish things were different. You were right. I'm running from a vicious killer who marked me with a knife. That's all I'll say. No one will find me. I've taken precautions. Don't worry about me. Try to think kindly of me. One woman to another, I know you figured out that I love Cort with all my heart. And you should know that he loves you in a different and very special way. I admire your courage. The ranch was my respite for the short time I was there. You will be in my thoughts and prayers as I try to make a new life for myself where I hope not to be found. The ranch gives Cort fulfillment and I hope he doesn't try to follow after me, for to follow me would be far more dangerous than he knows. I've taken some of your strength with me. When you see Wade, tell him he was bigger than life. Wish I'd have known him. Love to a dear friend . . . Always, Lark

Cort dropped the letter on the floor and cradled his head in his palm. "Jesus. What am I goin' to do, Sienna? I've got to find her," he choked. Sienna's hand moved to grasp his. Her fingers were cold and thin as twigs against his skin but her touch was filled with sympathy. "When . . . time's right . . . do what you must do. Letter to travel . . . in desk. Keep it."

"The snow is falling," Cort murmured as he raised his head and stared out the window. "Clouds rolled in."

"Same when Wade died." Her eyes closed and her chest rattled. But she still breathed, and he caught her hand between his to let her know she wasn't alone.

The afternoon waned and Zeke found himself standing on the other side of Sienna's bed. She slept. Cort sat slouched in the chair beside her. His eyes were closed and his hand lay beside his wife's. Sienna's mewling moan caught them both by surprise, jerking Cort to a sitting position. He rubbed his eyes and saw Zeke standing over Sienna.

"Sorry I woke you," Zeke said. "From where I stand, you've had a mighty rough day."

"Yep. What time is it?" Cort asked.

"Nearly five. She been awake?"

"Off and on. Theresa and Nita come in and check on her needs. They've given her more medicine to keep her pain down."

"Dammit to hell and back. Wish she didn't have to go through this. They put horses down with less."

"Zeke. All we can do, we're doin'. Don't talk so loud. Think she can hear. Anyway, glad you stopped in. You two go back long before me. Still. Don't think you should be up and around on that leg."

"My leg is doin' fine. Left the crutches in the hallway so I wouldn't wake her. I get around without them."

Zeke reached for a bench under the window and dragged it to the side of the bed. Silence stretched between them. Then Zeke spoke again. "Snow outside. An omen. Got men out keeping an eye on the cattle. Probably lose a lot this winter. Cold awful soon."

"I'm leaving the ranch operation mostly to Tangle, you, and Damon. My hands are full."

"Heard about that sweet gal. Lark. What got into her to leave like that?"

"Got some guesses and I plan to figure out where she went."

"When?"

"When the time is right. My wife has to come first."

"That's what I like about you. Wade and I saw the good in you. Couldn't ask for a better man to run this ranch."

"You'd do as good as me, Zeke."

"For her, I'd do anything. Sienna and I go back to the beginnin'. Trouble was, she loved Wade."

"And you loved her."

All Zeke could do was nod and tuck his chin. Cort imagined the old man's years of sorrow and adoration, watching another man with the woman he loved. She chose Wade. The sting was still there.

"Change name to Enders," Sienna mumbled. "Stop talkin' 'bout me. Goin' to be all right. Zeke. Stay. Take care of ranch."

Her dark brown eyes opened and she turned her head to stare at Zeke. He reached for her left hand and held it. When he lifted it to his mouth, there was a brief smile curving her dry lips.

"Don't cry for me, Zeke."

"Can't promise nothin'."

"Sleepy."

Cort took her right hand and squeezed it. That was where Theresa and Nita found the two men when they came in with platters of food.

Zeke's shoulders hunched and he shook with sobs as he knelt on the floor beside the woman he'd loved and lost. The last rise of her chest was followed by a long rattle of air from her mouth. Then came the stillness that only peace knows. Cort leaned toward her and placed a gentle kiss on her cold cheek.

Chapter 17
Bury the Past and Dig Up the Future

Five days later, snow whispered over the small gathering of cowhands, friends, and neighbors where they stood, on the hill overlooking the Circle H ranch house. Sienna had placed an iron fence around the patch of land where Wade lay beneath the sod. Now his wife lay beside him. The preacher and the lawyer had traveled from Ogallala. Even though Cort offered them room for the night, the guests had declined and made their excuses before leaving. He couldn't blame them. He wasn't fit company.

Preacher Micah Jeffers, a graying bachelor, provided words of solace and Scripture that only reinforced the finality of the moment. Cort stood stiffly, accepting condolences from the attendees, not really hearing what they said. He'd closed himself off from everyone. Only the bite of frost in his nose and mouth reminded him of his surroundings. His eyes felt frozen where flakes stuck to his lashes. Zeke stood apart from everyone, mourning the loss in his own private way.

All the ranch hands in their wool and fur coats stood in a long row. Tangle, Damon, Adoeete, Alonzo, Jude, and Juan had carried her casket to the final resting place. A sharp wind caught the heavy wool collar of Cort's coat and made it slap his jaw, bringing him back to search the silent faces staring in his direction. When the service ended, the guests formed a procession, shook his hand, slapped his back, and murmured words that felt like the flakes pelting his face. Most headed toward the house for some chicken and pie that the women had put together.

Cort stood there, unmoving. Something felt wrong in accepting their well-intentioned sentiments. A marriage on paper. A promise of work in exchange for freedom. He still owed time.

Marshal Peter Varnum waited nearby beside the lawyer, Marcus Layton. Were they planning to take him back in cuffs? They didn't know Cort Enders wouldn't go easy. Nothing would stop him from finding Lark Garrin. *Nothing.*

Cort turned and walked beside the two men and behind the mourners toward the house. Some folks had already bid farewell and made their way to wagons beside the barn. A few would stay in an empty bunkhouse. Others stepped inside the parlor to warm up and take refreshments. Nita and Theresa had set a large pot of coffee on the sideboard. Enticing scents of chicken and beef permeated the air, reminding Cort that he hadn't eaten much since yesterday. Sienna had died five days ago, and he hardly recalled the taste of anything he'd forked into his mouth since. His stomach growled.

He escorted Varnum and Layton into the office and offered them each a glass of bourbon before they sat down in the chairs set in front of the desk. Varnum was the first to speak. "Think we'll pass on the drink, as we want to get on the way. Might stop at the Jensen ranch if the weather turns worse."

"Halfway out, we got a line shack. Stocked with wood. Welcome to stay there," Cort offered.

"Thanks, Cort. We're mighty sorry about Sienna. She was one of a kind. Never met a woman knew so much about ranchin'."

"Agreed. Maybe you gentlemen will get on with what you want to tell me."

Marcus Layton cleared his throat. "She was a good woman who knew her own mind. Never did agree with the proposition between her and Judge McKenzie. That was her decision and I went along with it against my better judgment. Can't say as I know you well but you turned out all right."

"And?" Cort prodded.

"Well. I've got the will she drew up." He took a thick envelope from his pocket. "I told her it wouldn't be needed since you're her sole family. A husband, in fact. Maybe you already figured that about the time you married her back in June. She wanted it all legal."

"Look, *Mister* Layton." Cort clenched his fists to keep from lurching across the desk and punching the man in the mouth. He didn't like the suggestion that he'd married Sienna to get his hands on the ranch. Cort Enders might not be a choirboy, but he'd never sink that low. "I had nothing to do with these arrangements or this marriage. The marshal can attest to that. Don't much like your insinuation, so let's get that straight. Peter Varnum was there. You were there. Whatever she left me or didn't leave me, I had nothing to do with. In fact, I don't even give a damn. Guess she figured this way, she'd keep me here beyond the grave. My wife was apparently a manipulator with good intentions."

Layton cleared his throat and Varnum leaned back in the chair, eyeing Cort. The lawyer cleared his throat again before he continued. "Sorry you took it wrong. You now own a ranch and a bank account. All yours. Everything on it belongs to you. There's an exception for Zeke. He gets a house to live in, free, and his full pay for the rest of his life, working or not. She leaves you the option of changing the name of the ranch so long as you take a wife and raise a family on it." He held the will out to Cort. "You can read this yourself when you feel more settled down."

Cort set the envelope on the desk. "Thanks. Right now, I need to know whether Peter is here to escort me back to jail to finish that prison term in Lincoln. You haven't said."

Varnum sat straighter in his seat. "If that was so, I'd already have you cuffed. The terms that were worked out between Sienna and the judge still hold you to the promise of staying on the ranch at least three years. Can't see you leavin' on account of you own the place. But Tenner will be watchin'. You can bet he still has it in for you. That man checks with me from time to time."

"I've got good men and women working for me. I'm leaving the ranch in good hands to find a lady that went missing. I don't much care what Calvin Tenner thinks."

"That might be a problem," Varnum admonished him.

Cort jerked open the top desk drawer, withdrew a letter, and handed it across the desk to the marshal. He watched as the man read the words and then handed it to the lawyer beside him. Varnum's face was stoic. Cort watched the lawyer's face flush.

"Cort, sounds like your wife gave you all the more reason to find that lady," Varnum said. "She gave you this pass to leave. I got no quibble over this approval she wrote. Just make sure you come back. This ranch is a beauty. Zeke is gettin' too old to do it all himself."

"I plan to do that."

"When will you leave?" Layton asked.

"Might take a few days to a week before I get things settled here. I do have a favor to ask of you, Marcus. I'll pay you well. I need you to hire a detective to track the whereabouts of Lark Garrin."

"All right. Where do you think she is?"

"My first guess is that she took a train to Omaha. Start there. I'll pay whatever it takes to find her. So get somebody good."

"I'll talk to that depot clerk. Might have to squeeze it out of his mealy mouth," Varnum suggested.

"When I get to town, that's just where I plan to start. And then I'll be on the first train out," Cort warned them.

"We wish you luck, Mister Enders," Layton said as he and the marshal stood. "We won't keep you from your guests."

Cort nodded but didn't stand as the men walked from the office. Sooner or later he'd face whoever remained in the next room. Right now, he needed whiskey to dampen the anguish coiled inside.

Cort swigged from the whiskey bottle, still absorbing the fact that every book on these shelves, this desk, and everything else belonged to Cortland Neil Enders. For most men, that would be enough. The whiskey slid down his throat and burned. He'd been in here for, what . . . a couple of hours, at least. While he knew he needed to eat, right now Lark's musical laughter, lily scent, and poised walk floated through his head; taunting him, enticing him, and scaring the hell out of him. She had set herself up for trouble. She had no idea what could happen to a pretty woman drifting alone. Where had she gotten enough money to leave? That was a question he would figure out in Ogallala.

He opened the lap drawer, pulled out the wrinkled green ribbon, and held it in his fist. He lifted it to his nose and breathed in her scent, now so faded he was probably only imagining it. What a complete dumb donkey he was to live his life around a green ribbon. That's what he'd come down to while Sienna was alive. Now he was going to do exactly what Sienna had advised. Marry the woman who belonged to this ribbon, if he had to tear apart every wild, one-horse town from here to Texas. *I will find you, pretty lady.*

His fingers combed through his hair and he dragged his hands over his face. A sharp rap on the door brought his attention back to the here and now. Zeke opened the door, kicked it closed, and limped toward the desk. Cort read pure anger in his wrinkled face.

Zeke looked him over. "Ain't you a fine lookin' widow man? Gettin' drunk instead of thinking about this ranch and your own men out there."

"They all leave?"

"Yep. Figured you were distraught."

"Guess so." Cort picked up the whiskey bottle and swigged while he watched Zeke's face turn mottled red.

Faster than Cort thought the man could move, Zeke yanked the bottle from his grasp and heaved it to the floor. Cort jolted to his feet and the room spun.

"Yep," Zeke snapped. "Everybody left. I'm glad only Theresa and Nita are still out there clearing up dishes. Wouldn't want too many seeing you for the miserable feel-sorry-for-yourself kid you turned out to be. Thought you'd be able to stand up and take charge. Instead, you're in here cryin' over a lost love. Well . . . I can tell you a thing or two about that . . ."

Cort came around the desk and grabbed Zeke by the shirt front. "Go on. Tell me."

They glared at each other. "You loved that gal, Lark. Don't blame you. But you ain't going to find her sittin' here. Pick yourself up. Eat some food and make some plans. Drowning in whiskey won't help. I already tried that years ago."

Cort slowly released his grasp and nodded. "You got me pinned to rights. I'm wallowing in my damned stupidity. I should've seen it coming. I'm plain mad at myself. And it might cost her life if I can't find her before she winds up in a place I don't want to think about."

"Tangle's pretty good with a gun. Take him with you. Give us a few days to get your horses and gear ready. Then you head out and bring her back here. I can run this ranch same as you."

"Thanks, Zeke."

"Glad I'll be around for a while to give you the kick in the ass you need. You sure can be a stubborn mule."

The two of them laughed and headed toward the kitchen to pry loose some food from the women before they sorted through all the places where Lark might've gone.

Getting ready for this journey had taken more time than he had to spare. Sometimes he'd looked at the stars and prayed that Lark had lighted in a safe area and was tucked into a clean bed. If she'd been used, he'd never forgive himself. Killing Will Cardin would give him great pleasure. Nobody would hang Cort Enders for putting an end to that vicious animal. The man was wanted, unless the law and lawmen were stupid.

Now he sat in a room at Gast's Ogallala House, a scant few blocks from the train depot. Tangle was down the hall from him. They had all their gear stowed with extra horses and supplies. His entire body felt wired with an urgency that gnawed every nerve ending. Sleep wouldn't come and the glass of whiskey just made it worse. He lifted the ribbon to study it, imagining her wearing it in that beautiful gold-touched hair while his fingers ran through the silky strands. And then he imagined even more of her, until his heart nearly pounded out of his chest.

Think about how she thinks, you fool. That's how he would find her. Think. That depot clerk remembered her. She'd bought a ticket to Wichita, Kansas, by way of Omaha, Nebraska. The clerk had given her a warning about going on to Wichita. Damn. She was leading Cort on a merry chase to one of the roughest cow towns there was. If she decided to move on to Ellsworth, he didn't want to think about what would happen.

Pieces of a hazy puzzle were coming together. Theresa told him how Lark had been scared of Clay Brant and he'd suddenly disappeared. Lark also needed money. He'd poked around enough to talk Glory Sanderson into admitting she'd given

Lark cash. Cort covered her debt. At the boarding house, Ginny admitted to selling Lark a Colt Navy. A gun she probably didn't know how to use.

He was beginning to find out that the woman he loved was not only beautiful, but resourceful and cunning at covering tracks. But she wasn't good enough to throw him off. *Will Cardin.* Will Cardin must have found her and she was running for her life. And Cort was going to be the man to put Cardin out of his misery. *Clay Brant.* When Cort found *him,* he'd send him to Hell.

Cort rolled out of bed and went to the window. His hair and back were wet with sweat, and he shivered as he searched the darkness of the street and then the eastern horizon. The sun would be up soon. The snow had stopped, and all that was left were the white crystals on the windowpanes. A chill wind curled in around the sash. And he worried that Lark was cold.

CHAPTER 18
THE PIECES

"Miss Garrin? That you beneath that wool hood?" Gus Quaid's voice couldn't be mistaken for anyone else. That deep sound would shame thunder. Darn. He'd found her.

She turned to face the large man in buckskins, his rifle clutched at his side. She'd told him she was disembarking in Omaha. And she hadn't lied . . . exactly. "Why, yes. I've been waiting for the next train."

Gus looked her over from the tip of her boots to the top of her head. She'd hoped no one could identify her, but nearly the entire train heard him announce her name. The long buffalo robe he wore looked to be plenty warm against the wind, and she wondered if he'd killed many buffalo. She imagined his gun and holster were still strapped around his waist. Gus was every bit what she imagined a mountain man to look like.

"I believe you mentioned you were headed for Omaha. Now I figure you're goin' on to Wichita. That's not a place a fine woman should be headin'. I'd suggest you stay in Omaha unless you got a real good reason to be goin' to that rough town filled with gunfighters, gamblers, and women who aren't exactly ladies."

"I thank you for your concern, Gus. I have family to meet there."

"Uh-huh." His brows lifted. Lark was at a loss as to what to add. He must be mighty tired of being lied to.

"You said you had family in Omaha, if I recall. Still, it ain't my business. I'll bc on this train to Wichita and can see you safe that far. After that, I gotta head to Fort Leavenworth. Gotta lead some green troops north to the badlands. I hope you know what you're doin' before you step onto this train."

"I'm doing what I have to do."

"Have it your way, ma'am. Keep that gun with you every minute. Once you get there, I'll see you to Snitzler's Hotel. Might be one of the more decent places to stay. Got a good restaurant back of the saloon. That's where I'll be sayin' goodbye. If you change your mind, I'll escort you back to the train and head you to Omaha."

"Mister Quaid, I'm deeply thankful for your help. I assure you I won't be turning back."

"Gus. Just call me Gus. Let's get on board before they pull out without us."

They boarded, and the train got underway. November winds and a light frosting of snow on the endless brown grass and rolling hills kept her mesmerized, deep in thought about Sienna. By now, she guessed Sienna had gone to be with Wade. At least Cort wouldn't find Will Cardin and his gang on his doorstep. Instead, she'd send that devil on a lively chase and lose him.

The land flew by in a haze of frosty mist and then clear skies. Frost coated the windows and obstructed her view. She found herself rubbing the glass with her glove. Thankfully, the potbellied stove at the other end of the car gave enough heat to keep the few passengers somewhat comfortable. She looked across at her protector, his eyelids nearly closed. He had removed his coat to reveal those buckskin clothes and his holster and gun. His rifle lay snug beneath his seat.

"We'll be there in another hour," he said. The suddenness of his comment surprised her. She had thought he was sound asleep.

"I'll be glad to get into a warm hotel and have a hot meal."

"Just stay close to the hotel until you make other arrangements," he warned.

"My family will be there in a few days to get me."

"I don't believe you."

"Why do you have to be so . . ."

"Cantankerous? Nosy? I'm used to readin' folks. You got trouble and I wish I could help you out. Besides, you gave yourself away when I told you the best hotel to stay in and you agreed. Don't sound like you got family."

She laughed. No helping it. He was a nice man. Too astute for his own good. He wasn't Cort but he was sure a pleasant distraction. She missed Cort more with each passing day.

When they arrived in Wichita, Gus escorted her to the hotel and left her to her own devices, saying he'd check on her if he had the chance. After his departure, a new reality struck her. Money. The room rate of one dollar per night would run her out of cash before long. She wouldn't be able to buy another ticket to Ellsworth. Finding a job was her first priority so she could afford to keep moving.

The room was acceptable. A small stove in one corner would allow her to do a little cooking, and that would save her the cost of the restaurant. Thankfully, the room felt reasonably warm against the biting wind outside. Snow had been light, but she feared being forced to stay here when the tracks became impassable. Of course, that would slow Will Cardin and Clay Brant in their pursuit.

She looked in the mirror and saw a tired woman. If she pleaded her case, she might find a job in the hotel restaurant. It looked to be doing quite a good business, at least while the train was still getting in. The desk clerk had suggested she see Zuetta Stone in the back, and Zuetta might fix her up with a job. The train had cost her forty dollars. The meal had been four bits. And this room was going to be one dollar per night.

In a week, she'd be almost out of the money she'd borrowed from Glory Sanderson. Worse, she'd stolen money from Cort. He'd given her twenty dollars to buy necessities. That didn't include running away to a wild town in Kansas.

Gunshots erupted in the street. When she moved toward the window to see what was going on, it occurred to her that a stray bullet could easily make matters worse. She couldn't afford a doctor. Even as Gus had escorted her toward this hotel, gunshots exploded from one of the many saloons nearby. Gus had grabbed her and shoved her inside a doorway.

Now she stood mesmerized at the commotion below. Horses raced by in a blur. She saw men fire their guns into the air before they charged toward a bawdy house where women hung over a balcony, their scantily clothed bodies in full view. They waved the wild cowboys upstairs. A thought struck her with the force of a boulder. What if she had to become one of those women just to have a roof over her head? *No.* She would never stoop that low.

A soft rap on the door sent a new worry through her. That couldn't be Gus. By now, he must have left on that big bay horse he'd led down the train ramp. "Who is it?" She lifted the revolver, not sure how to shoot the thing straight.

"I'm Zuetta. Heard you was lookin' for work."

Lark slipped the gun beneath the bed pillow, smoothed her skirt, and slid the bolt back on her door, to face a very large woman. Black and red lace, blue satin trim, and a revealing décolletage filled Lark's vision. Just revealing enough to entice a man. The woman looked her over with a steady perusal, her black eyes trailing from Lark's boots to her face, pausing at her chest and then stopping at the scar. After a moment, Zuetta stepped inside the room and shut the door.

"So. You're lookin' for work, are you?"

Zuetta's nasal voice sounded like permanent ague. Without

warning, she reached for Lark and cupped her cheeks between her hands, turning her face this way and that. Then she stopped and traced the scar with a bony finger. "You been cut up by one of your customers?"

"Customers?"

"Yes. Course, you don't much look like any soiled dove I've ever seen. Sound too educated. But we can give you a try. I'll see what clothes I got and you can get started. This room will do until I see how you work out. Pay is one dollar a roll. Unless you do real good. We take half."

As Zuetta's meaning sank in, Lark felt like she was walking through a long tunnel. Heat crept up her neck and she felt her face flame. What this woman was offering her was offensive. This was no restaurant job, and Zuetta was under the wrong impression. *Thanks to that young clerk downstairs. Wait till I wring his neck.*

"Well? You look awful red in the face. You sick or somethin'?"

"There's a misunderstanding. I'm looking for a job in the restaurant. I can cook. Wait tables and serve. I'm not . . . a . . ."

"Prostitute. Well, honey. Guess you ain't. I'll talk with Snitz about a job here. I own the Dry Well Saloon but Snitz and I share this establishment. We could use a hand downstairs in the restaurant. I'm mighty glad for you. I was afraid you might be new, and these cowboys are pretty rough."

That night was the first of many when Lark felt hands touch her in vile, rude ways while she set plates on tables or bent to retrieve money thrown to the floor. The next few days, while repulsed by ill-mannered brutes and mule-faced miscreants, she grew numb to their unwanted advances and usually managed to slip away from their hands amidst their hoots and hollers. A roof over her head and food in her belly were the trade-offs. *Oh, Cort. I'm scared. Where will I hide if Cardin comes here?*

Gus said he might be back this way. She wished he would

hurry. Maybe he could escort her to another town. Tonight, her feet hurt and her hair hung in a loose braid as she moved around the restaurant. Just three days had gone by, and the last of the customers made their way out of the front door when Lark turned to find Zuetta standing in the kitchen doorway. "You look frazzled, honey."

"I am."

"After you help finish up the dishes, get somethin' to eat and go on upstairs and pack your things. Miss Rozzie Davis's Boarding House might be more fittin' a place for you to live than atop this saloon."

Lark wiped down a table and picked up a tray, thinking about this sudden proposal. Zuetta probably needed whoring space upstairs. She lifted the tray higher and marched past the woman into the kitchen, setting the dishes beside the soapy wash bucket where Jing Ton stood, settling wet dishes onto a rack.

Jing Ton glanced in her direction. "Missy go eat. Plate on table. No more customers?"

"I hope not. I'm done in."

She looked toward Zuetta. The woman was awaiting her response. "Think about what I said. I can guarantee a good rate from Rozzie. She can be a bit sour, but she's a good woman."

"I don't have much money to spare. I'll go look at it tomorrow, Zuetta."

Zuetta clumped away in her high heeled boots, followed by a slam of the door. Maybe it would be a good idea, moving somewhere else in town. She hoped cheaper than the hotel. Jing worked without speaking. Lark settled herself at the small kitchen table and lifted a slice of ham to her mouth. The bell jangled on the restaurant door. They were still open, and she had to see to all customers.

Jing Ton's face drew into his usual annoyed expression. "Customer late."

"I'll go take care of him." Lark lifted her tired body to a standing position, stretched her back, and walked into the restaurant. A medium-tall man wearing a fur-collared wool coat and a black Stetson stood near a table by the window, gazing out at the dark street. His hat was lightly dusted with fresh snow. His leather boots looked worn down. Cowman's work gloves protruded from his pockets. When he turned away from the window, she gasped in recognition. "Mason? Mason Lanning?"

He studied her as thoroughly as she'd studied him. "Is that you, Lark Garrin? I'll be damned. Man alive! I still can't believe my eyes. Maybe I should go outside and step back in."

His beard hid much of his expression, but his warm smile and white teeth she'd always remember. He looked older. He'd been quick to tease and always seemed happy back on the Circle H. They each closed the distance, and he slapped his hat off his head just before he lifted her from the floor and planted a light kiss on her mouth.

After he set her down, he studied her face. "Sorry if I was too rude in that kiss. I just, well . . . I'm still rattled at seeing you again. My tongue ain't even working."

"What are you doing here, Mace?"

"Last I looked, this is a restaurant and I'm a hungry cowpoke. Just came up from Dodge. Drovering cows up from near Amarillo. Now I'm heading back to Omaha to look for work. Sure enough won't find work with that temperamental boss man on the Circle H."

"Let's not stand here. I'll bring out a platter of ham and potatoes, and even apple pie if you've a mind for some. I was just sitting down for some supper, myself. We can sit here and you can tell me all about what you've been doing."

"I'm more interested in how you landed in Wichita. Ain't a town for a lady. If that son of a bitch Cort Enders fired you, I might go back and punch him in his self-righteous mouth."

"No, nothing like that. Take off your jacket and sit over there near the stove. Warm up. We'll talk after I get you something to eat and some coffee."

She caught sight of one corner of his mouth lifted beneath his scruffy beard while she busied herself with setting the table. Once the food was out, she took a seat across from him. As she nibbled on a piece of pie and sipped her coffee, Mason forked potatoes into his mouth. In between bites, he talked about the hard work chasing after cattle and picking their way around marauding Indians. He cleaned his plate with a biscuit, brushed crumbs off his hands, and lifted the coffee cup to his mouth.

Gunshots rang out and she jumped, instinctively leaning sideways to escape a stray bullet. He reached across the table and grasped her hand, smoothing his rough thumb over her skin. "Why do you stay here, Lark? You won't ever get used to the stray gunshots, saloons, and cowboys running roughshod all over town. This isn't safe. Way I hear it, Earp left and now there's nobody willing to stay put. Got a marshal doing several towns."

"I know. When I figure out where to settle, I'll move on. Saving up my money."

"Why not go back to the Circle H? As much as I don't like Cort for firing me, I know how jealous he was. Can't say as I blame him. Everybody knew he'd fallen hard in love with you."

Lark slipped her hand from his and settled it on her lap. "He's married. Sienna may not have long to live but I didn't plan to be a vulture. I liked her too much to do that to either of them. Besides, I was running from somebody and I didn't want Cort involved."

Mason's eyes narrowed. "What's goin' on?"

Avoiding an answer, she turned the questions on him. "Your turn. What did you do after you left the Circle H?"

Now it was his turn to squirm in the seat. "The truth is, I gambled and drank, then got into real trouble. I joined a gang that robbed banks and trains. Lucky to get away from them with my hide. I wanted to puke the first time I saw how vicious the leader could be. He even shot his own men if he thought they'd turn tail. Name is Will Cardin."

"Oh . . . my God! No! You? How could you think to join with him?"

"Stupid and bitter about losing my ranch job. Took the first thing that came along. I got out of it before I got too much into it. Found my way to Texas." He peered at her, curiosity clearly roused. "You look like you've seen a ghost. When I mentioned the name."

Before she could say a word, realization dawned in his face. "So. Cardin's the fellow you're running from." His gaze shifted to her scar. "Was him who cut you, wasn't it? Now it all fits together. I heard he likes to cut women. Jesus. If I'd known, I would've figured a way to shoot him."

"Will he come here?" she whispered.

"More than likely. He's been robbing trains lately. In fact, he robbed the Topeka and Santa Fe a week ago. Most likely holed up in Ellsworth. You gotta get out of here. Go to Omaha or back to Ogallala where you'll have protection. I'm heading north on the train tomorrow. Want to join me?"

"I can't. The money I had is almost gone."

"I'd like to help but I'm not very fixed. I'll send you money once I get a job up north."

"You don't need to do that. I'll figure something out."

"Go back to Cort. Did you tell him you were leaving?"

"No. One of Will's men got hired at the ranch to take your place. He was going to tell Will I was there. I decided to run before that animal came after me."

Mason leaned back in his chair. Eyes narrowed, he watched

her. Mason was a decent man and someone she trusted. She noticed he ignored his food and studied her. She knew he was trying to figure out an answer to her problems. His steady gaze and taut mouth revealed a lot about how dire her predicament. He sighed and ran a hand over his unkempt hair.

"If you hear gunshots, stay off the street. And if you hear Will Cardin is in town, lay low. Hide someplace. He's known to frequent saloons and hotels. You won't be safe here. And I will send you money as fast as I can."

Chapter 19
Found

Cort sat across from Tangle. The train rolled past the frozen landscape of frosted dead grass and distant low mountains. An occasional jolt signaled that they were speeding to make it over a grade.

"Hey, boss," Tangle said.

"Thought you were asleep."

"I can hardly sleep on a train with all the rattling. Worse than listenin' to bellowin' cows all night."

"We should reach Emporia by nightfall. With luck, we can get a train down to Wichita."

"What if she ain't there?"

"I'll be in a worse mood."

Silence stretched between them as the train rumbled over a wooden bridge with a frozen snaking river below. Might be a good idea to change the subject.

"Tangle. What's your real name?"

"Thomas."

"Wade and Sienna hired you on, so I don't even know your full name."

"I'll tell you if you don't laugh."

"Maybe. Depends."

"Thomas O'Dare. Folks kept callin' me Odor. So I decided to change it to O'Brien."

Cort couldn't hold back a chuckle. Tangle glared and then grinned.

"I see what you mean," Cort said. "How'd you come by Tangle?"

"Learnin' how to rope cows. That's all I'll say."

Before Cort could comment, the train lurched and they were thrown forward in their seats. The engine came to a slow, rolling stop and then started backwards before slamming to another stop. Cort stood. Tangle followed behind as they headed for the door with their guns drawn.

One woman clutched her child against her side, both of them visibly scared. Another man sat beside a window, gaping at the horses that had come up beside the engine.

"Looks like we got soldiers outside flagging us down," Cort said. "Wait here just in case it's a trick."

"Sure will. I'll keep watch from here. I'll get my rifle on them."

Cort stepped down off the train and studied the contingent of fifteen soldiers, all dismounted and apparently waiting for a mountain of a man who was conversing with the conductor and engineer. Cort strode past the soldiers and their mounts. Plumes of frosted air around the horses' heads told him they'd ridden hard. He'd recognize the mountain-sized man anywhere. This wasn't just any run-of-the-mill Army scout. Gus Quaid was legendary.

Cort holstered his revolver as he approached the group. Falling snow frosted his wool coat and hat, and ice crunched under his boots. "What's goin' on?" he asked when he reached the three men.

The engineer stood in his tattered and scorched wool coat and fur cap. His large leather gloves protruded from a pocket. "We got a problem ahead. Seems some robbers decided to stop our train and these soldiers here caught on. Chased them off. But the track is littered with dead cows, shot up on the tracks and burnt. The ones tried to run were shot and their carcasses dragged to the rails. Robbers set them on fire just for the fun of it. Thought they'd derail us. Just ain't safe to go on into Emporia. Not tonight."

Cort turned his attention to the fur-coated mountain man. "What do you think, Gus?"

Gus's eyes widened like somebody had swung a lantern at his face. "Sonofabitch. Cort Enders. I ain't seen you in a dog's age. I didn't recognize you right off."

"Got older. You look the same. Gray in the beard, is all. What're you doin' here?"

"Hell. Just leadin' these greenhorn soldiers out of Leavenworth to the train in Emporia. Goin' north to Fort Randall. These young soldiers shoot passable. But they sure are goin' to be in for a surprise when they get to Fort Randall with those miners. Seems like we got more trouble with train robbers around here. I figure we can pitch in and clear the tracks. Better than bein' sittin' ducks all night. Pretty cold to be out here for long. You up for helpin' out? Got me about fifteen strong backs and enough rope to drag these poor critters outta the way."

"If it'll get us out of here sooner, I'll pitch in. Got my horse on board."

"Got a spare you can ride. No need to get geared up."

The conductor shivered under his thin wool coat as he returned to the car to explain the situation to the scared passengers. The engineer's breath puffed into the cold air. "I only got enough fuel to Newton. Make it quick," he said over his shoulder.

Gus slapped Cort on the back, ignoring the engineer as he turned on his heel and left them. "Found a dead man by the burnin' cows. Shot through the head. Three of my men are over there by the cottonwoods with shovels. Figure on buryin' him."

"Jesus Christ. Let me take a look."

Tangle stepped down from the passenger car and Cort waved him over. Crouching beside the body rolled inside a blanket,

Cort lifted one corner and studied the blood-soaked head and face. Red ice dotted the man's beard. Cort sucked in a long breath.

"Tangle. Is this who I think it is?"

Tangle bent over the body and cussed beneath his breath. "Clay Brant. Wondered where he got to. Now we know."

"You know him?" Gus asked.

"He was one of my cowhands. Guess he joined up with this gang."

"Any guesses who runs the gang, Cort?"

"Will Cardin."

Two hours later, the cattle were dragged away from the tracks. Cort hunkered beside a campfire to warm his hands and grab some coffee while the engine began heading up some steam. The troopers chewed on hardtack and jerky. Gus crouched beside the flames, pulled off his gloves, and grasped a tin of coffee between his hands. Cort's thoughts wandered to riding on to Wichita. The weather was unpredictable. So was Will Cardin.

"Where were you headed, Cort? Emporia don't seem your kind of place."

"I got a ranch in Ogallala. Won't be stayin' once I finish business here."

"Don't say? I was through Ogallala about a month ago. What business?"

Cort drew in a long breath. "I'm lookin' for a woman."

A grin on Gus's face slowly melted into a frown. "A woman?"

"I want to take her back home and marry her when I find her."

Gus stared at Cort. "She has a scar along her jaw? Pretty gal with light brown hair and gold in her eyes. Named Lark?"

Cort slapped his cup down and stood like he'd been poked in the ass with a lightning bolt. "Where is she? When did you see her?" he barked.

"She was on the train from Ogallala. Alone and scared. I took a seat across from her and struck up a little conversation. Could tell she was runnin' from somethin'. And mighty scared. Told me she was gettin' off in Omaha."

"Did she? I got off there. No one had seen her. Depot said a woman like that went on to Wichita."

"Like I said. I tried to keep an eye out for her. Figured she lied. Next thing I knew, she boarded the Santa Fe to Wichita and I stuck near her. Was goin' that way. Guessin' she was out of money, else I think she was headin' for Ellsworth. A hellhole on a good day. I saw her to a hotel in Wichita."

"That was it?"

"Cort, I had to move on to Leavenworth to pick up these troopers. Hated to leave that pretty gal alone in that town. Warned her. Wish I'd known what was goin' on. I would've sent you a telegram."

"Was she all right? I mean . . . did she look well?"

"Looked peaked. Thin, maybe from lack of vittles. I left her at Snitzler's."

"Jesus. I hope she doesn't find trouble. You and I know the kinds of men that go in and out of that town."

"At least she's got a roof over her head."

"Cardin damaged her. Branded her like she was a cow. If he finds her, he'll use her and then kill her. Unless I find him first."

"I hear Cardin's crazy as a loon. And a straight, fast shot."

"I'm straighter and faster. I'd kill him with pure pleasure."

"If I didn't have this bunch to take up north, I surely would join you. Course, ain't nothin' sayin' we can't travel with you. Protectin' the train that's been under attack. Wouldn't want to miss seein' you use your forty-five in a gunfight one more time. You're a legend yourself."

"I'd prefer to stay out of trouble, Gus. This is the exception.

This varmint needs killing."

The train was ready to start up again. Horses and gear were loaded into empty cattle cars, while the soldiers crowded into the three passenger cars. Gus, Tangle, and Cort settled back and watched the passing of daylight into night while the crisp white snow slid by in the light of the train lanterns. The soldiers and passengers dozed, their snores competing with the clickety-clack of the train over the rails. Cort was too wired with worry to do much sleeping. The damned train couldn't move fast enough for him. The conductor walked by and told them it would take about two more hours to Newton.

"Newton?"

"That's where we gotta stop tonight." The conductor moved on down the aisle.

"Shit." Cort's eyes closed.

A judder woke him a short time later. Gus yanked his rifle from beneath the seat. "Got company."

Cort's eyes narrowed while he searched the darkness. Then gunfire erupted. Everyone dove for the floor as glass shattered. The train slowed.

"Tangle!" Cort shouted above the fracas.

"Boss?"

"I'm headin' up to the engine and get that mule-headed engineer to keep going."

"I'll have your back."

Gus and the soldiers were already taking aim at the shapeless forms firing from an outcropping. Riders came alongside, firing at the engine and passenger cars.

"Oh, my God! Is it Indians?" a woman shrieked.

Gus peppered the attackers with rapid firing through the shattered window. "No. I suspect they're bandits, ma'am," he shouted.

Cort made it to the engine. "Fire this thing up and move it to full steam!"

"We'll be killed if I don't stop and give 'em what they want."

"You stop and I'll shoot you. Keep moving, you stupid son of a mule."

Cort felt a sting along his neck and then heard a dozen pings as shells hit the sides of the engine. The engineer levered the throttle while a hefty fireman shoveled coal into the firebox. The engine whined. Cort fired multiple shots at the riders alongside the engine. Return fire missed him by inches. Of four bandits riding up, he managed to shoot three out of the saddle. Another attacker jumped onto the ladder and clung. Cort kicked the man's hands with his boot heel. With a shout and curse, the man dropped to his death beneath the train.

The immediate threat past, Cort made his way back to the second passenger car. Shattered glass crunched beneath his boots. Cold air, silence, and stunned fear swirled around the passengers, still crouched on the floor. Gus stepped through the door at the opposite end of the rattling car and the two men stood face to face.

"I've never been with you when there wasn't trouble, friend," Gus said with a grin.

"That's not something I'm proud of. Any of your men hurt?"

"Sergeant Springer checked on them. Got two winged. One shot in the chest but still breathin'. There's a doc in Newton and we're almost there. You got blood on your neck."

Cort had forgotten about that sting. He yanked a scarf from his pocket and pressed it against the graze. "Had worse." He turned to the frightened passengers. "Ladies and gentlemen. Stay down till we pull into the depot. Lights are ahead. The outlaws are either dead or scattered."

Gus cradled his rifle and looked around at the mess. "Looks like this train is stopping for a while at Newton. They'll need to have another train come in to take these folks on."

Cort clenched his teeth with frustration and pure hatred. He'd put an end to Will Cardin. He couldn't get to Lark fast enough. "At dawn, I'm makin' tracks for Wichita. Snow or not. Tangle and me will ride."

"I'll go along with you. Take a couple of my men and leave the others to wait till I make it back. I'm not lettin' you get into this alone."

"Appreciate the company. How far to Wichita?" Cort asked.

"Hell. Only about twenty or twenty-five miles. With rested horses, we'll get there in a day and a half unless snow stops us."

"I'm leavin' at first light. Cardin better not lay a hand on Lark or I'll carve him up for the buzzards."

Late on the second morning, lights on the horizon told Cort that Wichita was waking up. Plumes of frozen air rose from his horse's nostrils and the animal's hide twitched beneath his legs. They'd driven their horses to the limit but Gus, Tangle, and the three soldiers with them made no complaint. Everyone felt the urgency. Misty clouds rose from the hides of the six horses while they trotted down Main Street toward the livery. *Wichita. Where would she be? Gus left her at a hotel.*

Gus broke into his worried thoughts. "We'll get the horses settled and then find somethin' to eat. You look for Lark. I'll see my men bunked someplace."

Cort swung down and handed the reins up to Tangle. "Thanks."

The wind whipped against him in short, icy gusts. He headed toward Snitzler's restaurant and saloon. He'd been here in his wild days. Usually spent his nights in the Dry Well Saloon. His boots crunched over glassy ice. Once he found her, he'd made up his mind he wouldn't listen to her protests. She was leaving over his saddle, if necessary.

He hadn't planned on meeting up with a wall of a woman.

Zuetta Stone and the butcher, a knife-wielding Jing Ton, stood their ground at his questions. He'd met Lark's formidable protectors. After some quick explaining, they allowed her whereabouts.

His stomach groaned with hunger, but the only thing that mattered was getting to her. Kiss her until she melted into him. And then sweep her up into his arms to know she was safe. At the far end of town, he turned off of Main Street and headed down Fairview. A light snow drifted over him, blanketing his wool coat. Shivers and cold forced him to quicken his strides. He already planned out what he'd say, if he could get his frozen lips unstuck.

The white picket fence in front of the two-story house tilted with mounds of snow piled along the posts. Smoke from the chimney smelled of bread and bacon. He figured he'd best go to the kitchen in the back rather than face up with another sentry guarding Lark against the world. Maybe that would happen anyhow. Cort tugged his cowhide gloves from his numb fingers as he walked around the house, and he rapped on the back door. Quivers along his spine, numbness in his feet, and chattering teeth were his companions while he waited.

When the door was flung open, he caught his breath. Lark stood there, wearing a pretty blue blouse and gray skirt, her hair pulled into a braid and draped over her shoulder. She stared at him. Her forehead wrinkled as if in thought.

"Lark." His voice croaked. He wanted to back away and at the same time he wanted to charge through the door and pick her up, to feel the curve of her against his body. And make promises. "Lark," he said again.

"Cort? What are you doing here?"

"I'm about to freeze to death. May I come in?"

"Cort. My God. How did you find me? But I'm glad you did. Come in."

She reached for his hand and briefly squeezed his fingers. He'd forgotten how to move or to walk or to talk. Everything he wanted to say lodged in his throat. In his head. Could she hear the thudding in his chest? When he moved toward her, she closed the door behind him. Then she looked him over, her gaze trailing from his boots all the way to his hat. The beard and long hair had been a part of what he used to be. This was her first glimpse of the gunslinger with a bad reputation.

He removed his hat and hung it from the wall hook. Snow dropped to the floor at his feet. Sugary frost dusted his coat. In the silence, he imagined what she might be thinking. He'd failed her and he nearly sank to his knees, pleading for forgiveness. She looked as lost for words as he was. Stupidly, all he thought to say was, "Sorry about the snow on the floor."

"How did you find me?"

"It took me a while to figure out where you'd gone. You're pretty good at running. Hiding. I wasn't giving up, Lark. Had some luck when I ran into Gus Quaid."

"Gus? He's in Wichita?"

"Gus is here with a few troopers. Got Tangle along with me. Zeke is minding the ranch."

"For goodness' sake. Take off that coat and warm up. I'm just so stunned, I didn't think about manners. I can't believe you're standing in front of me. I never thought I'd see you again."

He shrugged out of the coat and hung it beside his hat. Then he turned and took her in, his eyes following every curve of her body. Every nuance of her expression.

"Sienna?" she asked.

"She passed on about two weeks after you disappeared."

Lark reached for his icy hand. "I'm sorry. So very sorry."

Her touch warmed him all the way through. "She's out of her pain. Quite a lady."

"If anyone can run her ranch, you can."

"It's my ranch. She planned it out from the start. A sweet, hard manipulator."

"Sienna will always have my admiration, Cort. Though I didn't agree with how she went about it."

"If not for her, I wouldn't have met you. That ranch. It's ours. Yours and mine. If you're willing to come home and marry a rough ex-gunfighter like me."

She didn't answer him. Instead, she moved on to ordinary subjects, avoiding an answer. "You look frozen. And probably starved. I'll pour coffee and fix you eggs and bacon. Sit down at the table." Did he have to shake an answer out of her?

He didn't move. "Lark? I need an answer. Forget food right now. I need to hear the word *yes.*"

She glanced away, then back at him. "I'm afraid."

"All right. For the moment I'll let that go. But we need to talk about this and everything else."

He sat down at the table and took in the dainty green curtains at the kitchen window. The smells of bacon and fresh bread felt like home. Without her, the ranch wouldn't feel like home. He didn't want to think about missing her smile, her scent, her defiance, and almighty courage. Not to mention living with a big hole in his heart.

She fussed with a plate and set it in front of him. When she turned to lift the coffee pot, he noticed she looked a bit thinner. The spark of happiness was missing in her eyes. He picked up a fork and poked the food into his mouth and watched her as she sat across from him.

"I hope it tastes all right. Not too many folks stop here in the winter."

He shook his head and lowered his fork. "Do you know how terrified I was when I found out you'd run off?"

That was all he managed to say before she stood and backed away from the table, swiping her hands against the ruffled apron she wore. He stood and took two strides toward her. Suddenly, she launched herself into him and wrapped her arms around his neck, burying her face against his skin.

He clutched her to him, using one arm to press her firmly against his chest where his wild pulse beat, while his other hand rubbed her back with the tenderness he ached to give her. He moved his hand to her hair and threaded his fingers in the silkiness. She leaned her head back and their mouths found and took each other with an ever-deepening kiss. Heat and demand consumed them.

The kiss ended and their eyes locked. She spoke the words he'd prayed to hear. "I love you, Cort. I love you. There could never be anyone else."

"You left me. Panic and fury and loneliness were all I felt when you didn't come back. The truth is, I was never married except on a piece of paper. A sentence to serve time. Since I claimed that green ribbon, you were mine. At least that's what I told myself. Don't leave me again."

"I'm sorry. I'm so sorry I left. I thought I had good reasons. Until I came here. Until I saw you standing in front of me."

"Damn. I know you thought you were keeping Cardin away from me and the ranch. Lady, you've got to trust me to know what I'm doing. That ranch means nothing to me without you. I'll take care of Cardin. But first things first. I love you more than anything in this world. Answer me. Come home. Grow old with me. Have my babies."

Tears rolled over her cheeks and she sniffled against his chest where she rested her head. If she didn't say something, his heart would burst wide open.

"Please?" His voice caught in his throat.

She tilted her head and studied him with childlike uncertainty all wrapped in a womanly body. Braced, he muttered an oath under his breath and waited. She nodded.

"Yes. Yes . . . if you think you can put up with my stupid mistakes and my scarred face for the rest of your life. Not to mention my temper."

"I'm scarred inside and out, sweetheart. The mistakes I'll make will keep you busy for the rest of our lives."

"Will Cardin won't let me go. I'm asking you not to go after him. I'm asking you to take me home and let the law have at the man."

"He'll let you go because he'll be dead." Her body stilled beneath his fingers. No longer cold, his body vibrated with a need for this woman. They'd put this moment off for too long. To hell with mourning. He couldn't wait any longer.

"Sit down and eat your breakfast."

"Food can wait, Lark. Ate enough to hold me. You got a place where we can finish this conversation in private?"

Chapter 20
Reconciliation

Lark put one finger across her lips. He tugged off his boots and followed her to the hallway stairs beside the parlor. Her hand felt so small within his. Ruggedly handsome with those blue-gray eyes, unkempt beard, and self-assuredness that fit the man, she wondered if she'd be woman enough to suit him. She knew where he was leading and yet she followed. Neither right nor wrong. Lark wanted to feel him and know they were truly one.

The old wood-planked floor creaked and they stopped. She held her fingers against her lips again, warning him to stay quiet. She didn't want Rozzie Davis to find them sneaking upstairs. Deep inside, she knew this moment would come. Still, she was naïve and he was experienced. There was the chance she'd be inept and unsatisfactory.

Just a few more steps and they'd be inside her room. Then a sharp voice snapped them to attention like they'd been found trespassing.

"Where you think you both goin'?" Rozzie snarled in warning. Lordy. This lady was as stalwart as an old oak tree.

The turned-down mouth and crossed arms were Rozzie's expressions of disapproval at something. There was no doubt at this moment what the something was. At her mortification, heat raced through Lark's face. She stood beside a man and faced Rozzie down.

Over the last few weeks, Lark had helped with cooking and cleaning in exchange for part of her room and board. Rozzie was married to the owner of the livery, Wes Davis, and neither of them took any guff. The innocent curve of Cort's mouth would've amused Lark if she hadn't been so damned ashamed. His eyes widened and his eyebrows lifted. A former gunfighter being confronted by the sour expression of the formidable Mrs. Davis, who looked him up and down with disdain, was something to witness.

"Ain't got no room upstairs for him. Meals in the dining room. You plannin' to stay, mister?"

Cort cleared his throat, dropped Lark's hand, and straightened his back. Lark bit her lip at what he might say to extricate them from embarrassment. Still, she doubted Cort was quite as humiliated as she was.

"I'm just having a private moment with my wife, Mrs. Davis."

"Wife?" The woman snorted and stepped closer as if inspecting Cort, her deep brown eyes narrowing in her dark face. Lark felt faint at his bold lie.

"She left me over a misunderstanding. I'm here to take her home. Reasoning might work out," Cort added.

"I got a husband and three grown kids. Reason ain't what you intend, Mister . . . ?"

"Cort Enders."

"Know that name. Heard o' you. Remember you bein' in Wichita a time or two afore."

Lark heard his breathing but was afraid to look toward him. She imagined his jaw taut.

"Well now, Mrs. Davis. I'd just as soon forget those times. Got a home now and want to have kids. Just passing through and takin' my wife with me."

"I overheard some of what you were sayin' in my kitchen. Got good ears. I advise you to stop at the Presbyterian church afore you leave with your *wife*. In the meantime, I'll look the other way this one time. Seems like you need settlin'. I'm thinkin' the sooner the better, what with your reputation with that big gun you wear."

"Now . . . just—" Cort began.

"Git up the stairs and don't take all day."

With that, Rozzie turned in her big boots and marched away. Cort looked toward Lark and his mouth curved into a grin. "Not sure I like her."

Lark drew in a deep breath. "She's blunt but a good woman. Are you coming along, *husband*?"

"Bet on it, *wife*."

Inside the little slant-roofed room at the back of the house, the scent of lilies pervaded the air. A few dresses hung from the nails on a wall. The raw wooden walls had never been painted, but the gray tufted chair and the big bed with a patchwork quilt made the room feel homey. He'd shared a room like this with his brother. A small mirror hung over an oak chest of drawers. Lark's carpetbag sat on the floor in the corner of the room. A wool coat and fur hat hung from the back of the door.

He felt her eyes on him while he took in the room. "Warm enough."

"Just above the woodstove. Heat comes up through a vent in the floor."

He nodded. In fact, he wanted to ask more questions just so he could hear her musical voice. He'd missed it these last months. Cort swallowed. Suddenly he felt like a man with his first woman. She stood in the middle of the room, her hands clasped in front of her. It seemed he was always scaring her in some way. When her eyes traced his face and then stopped at his gun, he knew exactly what she was thinking. That if he were prodded, he'd kill. And one man was at the top of the list. She was right. No amount of convincing would change his mind.

"Honey. As much as I want to have you in that bed, I can wait. We can talk." Sure, he'd wait . . . even if it killed him.

"I've never been with anyone like this. Just the branding."

Mention of that horror she'd endured at the hands of Will Cardin nearly sent his fist into a wall. He'd like to peel the man's skin from his body just before he cut out his heart. She had no memories of tenderness or even rapture. Except for the stolen kisses between them. Damn. He had to change all of that. Erase the horror. Because he loved her so much, he had to show her how it could be.

In two long strides, he reached her and pulled her against him, lowering his mouth to hers softly, and then with more urgency. He parted her lips with his own, his tongue tracing hers with gentleness. Their breath mingled. Under his roving hands, he felt her heart racing beneath her blouse. When his fingers loosened the buttons, she quivered.

His lips moved along her neck. He nipped at her earlobes and felt her shudder under his touch. When her hands moved to curve around his neck, she tilted her head to allow him freer access to her skin. Her pleasure melded with his. Slowly, her blouse opened beneath his fingers while his mouth caressed her lips, then followed to her chin. When he returned to her neck, he slipped the blouse from her arms, lifted it away and dropped it to the floor. As he slipped the camisole from her shoulders, he leaned away and took in the pink softness of her breasts. He bent to capture those pert nipples between his teeth. Sinking. He was sinking into the invitation of her roundness while she whispered his name.

Without waiting, he lifted her into his arms and stood her beside the bed where he slid her skirt from her hips. He set her on the bed, rolled her stockings to her ankles, and proceeded to unbutton and tug away her boots before divesting her of her winter stockings. Along with his pleasant arousal, the reminder nagged that Rozzie might arrive armed with a broom should they make too much noise. He wasn't about to stop. But he knew this was new for Lark and he intended to give her pleasure.

"Cort? What should I do?"

Her innocent question prompted him to handle her differently. Her beautiful skin took his breath away. Her innocence was too precious as she rested on an elbow, with a twitch in her lower lip. And her fearful eyes warned him to slow. He surfaced from his own needs and slowed his breathing.

"You don't need to do anything, sweetheart. I'll teach you. This will all become so much better. For now, stay with me. I'll make this good."

He waited. She nodded. He unfastened his gun belt and hung it over the bedpost. His buttons unfastened, he shucked his shirt and pants, dropping them into a puddle beside the bed. Her eyes widened while they trailed over his body and then settled on his face. Waiting, he gave her time to adjust to him and prayed he did this right. Sooner or later she would be his. This was the moment, and he'd waited too long for this day. Talk was for later. Right now, he needed to claim her in the gentlest way he could muster.

The bed sank beneath his weight as he lay beside her, taking her into his arms. She looked toward him with a question in her expression. He straddled her. His arms holding him above her. She closed her eyes. "Open your eyes," he said. "Please."

She made a feeble attempt at a brave smile through trembling lips. He lowered his mouth to hers, crazy with need and struggling to slow his claim.

"You know I love you," he said against her mouth.

She nodded beneath his kiss. He lifted his head and took her chin between his fingers. "Say it."

"I love you."

"Good. I will never hurt you intentionally. Only this one time." He swallowed the lump in his throat. "I can't stop the hurt, but I'll do my best. After today, no more fear. You'll know how love feels."

"I trust you, Cort. And love you. No matter what."

He ran his thumb over her scar and knew how much that admission cost her. She'd learned trust could be deceiving. Deep down, she had every right to be afraid. She'd never learned real love. Neither had he. They were more alike than she realized.

"Your neck," she murmured. "What happened?" Her fingers brushed the graze.

"Nothin' to worry about. Forget that. Just think about you and me. I can't hold back much longer, sweetheart."

He lowered his head again and took her mouth with fierce possessiveness, slanting his lips over hers. Then he trailed kisses along her throat as she lifted, giving him access. He kissed her breasts and his mouth traced the curve of her stomach where she arched. Even lower, his lips moved until he heard her moan and felt her fingers tangled in his hair, tugging him closer. When he looked up, their eyes locked. Hers were glazed and imploring.

A moment later, he drove her to a pinnacle where she called out his name and thrashed beneath the hands that pressed her hips against the bed. He stroked, laved, and soothed her with gentle touches while she offered herself, body and soul. The shudders where his damp skin touched hers told him he'd taken her where she needed to be.

Straddling her, he held her face between his hands and brushed her mouth with his. His hips moved and she became his. When her fingers dug into his shoulders he held himself still. She gasped. Her arms stretched above her head, searching for something to hold. When she tumbled outward into the starry space they shared, he moved to catch her before she fell without him. The stars burst around them as with lovers. Then, cradled in his arms, he kissed her and sleep took them both under.

Cort jolted awake at an abrupt rap on the door. He rolled to his feet, reached for his gun, and cocked the hammer all in one fluid motion. He'd learned you didn't live long in places like Wichita if you didn't shoot first. At first, he had to shake his head to remind himself that he was in a bedroom and that Lark lay beside him.

Rozzie's sharp voice sounded through the door. "Both of you fools need to do what you came here for and get yo'selfs downstairs. Got company. Yo' friends are here. They mean business."

Cort drew in a breath and looked to where Lark sat up in bed, the cover pulled up to her neck and her eyes wide with humiliation. Hell. Men didn't care about what some prissy boarding house owner thought. But he knew Lark cared. And she belonged to him now, and no one better get in his way. Simple as that. "Be down," he called out to Rozzie. "Tell them I'll kick their asses if this isn't really important."

All they heard were the thumps of Rozzie's leather boots and her cantankerous mumbles as she trod down the stairs. Cort slid his gun back into the holster and leaned over to haul Lark against him where he planted a lingering kiss on her pouting, swollen lips. "Mmm. You taste too good, Mrs. Enders. Do you know how beautiful you are?"

"Oh, Cort. How can you be so cavalier? I'm already embarrassed enough to last the rest of my life. And now more people are downstairs figuring what we're doing up here. Let me remind you that I'm not your official *wife*. I'm not much better than Pansy, Zuetta, and all the others in the saloons."

"Just how do you know the *others*? Besides, you are *not one of them.* I better not hear you say it or we'll have our first big argument. I'm taking you to that Presbyterian church and we'll say those vows. I'm making it official. Here and now."

She leaned against him and buried her face against his neck. "I'm scared. He won't stop. If anything happens to you because of him."

"Rozzie said we got friends downstairs. Tangle and Gus. Probably here to tell us to get our tails moving. I'd rather have it out with *him* once I have you somewhere safer." He kissed the top of her head. "Stop worryin'."

He knew her well enough to know what she was thinking as she gazed at him. The lines and creases on his face were evidence of years of hard work and living wild. Prison time and gunfights. Tumultuous years written in his eyes and the way he held his gun. And now she figured she had brought him more trouble. "Let's get dressed and find out what our friends want." Leaning toward her, he kissed the corners of her pouting mouth.

In a flurry of gathering clothes, they washed and stood beside each other, ready to face the rest of the day. Cort felt himself transforming into that hardened, determined man who'd fight to the death to keep her safe.

Gus and Tangle scooped eggs and bacon into their mouths while Cort took a seat at the table. At first, they didn't say anything. His having Lark upstairs alone left even these grown men feeling awkward, he guessed.

Rozzie slapped Cort's plate in front of him with a thump, then sliced down a loaf of bread for the hungry men at the table. Lark busied herself pouring coffee into their cups before setting the pot on the stove. The only sounds were of men chewing and grunting with satisfaction. The clatter of forks and knives only added to Cort's sense that something wasn't right. Tangle and Gus were avoiding the bad news. Cort shoveled eggs into his mouth. He hadn't eaten in so long, his stomach must have shrunk to the size of a grape. Between chews, he decided to break the silence and step into whatever trouble was brewing, even at the risk of losing his appetite. "All right. Which of you wants to tell me what the trouble is?"

Gus set his fork down and sipped his coffee. Tangle chewed slower and waited for Gus to speak. "We got company," Gus said. "Sorry to say this right out loud in front of the women. Will Cardin rode into town. A few of his men were shot up. Probably the train robbery. They're spread out in the saloons and in the hotel, most of 'em sleepin' off a drunk. They got their horses in the livery corral. I counted at least fifteen."

Lark turned and dropped the spoon to the floor. Her eyes were wide as saucers and her face paled. Cort stopped chewing and set his fork down, then stood and reached for her. She trembled in his arms.

Tangle spoke. "We got six of us. Better shots than any of those varmints."

"Rozzie, I need you to keep Lark here," Cort said. "You got a gun?"

"Sho' do. I'll shoot any bugger comes through my door. Wesley will, too. He'll be along for his coffee. Guess he put up those outlaws' horses."

"I have a gun," Lark said. Chin up, she stepped away from Cort's embrace and looked each of them in the eye. "I'm not going to be his victim. I can shoot. All I need is to see him and I'll pull the trigger."

Cort was proud of her determination. Pride. Courage. Loyalty. Beauty inside and out. They'd fight together and come out on the other side. They had no other choice.

Rozzie shuffled around the kitchen while Lark sat watching from the front window, the revolver resting on her lap. The sun lit the sky, melting what was left of the thin November snow. The two women had bolted the doors and windows once the men left. Wesley had come home and gotten his ear full before he charged back to the livery. No black men would dare shoot at white folks, but he damned well would try to protect his property. White or not, he'd have his guns handy.

Tick. Tick. Tick. The sound of the clock in the hallway beside the front door nearly drove Lark crazy. She was already so tense that her teeth hurt from gritting them.

Rozzie came into the room, a rifle in one hand. "Them men sho' enough can take care of themselves, Miss Lark."

"I know Will Cardin. He's a cruel, sneaky snake."

"I got a hiding place in the attic. He comes along here, you goin' up there."

"Rozzie. You don't know this man. Hiding? He's been killing and stealing his way westward, always taking whatever woman caught his fancy. He never lets his property go. He'd find me or rip apart this house to do it. If it comes down to it, I won't let that happen."

"My mama lived that way. I figure it's time somebody blew that man to kingdom come. If Mister Cort don't do it, I'll do it. Marshal Smith ain't worth a rusty nickel. If Earp was still here, this mess wouldn't be goin' on."

Lark bit her lip. "Where is the marshal?"

"When he sniffs trouble, he goes off to Newton."

Once Rozzie left the room, Lark knelt at the front window and scanned the few trees near the house. The Devil was out there and about to meet his match. The only sounds were the drip of melting snow, ice sliding from the roof, and the pounding of her heart. And the incessant ticking of the hall clock.

Cort and Tangle made their way to the back kitchen door behind the hotel, expecting to find the Chinese cook wielding his knife and Zuetta guarding the doorway with her steely eyes and large frame. Instead, the door was partway open. Cort nudged it with his boot and lifted his revolver. He signaled Tangle to wait outside.

He stepped into the room and swiftly gazed around. The stove felt cold to his touch. When he caught sight of a thin river of blood on the floor, he followed it to Jing Ton's lifeless body. Blood ran from the deep slice in his neck, and his own knife lay beside his corpse. Cort clutched his gun and moved toward the next room, then halted at a low moan from what must be a storage room. When he flung open the door, he found Zuetta lying in a bent heap on the floor, her head bleeding from where she'd been bashed.

He squatted beside the woman and felt the back of her head. A large bump. His hand came away with a smear of blood. Just as he started to stand, a creak of the floorboards warned him that someone was behind him. Before he could turn, a sharp pain sent a shattering shower of light across his vision. He had enough time to see the vague outline of a man dressed in a fancy black topcoat. *Cardin.* Then there was nothing.

Cort's next foggy thought, a long while later, was of pain shooting through his back, arms, and legs. Something was yanking him through the dirt. A rope, beneath his armpits. His shoulders strained as though his arms were being ripped off. His head pounded with a fury like something in his brain was trying to escape. Mouth dry, he tried to call out for Tangle but his throat constricted. He forced his eyes to open a sliver and saw dim waves of light. Convulsive retching sent his breakfast out of his mouth and over his chin. A bitter taste urged him to beg for water. He had no voice. Just dim light and pain.

Someone spoke. Told him to grasp the rope or he'd surely lose his arms.

"*Jee . . . sus.* Who?" He turned his head slightly, only to be punished with brutal pain and more waves of nausea.

"Justliequiet. Youmight live a littlelonger."

Jumbled words. He was out of focus. *"Lark. Tangle."*

Stinking breath as someone leaned close to his face and whispered, "Thatman outside? He's in jail. Sameasyou. Got a badheadache. And prettyLark. She's with herman. Will Cardin. Mightyglad to come across her."

The words kept disarranging in his head. Time, too. No more rope, no more dragging. Where had they gone? Cort tried to move his arm but it was fastened to something he couldn't see. He tried to move a leg. It jangled. Felt heavy. *Lark.* He had to get his gun and get to Lark.

"Got somethin' for you to drink. Boss wants you kept alive for now. And asleep."

Cool liquid was drizzled into his mouth. Bitter taste. Tried to spit it out. Tongue too numb. *What did they give him?*

"That'll help you forget. Helpyou. Helpyou." The words kept ringing in a cluttered mess. He clawed at the cold stone floor. Thought of Gus just before he sank into nothingness.

The Devil was at the door and he sat on a gray horse. Surrounded by his outlaw friends, he wore his fine-looking black coat tucked behind his holster. A black Stetson shadowed his cruel eyes. If Lark squinted, she could see his knife sheath tucked against his belt. The row of men on either side of him aimed their rifles at the front of the house. At any moment, she expected Cort, Gus, and all the rest to shoot them all from their saddles. Instead, Cardin nudged his hat further back. With a smug stare, he waved his hand and his men shot out the front windows, leaving only the one in front of her intact. Shards of glass lay strewn across the room. The clock no longer ticked.

Rozzie charged into the parlor, her eyes wide with terror. She lifted her heavy old Henry and took aim.

"No, Rozzie. Put it down. He'll kill you. Go upstairs and hide in that hidey place."

"You come along, too."

"He'll only tear the place apart to find me. Then he'll burn it down. I know him. I know what he wants. You hear anything down here, you run out the back as fast as you can." Lark stood and lowered the revolver to her side. Where was Cort? What had they done to him?

"I can't let you go out there, Miss Lark. He might hurt you."

"He's already done that. You see it on my face." She slipped into her cape, lifted her chin, and walked slowly toward the door. Once she opened it, she knew her life would be over. He'd take her and use her however his crazy mind meandered. If Cort was still alive, she'd fight. If he was dead, she'd have no more reason to fight.

A gasp behind her, the brush of a hand on her shoulder, and Lark walked out of the house toward the Devil in black. One foot in front of the other, still gripping the revolver at her side. Ever closer, she took in the grinning gang members with their rifles in their hands.

When she was near enough, her mouth twitched with nervous fear. Her mind wanted to sink into darkness, but she wouldn't let it. Not as long as she breathed. Her fingers around her gun were slick with sweat. She itched to raise the weapon and fire. But then they'd kill Rozzie and burn the entire town. And force her to watch. And maybe kill Cort if he was still alive.

Broker a deal. His life for hers. "Where is Cort?"

"So you do have a voice, Lark Garrin. How about you hand me that gun before we talk," Will Cardin said calmly.

She shook her head. "Where is Cort?"

For the first time since she'd stepped outside, Will didn't seem as confident. In fact, he looked surprised. His jaw tensed and he flushed. That gave her some satisfaction.

"You got a lover, huh? Cort? Well, I'm glad we hauled him to jail with his other friend. They won't be able to help you. They're sleeping like babies."

"They're alive?"

Will leaned lower in the saddle as though only she should hear his words. "Alive as long as you give up that gun and come with me, without giving me any fight. I *won* you. You're my property."

"You will let him live. And the others. And—"

"And, and . . . and. Darlin'. You're mine. I have all the aces. No deals. Guess I can let him live. But it'll be in hell each day he wakes knowing you're with me. How's that?"

"I hate you. I despise you. You can rot."

She handed up her gun. When he reached for her, she backed away. Without warning, he grabbed her hair and walked her alongside his horse while she stumbled, trying to reach for his hand. He laughed. All at once, he stopped and hauled her up to sit in front of him. She heard shouts from outraged townsfolk. People she knew. Innocent people who scattered out of Will Cardin's way as he rode by them. Slumped against him, his firm arms held her. With unexpected gentleness, one gloved hand caressed the scar along her jaw, reminding her that he had put it there. And she cursed her father.

The smell of burning wood filled her nostrils. She turned her head and saw flames shooting from the boarding house. *Gus, Cort, Tangle, Rozzie. The troopers.* Were any of them still alive? *Rozzie. Did you get out?*

Chapter 21
Helpless

Piercing bright light came from above him. Slowly Cort opened his eyes. Jail. The bars made a crisscross gray pattern on the cracked ceiling. He blinked to try to focus better. He remembered. He'd tried to move before and couldn't.

He lifted each arm. Free. He moved his legs. His boots were gone. When he turned his face toward the bars, an ache roared through his head and forced him to close his eyes against the bothersome light.

Footsteps. Solid, forceful footsteps came nearer. It sounded like a chair was dragged up beside him. "Good to see you coming around. You got quite a knock on the back of the head."

Cort opened his eyes and squinted into the blinding light. A shape sat beside him. He blinked until it came into focus. A man with graying hair looked at him.

"Who are you?" Cort flopped his arm over his eyes and waited for his own words to stop ringing in his ears.

"I'm Doctor Yates."

"Where am I and what happened?" Was that his voice? It sounded like a saw cutting wood.

"You're in a jail cell. It's where your friends found you out cold and locked in shackles. The blood from your head did a good job of soaking into your hair. You were cut from your face down to your legs after being dragged behind a horse on Main Street. Had to do some fair amount of stitching. Most of what you were wearing was in tatters and blood soaked. Rozzie and the pastor came over with replacements. As to what happened, I'm not sure you're up to hearing the rest. You got a concussion and need to lie still. We didn't want to move you."

"Jesus. How long before I stop hearing the echo of my own words? I need to find Lark."

A throat cleared from somewhere to his left and the chair slid back. "I'll leave you to your visitors as long as they keep it short. Don't even think about getting up for at least a few days. Then you need to stay in bed and not move for a month. That head took a hit. I cleaned and bandaged the cuts and scrapes. Nothing appears broken. See you in a few hours." The scrape of the chair and the receding sound of the doctor's boots told him the doctor had left.

"You look like hell," Gus said.

Cort slowly moved his arm from his face and turned enough to stare into Gus Quaid's eyes. The mountain man was wearing a chambray shirt, vest, and Levi's. "Thanks. Where'd your buckskins get to?"

"Got a bit bloody when I held you up so the doc could stitch up your tough head. Had to get you into some new duds. Cardin's men had a good time dragging you down the street behind a horse while you were half conscious. By the time I realized what happened . . ."

"They gave me something. Tasted bitter. Poison?"

"An opiate, accordin' to Doc Yates. We had a helluva time because they gave you enough to send you into hallucinations. Had to hold you down. Tied you down once. When you started wakin' up, you begged for more. Had to get that stuff out of you. You sweated through the night. Lucky they ran out of the stuff or you'd be dead."

"Remember retching. Stomach felt like it was in my mouth. My food shot out."

"Accordin' to doc, puking up that stuff worked in your favor."

"How long?"

"A little over two days."

"No! Christ! Where's Lark?" Cort jackknifed from the cot. The room spun. A hand pushed him back down.

"You need to take it easy for the rest of the week. Then we can talk about Lark."

Cort gritted his teeth while his spinning jail cell slowed and came into focus. "Tell me, dammit. Where did he take her?"

"Cardin found out she was in town. He forced Zuetta to tell him where she was."

"The cook is dead."

"Dead. But Zuetta is all right. Mad as hell. She'd like to kill Will Cardin with her own hands. On top of that, he took up residence in her saloon. Him and his men."

"Tangle?"

"He's all right. He's keeping watch on the door. I got one trooper watchin' the Dry Well Saloon."

"Jesus Christ. I've got to get up and go after her. Kill him." Cort forced himself up into a sitting position and waited for the room to quit moving. "I've got to get her or die tryin'."

"I sent two of my troopers to Newton to bring reinforcements. They'll get here any time. Orders to requisition the train. And I got another surprise up my sleeve on that train. Then we'll give 'em hell."

"I want to be the one to kill him. No one else, Gus. I promised to keep her safe. Did he find her at Rozzie's place?"

"Yep. Shot it up good before she gave up. I watched and couldn't do anything. I never felt so helpless in my life. He took her to the saloon and we ain't seen her since then." Gus huffed out a breath. "They burned Rozzie's boarding house to the ground. She got out. Her and Wes and half the town are holed up at the church. Waitin' for this to blow over. Everyone in town is scared and either hiding or staying low. About five men offered their guns and are watchin' from windows across the street from the saloon till my men get here."

Cort leaned back against the wall and closed his eyes as if to banish the vision of Lark in the hands of Will Cardin. "What he must be doing to her. I'll tear him to shreds."

"Is the room still spinning?"

"Settled down. I think if I sit up for a bit, I'll be all right. Where's my gun?"

"Found it on the sheriff's desk. Nobody knows where Marshal Smith is."

"Don't need him. How about helping me to the livery. I can't wait till tomorrow. I'm goin' to need my horse. My gear."

"I didn't want to tell you this."

"What else could go wrong?" Cort snapped.

"Zuetta marched into her saloon madder than a wet old hen. She's goin' to try to see Lark by cozyin' up to that pissant, Cardin. Hope she knows what she's doin.' Don't much like dependin' on a woman when she's on the warpath. If we wait for reinforcements, it'll even us up."

"He'll kill her. Both of them."

"Unless Zuetta has some tricks sewn into her dress."

Cort thought about that. *Just maybe that might work.* "Would you wait? If she was your woman?"

"No. I wouldn't. I watched the woman I loved get taken by a band of renegades while I held onto my horse chasing them down. Three arrows in me. Kept goin' till my body and horse gave out."

"I remember that. Remember how you drank yourself nearly to death."

"Till I found out that I was still alive and each day got a little easier."

"She's been through too much, Gus."

"Cort, listen. You're the best shot I know. But if you're seein' double or you bend over in pain he'll put you in the grave."

"I plan to take him on with or without your men gettin' here. I can't wait. I gotta go get her."

"My wife. Figure she died. You got a good chance of gettin' Lark back."

Cort figured there probably wasn't a day he didn't remember what happened. But he couldn't let Lark go without a fight. "Got something around here to drink?"

Gus turned his head. "Hey! Tangle! Cort needs water."

A contrite-looking Tangle ambled into the room with a pitcher of water in one hand and a small tin cup in the other. He handed the cup to Cort but didn't look him in the eye.

"Hey. None of this was your fault," Cort said.

"Caught me by surprise. It won't happen again."

"Shit. Caught me, too. Wasn't thinking. I'm thinking now. And we know where they are and how many." Cort sipped the liquid in the cup and grimaced at the taste. "You wouldn't be trying to drug me?"

"Doc said it would ease the headaches. He'll be back later to check you. But he advised you to get out and hide. These outlaws took over most of the town. Seem to be celebratin'. They might be back here once they get liquored up. Probably figure you might've died. You got pretty banged up."

"I'm tough. Been through worse." Cort swallowed the foul-tasting water and stood, then waited for the flash of pain in his head to subside. Tangle handed him his gun belt. Cort buckled it on and then spun the cylinder of his revolver to make sure it was loaded before seating it in his holster. He felt their eyes watching him while he snugged the leg ties. "Let's go. I'm not waitin' any longer. I made a promise to keep her safe. I've done a piss-poor job of it. That's about to change. I'm goin' to need my rifle, too."

★ ★ ★ ★ ★

Lark leaned against a wall and searched her mind for a way to escape. Her plain blue muslin gown was torn and dirty. Will had walked in, taken one look at the way she was dressed, and left her there. He'd slammed the door so forcefully that the window rattled.

Her body shook. She bit her lip, imagining what he had in mind for her. He'd told her Cort was in jail and badly hurt. His maniacal laughter played over and over in her head. The pleasure he'd found in Cort's hallucinations, as he described them, sent chills through her. She'd pleaded for Will to let him go. Instead, he'd grabbed her hair and yanked her from the bed and flat-handed her backwards. When she heard the click of the lock, she knew she'd just heard her death sentence. She pressed a hand to her jaw.

At a quick, light rap on the door, she jerked her head up. Fear sliced through her. Someone was jiggling the lock. She slid to the floor, flattened herself against the plaster, and drew up her knees. There was nothing to use as a weapon. But she would scratch his eyes out.

With a sudden whoosh, the door opened. Zuetta Stone filled the doorway. The last person she'd expected. The woman slammed the door. A dress of green and dark blue satin and lace was draped over her arm. "He sent me up here to make sure you put this on. More to his taste," she sneered. "Damned if I don't hate that animal."

"I'm not wearing that," Lark snapped. She stood and crossed her arms.

"I'm here to hurry you out a back window. Don't got time to argue. He might just decide to come up and check on you. See if you cooperate." "

Lark didn't trust Zuetta. Then she saw the swelling on the woman's head when the nervous woman looked back at the door. Zuetta was so flustered, she looked about ready to tear out her own hair.

"He in here last night?" she asked.

"Yes. But he didn't do what you think. He just stroked my face and whispered crazy nonsense. Then he left. Mumbled about my dress."

"He doesn't trust his own gang. Thinks they'll turn on him. He's out of his mind. I'm bettin' the rest of them take off and leave the bastard to fend for himself. I wouldn't mind killin' him. He killed Jing Ton. I won't forget that. If we get outta this room quick, we can get you out a window down the hall. Just in case he finds us sneakin' out, I hid a derringer."

The shrill whistle of the train cut through the air. A commotion arose from downstairs, the thud of stumbling boot heels and the dragging of chair legs over the wooden floorboards. Furniture crashed to the floor and then glass bottles broke. Several minutes passed before the sounds of thundering hooves and bellowing cattle filled the north end of town. The crystals on the lamp swayed.

Zuetta went to the window. "Come on. This is our ticket out of here, honey. I think we got help. We don't get cattle here much anymore."

"Do you know if Cort is still alive?"

"He was in bad shape, honey. I don't know. Come on. They'll be busy downstairs tryin' to figure out what's goin' on. I think we got a genuine stampede headin' this way."

Lark followed the woman out of the bedroom to the end of the hallway, the dress forgotten. A door on the left led to a short landing and a set of steep, narrow stairs. They came to another door, but it was bolted on the other side.

"Where's the key?" Lark pleaded.

"Darned if I know. I never saw this bolted. Just a storeroom." Light streamed through a window about five feet away from them. Thankfully, a crate sat beneath the window. They looked at each other.

"You'll have to drop down on the other side. Since I won't be able to get my considerable weight up on that crate and over the sill, I'll need to go downstairs and sneak out. I'll make excuses if it comes to that. Main thing, let's get you out. Come on. Get on up there and shove it open. I'll push you from below."

Gunfire and hoots and hollering pierced the morning. The building rattled. Lark heaved herself upward, Zuetta's hands shoving from behind. Lark pushed at the window and it creaked open. She threw one leg over the ledge, heaved her body onto the casement, and managed to swing her other leg up and over. She found herself sitting on the ledge, studying the ground below. This would mean a broken leg or worse, but she had no choice.

Gunfire from the street shattered windows nearby. Horses galloped down the street to her right. A bullet splintered pieces of wood from the corner of the building, nearly hitting her in the face. Looking down, she estimated she'd have to drop four or five feet to the ground. She ran her tongue over her parched lips while cattle charged along the street, their hooves pounding the dirt. A dark maned horse appeared, trotting from the corner of the alley. Cort. He looked up toward her with his gun drawn. His face was shadowed beneath his dark gray hat. Her rescuer. More. He was alive and able to sit his horse.

"Hang on," Cort ordered. He nudged his horse close to the wall and reached upward, grasping Lark around her waist. She slid off the ledge, trusting his hold. He seated her in front of him, wrapped his arms around her, and turned his horse toward the back alley behind the buildings while cattle charged down the middle of Main Street, slamming into porch pillars and tearing up hitching posts. Pure chaos broke out as the cows filled the air with choking dust and frantic bawling.

Rapid gunfire along with shouts blended with squeals of panicked horses as Cort guided his mount beyond the commotion. Cussing outlaws were running in between the buildings to catch their wild-eyed horses as the two moved toward the church. Blue uniformed troops charged behind the cows, dismounted, and blasted their rifles into the fracas.

Once out of the alley, Cort pressed his mouth against Lark's hair and kicked his horse into a run. He guided Lincoln behind the charging herd and skidded to a halt in front of the church, where a group of armed and angry citizens had gathered. Rozzie and Wes stood out among them. The pain in his head rose and fell in sickening waves as though a pressure was about to explode. He blinked to bring back his focus. With one arm, he lowered Lark to the ground.

More shots rang out further down the street. Volleys of gunfire between buildings sent acrid smoke swirling into the air. The cattle had run to the far end of town and scattered out onto the plains, the sound of their hooves fading. Very little would hold them back once they headed for the river. Cort dismounted and drew Lark against him. There was no time to talk about the anguish or to answer questions better left for later. And her trembling sent the need for revenge through him that wouldn't be quenched until Cardin was dead. Her dirty, torn dress added to his rage.

"Stay here. Once this is over, we'll scrounge up some clothes and get outta here."

One of the church women stepped forward and curved her arm around Lark's shoulders. "Come with me. My house is just across the way. I'm Doctor Yates's wife, Dorothy. I'm sure I've got something that will do."

Lark looked into Cort's face. He knew by her worried expression that she was eyeing his cuts and bruises. "I'm fine. Stay here, Lark."

"What have they done to you?"

"Nothin' for you to fret about. Keep a gun handy and don't follow me."

With that, he looked toward the crowd of about fifteen men, women, and children who'd taken refuge at the end of town. These were ordinary folks used to wild cowpokes, not deranged killers. "All of you, take cover inside the church. Keep your guns ready. Shoot the varmints if they come this way. And don't think twice."

Chapter 22
Gunfight

Cort winced when he swung into the saddle. He gritted his teeth, knowing that his vision came and went. He yanked the reins and kicked his horse into a gallop toward the center of the town. Gus, Tangle, and some of the troopers had driven the cattle through as a diversion. And it worked. Now the time had come to face down Cardin.

Dust still drifted over the street. Hitching rails and porch supports had been knocked down and broken apart. Glass lay strewn along the boardwalks where windows had been shot out. Gus hollered from the doorway of the Dry Well Saloon, and Tangle waved a rifle in the air in front. Cort trotted up and dismounted. Eight soldiers in dust-covered uniforms stood facing the street, divided on both sides with their rifles aimed toward the shop windows.

Tangle was the first to speak. "Cort. We got some varmints you might want to have a look at before we finish them off."

Cort stepped into the shot-up room. Chairs overturned, shattered glass everywhere, and the smell of whiskey mingling with the smell of sulfur told him there had been a fight. Five of Will Cardin's men were standing against a wall, their weapons piled on top of the bar. Four soldiers trained their rifles on the sorry group. One of the outlaws stooped, bleeding from his chest. Cort watched as he slid to the floor.

Cort stopped in front of one of the captives, his revolver aimed at the man's sternum. "Where's Will Cardin?" he barked.

The silence was broken only by the tinkling of glass, dropping from the cracked windows with each gust of breeze. "If I don't get an answer, I'll shoot each of you, one at a time, until somebody speaks up," Cort snarled.

One of the men glared in his direction. "You won't do that. Hear you're a law-abidin' sonofabitch now."

Cort leveled his revolver and fired. The man crumpled, blood running down his pants leg and soaking through the denim. No one spoke. When Cort turned his gun toward the next man, the room fell into silence. Cowards who'd ride with a crazed outlaw. His vision blurred and he shook his head.

"Cort. Maybe you ought to ease up," Tangle suggested.

Cort bristled. "I'm not the easygoing kind when someone hurts people I care about. If you don't like it, walk outside."

Gus stopped him from firing at the next man in line. "Think I know where Cardin got to, Cort. I see him comin' this way. Must've found a horse."

"Watch these mule's hind ends," Cort growled. "Shoot them if they move an inch."

He no longer felt his stiff sore legs or the pain in his head. All he felt was uncontrollable anger and resolve inside where his demons lived. Some men might be capable of letting the law dig out the vermin. For him, the law had usually failed. This time, he'd make sure this outcast of humanity didn't walk away, for everyone's sake.

He walked outside to where Lincoln stood and stepped into the stirrup, nudging the animal into the center of the street. He didn't have to wait long. The madman on his gray horse rode toward Cort. For a moment, Cort's vision clouded. When he saw two horses, he blinked. He shook his head and his vision cleared. Gritting his teeth, he prayed his eyes would hold out just long enough.

The gray horse and its rider walked in his direction. Once

Cardin was within shooting range, Cort would exact his retribution. He tucked his coat behind his holster and watched the outlaw sitting impassively in his saddle, his black Stetson hiding his eyes. Boot steps to Cort's left told him that Gus, Tangle, and maybe a few townsfolk waited. Finally, Cardin drew up his mount and they faced each other with only about fifty feet separating them.

"So. You must be the fast gun I heard about. Cort Enders," Will shouted.

"Yep."

"Heard about you from Clay Brant. He worked for you."

"Did you hear just before you shot him through the head?"

Will laughed. He tossed his hat onto the street. Cort watched and waited. Cardin's black coat was tucked behind his holster. The man shrugged. "Clay was stupid. Didn't follow my orders. Heard you killed more than me."

"We've got something to settle, Cardin."

"Ah. *The woman.* I won her from her daddy. She stays with me. Lark surely felt good curled against me last night."

That taunt was meant to unsettle him, force him into making a mistake. Cort clenched his teeth, sat straighter, and imagined the hole he'd put in Will Cardin's chest. The need convulsed through him like a plucked fiddle string. Goading was Cardin's way of distracting. And that wasn't going to work today.

When Cort saw the wild-eyed man kick his horse into a gallop straight for him, he hefted his rifle from the boot of his saddle. His heels sent Lincoln into a powerful charge.

Cardin lifted his revolver but Cort bent over Lincoln's neck. With one mighty swing, he slammed the butt end of his rifle into the gray horse's chest, sending the animal into a rearing skid and throwing Will to the ground. Cardin rolled to his knees only to be met by a hard kick in his side as his riderless horse galloped away.

Cort dismounted and stood over the writhing man. One shot to Cardin's miserable head would give him satisfaction. Tangle's words bit him in the conscience but the sight of Lark in those torn clothes couldn't be forgiven. Cort reached for Will's revolver where it lay in the dirt.

Standing over his enemy, Cort took pleasure in the man's gasps of pain and the look of dread on his pale face. There was nothing redeeming in the cold blue eyes that looked upward. No pleading for forgiveness. No remorse. Killing this madman was the only way Cort could make sure he didn't come after Lark again. And Cort had the stomach for it.

A group of women and men had taken up places on the boardwalk. Revulsion, hatred, and conviction all took turns at his determination to finish the job. He was the gunfighter inside now, not the rancher and husband. And the good folks would be witness.

Lark was there. He sensed her watching. Not even for her would he offer reprieve. Not after all she had suffered.

"Go on. Kill me. You and I are more alike than you admit, Enders." Will coughed and struggled partway upright.

"Cort." Lark's voice. He glanced in her direction for a split second. Gus stood beside her, his rifle in hand. He leaned down and whispered something and she melted into the crowd.

Cort looked back at Cardin and shook his head. "No. You've got one shot. No one will say I didn't give you a chance. Deserved or not." He dumped bullets from the cylinder of Will's gun, each thud a decree of rules. "One left." He tossed the gun to one side of the street, then backed away a few yards and waited. Staggering onto his feet, the man in the dusty black frock coat coughed, then bent at the waist and picked up the gun. Cort allowed him to shove it into his holster.

"A fair fight, Enders. Gentlemanly of you." Those cold eyes flashed with years of evil. Blood stained Will's arm where he'd most likely been shot in the street fracas. He swayed with weakness. "I'm faster, Lark. You hear that?" Cardin called.

Cort blinked and straightened. "I'm better."

Silence fell. Just two men, both good with guns. One was about to die. And Lark watched.

A glint in Will's blue eyes brought Cort's gun sliding from his holster as though it were part of his hand. He squeezed the trigger. A burst of orange-white flame shot from the end of the barrel. The feel of the hot metal and the smell of sulfur plumes reminded him of all the others he'd faced. Two booming blasts set his ears ringing, thundering through the bones of his chest. The black frock coat lay in the street, the legs beneath it bent and oddly twisted. Red blooms soaked the dandy white dress shirt and seeped into the dirt. A fitting end.

Heat radiated through Cort's fingers where he still clutched the gun. He'd bragged that he was faster. For a moment, he wondered if it were true or were these things a matter of pure luck? He was still wondering when Gus, Tangle, and a tall man in a duster stood beside him. The doctor set his bag beside the sprawled body and felt the neck, then looked upward, shaking his head. Other men came forward and lifted the body and carried Will Cardin away as though to quickly erase the terror.

"I'm the town marshal," said the man in the duster. "Jake Smith. If you got time, I'd like to have a word about what went on here. Lots of lawmen would thank you for what you did. I'd most likely be a dead man if I'd have stood up to him."

Cort eyed the fellow cautiously. "Where've you been?"

"I was needed over in Newton. Got in on the train with the troops when I heard what was goin' on. Helped with the cows. That was some fast shootin', Mister Enders. Still, I gotta follow the law and get your statement. Before you leave. Might even be a reward."

"Give the reward money to Rozzie and Wes. They lost their

house to an outlaw. I'll stop to your office in the morning."

The marshal nodded and walked away down the street.

Cort's eyes were still on the spot where he'd claimed Cardin's life when he caught sight of Lark at the edge of the street. Most folks had gone home or to the saloon. She stood watching him. His long strides took him to her, his arms open. She ran into his embrace and tucked her head against his chest.

"Did he hurt you?" Cort asked her.

"Not the way you think. His hands. His touch. Those eyes. They'll always be with me."

Cort leaned away and lifted her face with his fingers. His vision clouded. Still, he made out the bruised area on her cheek. "He hit you."

"Only once. Mostly he stayed downstairs and kept an eye on his drunken gang members."

"I'd like to put more bullets into his worthless hide."

"It's over, Cort," she whispered.

"You saw it?"

"Yes."

"Killing. It does something to most men. I shot one of his gang. First time I ever shot someone who wasn't wearing a gun. I'd have killed them all if Tangle hadn't reeled me in."

"What's wrong? There's more bothering you. You don't look well. Please let me help you."

"If you want to help, I need you to go on to the hotel. Get a room while I get a whiskey and settle down. I'll be along after I see about the soldiers."

"You aren't going to tell me. I know you. You haven't been seeing right."

He drew a finger over her lips and leaned down to kiss her. "Give me time to come back from the man who just killed another man. I have to step back."

He looked into her questioning eyes. Pain stabbed through

him and his vision blurred. He was losing his sight. For a second, he'd seen Cardin double. *Blind.* How would he run a ranch dead blind?

He turned and strode away from her. Pride twisted him into knots.

"Cort. If it's your eyes or head, let's go to the doctor," she called after him.

Cort ignored her and kept walking. Damned if he'd tell her he was most likely going to be a useless burden. Doc Yates had warned him. His head and his heart pulled him in two directions. Swallowed by the hoots and hollers, the smell of whiskey, and the sound of the tinny piano, Cort joined the revelers at the bar.

She waited, staring toward the batwing doors, thinking he'd change his mind and come back. After a while Gus approached her from the hotel, following her stare. So lost in misery, she hadn't even heard him.

Glancing up at him, she said, "He's gone in there. Gus, I can't reason with him. He won't tell me what's wrong."

"I'm sorry 'bout that. But don't put too much stock in what he's sayin'. He's riled up and worried about a lot of things. He'll ease up and find you quicker than a hound after a rabbit. Men like Cort live between two worlds. My guess is, he didn't like you seein' what he was capable of doin.' Most likely didn't like the woman he loves seein' the kind of man he used to be. I understand that thinkin'. Leaves a man exposed, so to speak."

"Besides that, Gus. Something isn't right since he got hit on the head. His eyes. Haven't you seen the way he blinks his eyes?"

"Cort's tough. You won't help nothin' by gettin' yourself sick standin' out in the cool night air. Let's get you to a room in the hotel. And a hot meal."

"He didn't like me seeing the gunfight. He admitted that."

"He's fast."

"We owe you our gratitude for what you did. Running cattle down the street gave me time to get away."

Gus laughed. "Old trick. Borrowed those cows. Tangle and my men are roundin' them up. Bet those greenhorn troopers are learnin' the difference between the front and hind ends of a cow about now."

"You're trying to distract me."

"Is it workin'?"

"Not exactly. He's slipping away from me. I can't put my finger on it. There's women in there he can turn to."

"He wouldn't do that. No woman could ever take your place for him. Sides, I'd beat him into a bowl of stew if he did. I'm goin' to join him for a beer. You go tuck yourself in. And eat."

"You don't have to look out for me. If he isn't on the train tomorrow, I'll make my way. You have to take those troops north."

"Well, it so happens that Fort Randall is north. I plan on stickin' near. So will Tangle. That mule head will come back down to his senses."

"I hope so. Thank you. Goodnight, Gus."

She raised her chin and stepped up onto the boardwalk, and then into the hotel. Sleep wouldn't come easy with a hurt heart.

Lark's face haunted him while he slugged the whiskey in his lonely corner. One of the well-used whores plunked onto his lap. He'd given her pouty face a kindly pat and sent her on her way, but not before he smacked a silver dollar on the table. She snatched it up and sashayed toward the bar. His thoughts were centered on Lark.

Leaving her behind was what he would have to do. Him facing this blindness alone would give her a chance at a good life, without the burden of a blind husband. Remembrance of her warm body against him sent heat to his loins. Damn. She could be in a family way. No baby of his would go without his name. He should have thought of that. *Cort. What a reckless fool you are.*

"Feeling sorry for yourself? Or just plannin' on how best to hurt that gal again?" Gus straddled the seat across from him.

Resentment struck just before guilt washed over him. He didn't like being lectured. Gus usually minded his own business, but just maybe he deserved a kick in the ass. Gamblers guffawed from another table. Bottles and glasses clinked. The piano pounded out a raucous tune, and cigar smoke nearly choked out the breathable air. Cort had nearly lost himself in mindless self-pity before Gus took aim.

"Needed time alone. If I made her cry, I won't mind if you punch me in the mouth. Just don't knock my teeth out."

"I might just do that if I don't like how you play this. She figures you're stirred up about your eyes. Or maybe havin' second thoughts about her. Started her thinkin' about why you'd come to a saloon where prostitutes offer a man plenty."

Cort swigged his whiskey, swallowed, and glared at the dim shape across from him. "Jesus Christ. No other woman could take her place in my bed. Ever. Dammit. She could be carryin' my baby, Gus."

"A baby, huh. That just caps it. If you're finished with boohooin,' I'd suggest you talk to her. She's tucked in at the hotel."

"I plan to."

"You gonna tell me what's goin' on with them eyes?"

"Saw the doctor about my eyes blurring. Sometimes, I barely see at all. Comes and goes. He said I could wake up and my sight could be gone. Or they might get better in time. From the size of the knot on my skull, he guessed it did something in my head that's affecting my eyes. Said there might be bleeding inside, but he'd have to send me to Philadelphia to figure it out. How am I going to run a ranch, bein' an invalid? A husband needs to take care of his wife. Instead, she'd be takin' care of me."

"Have you told her this?"

"No. So keep your mouth shut. Don't want her pity."

"Well, now. Thought I'd heard every sorry excuse there was till you started whining. You're book-learned. You can still make decisions and hold her in your arms. You don't know if tomorrow you'll see or not."

"How will I defend her? Will she have to dress me? Feed me? I can't live like that."

"Come tomorrow at noon, you'll be on the train with her. Or I'll hunt you down. That woman loves you. Sides, you ain't got no choice. Where do blind men live? You willin' to live in one of them hospitals on charity? Maybe you sweep floors for a nickel. What the hell kind of life is that?"

"I'll decide for myself."

"Suit yourself. Figured you to be tougher. One more thing, Cort. You best not hurt that gal or you might find my fist in your mouth."

Once inside the hotel lobby, Cort swung the guest register around. Lark Garrin. Room Five. The clerk looked to be sound asleep on the only settee. Cort took the stairs two at a time. When he found Room Five, the point of his knife released the lock. The door gave way. Inside, he set his gear on the floor as quietly as he could.

In the dim light, Cort watched Lark curled like a little girl beneath a patchwork quilt, her arms bent and one cheek cradled in a hand. He knew for a fact that her body was all woman. Pure, beautiful, and lusciously woman. Recalling the way she fit against him made his throat go dry and his heart trip. For just a moment, his eyes blurred again. Blackness filled his vision and then cleared. Would it always be like this? Being helpless didn't sit well. Leaving her without his name didn't sit well, either. For tonight, he'd have her once more to feed the fire of his soul when she became a sweet memory.

Chapter 23
The Last Taste of Fire

The smell of whiskey and leather found her in her dreams. She wrinkled her nose and stretched her legs. *Warmth and hair and a man pressed against her.* Before she could muster a scream, a hand clamped over her mouth. "Shh. It's me."

She jackknifed into a sitting position and took in his firm chest poking above the cover. A slow fire crawled along her face. How had he managed to get into her bed without her feeling something?

She leaned toward him, wrapping her arms around his neck. "Oh, Cort! I wasn't sure you'd come."

That boyish grin of his made clear that he enjoyed her surprise. He tucked his arm around her, and with a tug he lifted her to lie against him, their mouths inches apart. "I'm here. I'm sorry I left like that. I'm here now," he said hoarsely.

"Do I smell whiskey?"

"A little. Didn't know you were so prudish, Miss Garrin."

"There are women in that saloon. They . . ."

Cort touched two fingers to her mouth to silence her. "Not for me. I'm a man who loves only one woman. She's right here. I'll never betray you."

Lark shook her head and traced his lips with her fingers. Their mouths took each other where there were no more unhappy thoughts. When he lifted his head, he set her back and tugged her nightgown. She lifted it away, dropping it to the side of the bed. He rolled her to his side where they faced each other, a breath apart. He blinked several times as though he were trying to see her. He smoothed her hair beneath his hand and held a strand in the dim light, as if to remember it. Her eyes stayed on his.

They lay together, the moonlight through the window shining on their damp skin. Touching. Exploring. A quiet, peacefulness. Their mouths touched softly and they kissed. And kissed. Then the kisses grew deeper. Until they needed to be closer. Their tongues danced together and their breath mingled. His mouth left hers and moved over her silky skin to where her breasts rose and fell with the beat of her heart. He moved lower. She cradled him. With the sound of his name still on her lips, he took her with him to the depths that only they knew. Where no other could follow. And the night locked away their secrets in a place where their bodies joined and made them one. Skin to skin.

When they awoke, a dreary light filtered through the room from the dust-coated window. Cort touched her smiling face, alight with the sweet blush of a satisfied woman. "Mornin'."

"Morning to you, Mister Cortland Enders."

"I hope you like that name because I want to give it to you. Will you marry me?"

"To make an honest woman of me?" she teased.

"You are an honest woman." He dragged his finger over her nose and down to her lips. His fingers trembled. "In every way."

"Do you love me? And don't look away. I need to know for certain. I don't want a man who feels obligated or pities me."

"I've loved you since I danced with you in Ogallala at that God-awful spectacle called a Ribbon Cotillion. I'm just glad I found you before someone else took you away. Just how do you figure I'd feel obligated?"

"Most men wouldn't want a scarred woman."

"Honey. You just don't understand how beautiful you are. I

see how other men look at you. Makes me damned jealous. And another thing, your scar isn't as bad as you make it out to be. I hardly see it. And neither do the people we care about."

"That's because you love me."

"No. It's because it is true."

"My answer is yes, then. I'll be your wife. I love you more than I can ever say. I can't imagine my life without you."

Those words jolted him. His sight was blurred this morning. And it didn't clear as much as before. To never see her face again was unthinkable. Plunged into darkness, he'd have no life. Cort squeezed his eyes closed. A flash of what her father might look like crossed his mind. He'd like to put a bullet in her father's head. If he ever found him.

He opened his eyes. For a moment, fog distorted her beautiful face. "I've known men who don't treat women right. That's why I had to serve time in prison. If it wasn't for Sienna, I'd be behind bars in Lincoln and most likely just skin and bones. That was over a woman."

She levered up on an elbow. "Tell me what happened."

He sighed, sat up, and leaned against the headboard. Lark moved to sit beside him, one hand resting against his thigh. He could hardly think straight with her this close. He had no doubt she'd see his reaction.

"I showed up on the Harris ranch in about April of 1875. I'd been wandering and holing up wherever I found some work. Got into a gang of robbers. After prison, I wasn't in a good mood."

He paused. The pity and pain in her eyes almost made him stop. "You deserve to hear this from me. I hired out my gun, drank, and everything else that goes on in a saloon."

He felt her stiffen against him. "Go on," she whispered.

"I was with a gal named Sally. A prostitute with a kid to raise. Just a woman trying to take care of her little boy. A few days later, I heard a scream when I was getting ready to head out of town. I ran toward a side alley and found her pinned against the wall, a man punching her in the face while she slid to the ground. She wasn't dead, but her face looked like raw meat. I turned and caught sight of where the damned attacker was heading. If I hadn't come along . . ." Cort rubbed his hands over his face.

"Did you catch up to that miscreant?"

"I did. By mutual agreement, we decided to find out who was faster with a gun. I didn't aim to kill him. I aimed to hurt him. I was faster. But it left Mark Tenner's arm paralyzed."

"You should have been given an award, Cort. How could they have put you in jail for defending a woman?"

"Accordin' to the *law,* I took matters into my own hands. But it was worse than that. That spoiled piece of dung is the son of Calvin Tenner, who's looking to be governor. And he used his influence to have the law herd me to jail."

"That's when Sienna stepped into this?"

"Yep. One thing about Sienna. She was persuasive and had her own powerful friends. I'd been made ranch foreman while Wade was still living. Judge McKenzie, a friend of Sienna's, heard my case. They concocted a plan to have me serve my sentence on the ranch. You know all the rest."

She rose up on her knees and kissed him. When she wrapped her arms around his neck and nuzzled her face against his galloping heart, he knew leaving her would be the toughest thing he ever did. If only he could keep his sight, he'd never let her go.

"I'm proud of you and what you did. I'm mighty proud to become your wife."

He swallowed against the raw pain in his throat. Their time together was going to be short. And he still hadn't figured out where he'd go. Maybe he could find a doctor in St. Louis or

Omaha. "Sweet lady. We better get cleaned up and dressed. That church down the street looks to be a likely place to say our vows. What do you say?"

She pressed her lips to his. "I say we get dressed and get moving. I want to be Mrs. Enders."

"Uh. One other thing. There will be talk. Marrying me before that one-year period of mourning. But I guarantee none of my men will utter a word or they'll be collecting pay."

"I can survive wagging tongues. I've lived through a helluva lot worse."

"Rushed. That's what I think of this. That man needs to give you time enough to have a nice dress sewed up."

"Rozzie. I'm just so glad to become his wife in that Presbyterian church that I don't care if I'm wrapped in an Indian blanket. This dress will do just fine."

"Thin as you are, it needs a few tucks. Just hold still so as I can fix it up some."

Lark looked down at the black-haired woman with a large pin sticking out from between her lips. She tugged the thread through the blue calico dress sprigged with little yellow flowers. "I think this dress is fine."

A long harrumph engendered a laugh. "I thank you for all your help with this, Rozzie, I'm so sorry about your house. I sure brought trouble your way."

"That house needed to be bigger anyhow. Wes says he'll build me a big boardin' house fit for a queen." The woman stood and wobbled a little, then looked Lark over from head to her shoes, as if appreciating her own work. "Pshaw. You could make a potato sack look pretty."

Lark reached for her and they hugged.

"Lands. Let's get to the preacher before you start to cryin' and ruin that pretty pair of eyes. Got a whole town out to see you two get hitched. Even them soldiers. Except the few of them makin' sho' that train don't leave without you. Those outlaws is bound up in a cattle car, layin' in cow dung where they belong."

Dorothy Yates handed her a bunch of dried lavender to hold before Lark stepped from the rear office of the church. *Stunned. Scared. Excited. Anxious. In love.* Those were some of the things that coursed through every thought at the sight of the packed pews before her. Then her eyes settled on Cort. He'd changed into a crisp white shirt and dark blue wool pants. His holster and gun belt were on the floor near the oak altar.

His hair had been trimmed and his face clean-shaven. When she took her place beside him, she smelled bay rum. Cort stood straight, not taking his eyes from her. He winked and took her hand between both of his. The preacher took his place and began his opening lecture about what marriage should mean between a man and a woman. The words were far away. All she could do was look up into Cort's face and believe their lives would be wonderful. Their fingers laced and he grinned.

Lark heard, *"Do you take this man to be your wedded husband?"* She answered, "I do."

At Cort's turn, he barked, "I do" with such force, there was laughter. Gus stepped forward to hand over the gold ring. Cort slipped it onto her finger, then pressed her hand against his mouth.

There hadn't been many times in her life that she hadn't listened carefully to what was being said in church. She had a feeling of time standing still and of her body floating through air with hopes and dreams. The thought occurred that she might be dreaming.

"I now pronounce you man and wife. Mister Enders. You may kiss your bride."

Cort hesitated. Gus stepped forward and leaned toward him. "Best do that before I do it for you."

Cort scowled. When he took her against him, his mouth possessed hers with a jarring kiss that might be considered ill-mannered inside a church. "For as long as I draw breath, darlin'. I'll love you," he said.

Farewells were painful. Wichita had become home. Cort had found her and destroyed the devil who'd chased her here. Rozzie, Doctor Yates and his wife, Wes, Zuetta, and everyone in town stood outside the train car as she and Cort took their seats. She would forever remember their faces.

"No sadness today. You're going home. Where you belong," Cort admonished her while the train lurched northbound. He kept tight hold of her hand. Something niggled. What had he said just now? *You're going home.*

CHAPTER 24
SACRIFICE

Mid-March 1877

Cort set his Stetson on the seat across from them. He clutched her hand, rubbed his thumb over her fingers, and wished to God his eyesight was clear. Nothing felt right. Things had slowly gotten worse until he was afraid that if he stood, he might bump into one of the seats. His teeth clenched. Maybe if he dozed, he'd wake up and his vision would clear. Finally, he managed to sleep until someone nudged him from the darkness. "Cort. The train is slowing."

Cort woke with a start and took in his surroundings. His vision was clouded but he could make out the approaching buildings from the window. When he looked toward his wife, her beautiful face dissolved into a watery pool. Damn. He was losing his sight. She squeezed his hand. He felt her wariness flood through him.

Tangle came up beside them and nodded. "That there is Emporia. Guess we'll be stoppin' here for a spell. Been travelin' about three hours. Might be a good time to eat in a restaurant. Got a good way to go to Omaha before we can get to Ogallala."

"Thanks, Tangle. How's Gus doin'?" Cort asked, his voice hoarse from his long sleep.

"Like you. Been snorin'. Some of them troopers near him took off for another car, it got so loud."

Cort had to chuckle. "I'm goin' to see Lark to the restaurant. Guessin' you boys have another place in mind."

"Ain't goin' to lie, boss. I need a drink. But I'll get me some vittles. Got a little place in mind for that. See you back here before the train leaves. The conductor said it'll give us two hours."

With that, Tangle turned and moved with a jangling of spurs toward the other end of the car. When Cort turned toward her again, Lark was staring at him as though she could see through him. Her eyes were golden brown in a sea of rippling waves.

"Cort. Something is wrong." The anguish in her voice hurt. Worse, he knew he'd have to hurt her even more. There was only one thing he could do. He'd have to leave here and find a doctor who might or might not fix him. One thing for certain, his pride refused to let him be a burden.

Lark was far too observant. If she suspected he was in trouble with his eyes, she'd try to get him to some fancy doctor. What if there was nothing they could do? He refused to be led, fed, and dressed for the rest of his life. Doc Yates had already told him all he needed to know. No way in hell was he going to subject his wife to caring for an invalid the rest of her life. Bumping into furniture and sitting on a porch rocker wasn't how he wanted to live.

They waited for Gus, Tangle, and the other passengers and troopers to file out of the train car toward the depot platform. Cort stood and she followed him. Just as they got to the doorway, it swung open and the outline of a man in a black suit and cap bumped into him.

"Pardon. Guess you didn't see me coming toward you, sir." Cort nodded as the man moved on.

"Cort? Tell me what's wrong," Lark insisted.

He searched her face but her features were so blurred, he could no longer make them out. A blackness was closing in around the edges of his vision. He cupped her face between his hands. "Nothing, pretty lady. Nothing for you to worry about.

Let's go get some supper or we'll miss the train."

Lark didn't move. "Something's wrong. Sooner or later I'll need to know."

Cort leaned down and took her mouth in a searing kiss. One that he hoped would last him for the rest of his lonely days. Where did a blind man go? She would find someone new and raise a family on that ranch. He wondered how he'd live without her.

When he lifted his lips from hers, he could barely make out the tears that swelled in her eyes, but he felt their warmth beneath his fingers. "Let's put on our coats. Mighty cold out there in the wind," he suggested.

Those words would replay over and over in his head as he rode toward anyplace that had some whiskey, a warm fire, and a bed. When and if he no longer could see, he'd have to find a doctor. Maybe there was one right here in Emporia. He never figured he'd die inside his own head like this.

The soldiers boarded the train. Standing beside Tangle, Lark watched for Cort. When Tangle offered her a hand up the boarding step, she shook her head. He nodded and went inside the train. *Where was Cort?* He said he'd just buy some tobacco and be along. When she saw Gus coming toward her with that long, shuffling gait of his, his usual smile was missing. Cort wasn't with him. She felt faint.

"Best we get aboard. They're about to pull out," he said as he reached her.

"No. Not without Cort. I knew something was very wrong. We had a nice dinner. He paid the waitress. Then he said he had to go get some tobacco and cigarette rolls. That he'd catch up. He keeps his word."

"Lark. Please get inside out of this cold afore you get yourself sick," Gus pleaded.

His head tipped downward. When he glanced up again, he looked aged. His expression was forbidding and hard as though carved in stone. Her world spun. Running was all she could think to do. She guessed that's exactly what her feet had done, until strong arms lifted her and carried her against a hard chest into the car. The conductor stepped up behind them and lifted the stair. Gus set her on the same seat where just a while ago she had sat beside her husband.

"You know he's gone. You knew." The harsh words were meant for herself. She should have known.

"I saw him mounting his horse with his gear. His rifle in the boot. I tried to stop him."

"Why? Why?" she cried. She was barely aware of Tangle standing up and coming toward them until Gus waved him back.

"Because he loves you. Because his eyes are bad. Doc Yates told him he could go completely blind at any time. Probably that knock to his head. Cort felt less of a man and more of an invalid. Not that I agreed, but he figures you can have a good life with that ranch. It's all yours now. Sometimes you got to let someone go so they can figure things out. Expect that's what he'll do. Said he'd look for a doctor and if things work out, he'll come home."

"I could have gone with him to find a doctor."

"And if he goes blind, how would you convince him to let you give up your life to tend him? That's what he thinks in his fool head."

"Will you look for him?"

"Do you want me to?"

"Gus. Yes, please do that for me and I'll never ask another thing."

Gus touched the tears streaking along her cheeks. "I'd like to give him a flailing for makin' you cry. After I get my troopers to Fort Randall, I'll see what I can find out. I know some places he might hole up till spring. Fool. Don't think he's so stupid as to live in the dark. He'll get to some hospital."

"Find him."

"Findin' him is one thing. Getting him to come back to his ranch is another thing. If he goes blind, he won't be wantin' you to know. Guess he didn't think this all out."

Lark sat back, leaned her head against the seat, and stared out at the stark landscape that was Kansas in winter. The long sloping plains stretched out, dotted by a few cows here and there, grass caked beneath a coat of frost as though God had dropped sugar from the heavens. All of a sudden, she thought she saw a rider in the distance wearing a Stetson. A brief wave of his hand and then he was gone.

The minutes ticked by. The hours turned to a day. And when they reached Omaha, she had cried until nothing was left inside. Just numbness as once again, she had to say goodbye to Gus. Before he left, he pressed an envelope into her hand along with the folded marriage document. Gus's last words replayed in her tortured thoughts while the Union Pacific clacked westward along the rails.

He wanted you to have this legal marriage document so as there would be no doubt you now own the Double E, that was the Circle H. And he put a note in that envelope to read once you got down the tracks. He's hurtin'. I know that. Keep your chin up, pretty lady. I'll be along one day to see how you're doin'. And I'll look for him. Maybe drag him home if I have to.

She looked up at the sound of jangling spurs. Tangle took his place across from her. He didn't seem able to express the sorrow written on his face. But she saw it in the way he rubbed his eyes, searched the grasslands, and turned his face away to find solace in nothing. Just before his eyes closed, he looked toward her.

"Good to get home. The ranch needs you. The boss, well,

he's gonna think things through like he always does. In the meantime, I'll see you get there safe. Sent a telegram on to Ogallala so as they know we're on the way back. Bet Theresa and Nita are fit to be tied."

Lark couldn't muster a smile. She reached across and touched the hand that lay balled in a fist on Tangle's lap. He uncurled his fingers and grasped hers, squeezing them with reassurance, and then he released her and patted her hand. Leaving her to think about what she would do. *A private detective?* Gus? Someone would find him.

Early April 1877

Smoke, clinking beer glasses, and hoots and hollers surrounded him as Cort swallowed his fourth whiskey. Hell, he'd bought the whole bottle so he might as well finish it. Maybe it'd kill him and take away the God-awful pain knifing his heart. By now, Lark was tucked into the house on the ranch with Theresa, Nita, and Zeke consoling her and cursing him. Which he deserved.

The damned glass was a filmy outline. A local doctor had told him he didn't know enough about Cort's head injury to pursue treatment. Instead, he recommended going to an Eastern doctor. However, he'd told Cort to stay in bed. What kind of answer was that?

A big bearded hunter beside Cort was taller than him and mouthy, and kept the bartender busy with complaints about the watered-down whiskey. From the cut of the wool robe, Cort guessed the man was a buffalo hunter. Sure did smell like one. Cort was game for a fight, just to relieve the hell boiling inside.

After he swallowed his whiskey, he turned to take in the room full of gamblers, whores, gunslinger types, and want-to-be gunfighters. From what he could make out through his bleary, colorless world, he was smack dab in the middle of mostly cut-throats. More often now, everything was black. He'd spent days lying in his hotel room until he knew he had to figure out where to go and how he'd get there. Stay in Emporia. Or maybe he'd try to get to St. Louis. No. He was going home. There had to be a way to make a life there.

"What you starin' at?"

Jesus. The buffalo hunter wanted to start a fight. Maybe another shock to the head would kill him. On second thought, he probably should avoid more shocks. He turned toward the vague shape beside him and trailed his eyes upward to the man's face, lost behind a watery veil. He didn't think he'd swallowed enough whiskey to actually be drunk. Not yet.

"Nothin'. Just tryin' to mind my own business," Cort replied.

"Keep that look you give me to yourself afore I decide to teach you a lesson."

Cort never backed down. Never. This time, he gave it a thought. No sense in trying to fight this hunter unless it could be fair. He had to see to fight. Just then, all of his vision blinked away. He felt a big fist grasp his coat, jerk him around, and shove him backwards. Cort landed on his back, desperately searching for any glimpse of the room. There was nothing. Blackness.

"Hey. That man can't see. Best leave him alone," a voice shouted.

Cort didn't know who'd spoken, but his ears told him it must be the bartender. This was the helpless feeling he'd most feared. Without his eyes, there was no sense in living. What the hell did a washed-up gunfighter do for a living when he couldn't even see his hand in front of his face?

"I ain't pickin' no fight with a man that can't even suck a tit without help."

Cort heard boots stride away from him while he heaved to

his feet. His vision always came back. Just a few more minutes. The room was quiet. Then, distant voices. It sounded like two or three men were marching toward him. He blinked to clear his eyes. A little light, and then faint shapes stood near him. The darkness hovered on the edges of what little vision he had left.

"Hello, Cort Enders. Maybe you can't see me. But I remember you."

"Who are you?"

"The man you shot in the arm. Paralyzed me. No doctors can help. Thanks to you. Now you got no sight. I'm thinking that's retribution."

Cort squinted. A man with a mustache took foggy shape in his vision. He blinked again. "Mark Tenner?"

"The same. My pa is standing over there. You remember him. He had you arrested. Never could understand why you didn't serve three long years in prison over in Lincoln. Except for that ranch woman who interfered, you'd be in a hellhole right now. Instead, I come across you in a nice town like Emporia. Right near Pa's ranch."

"What's done is done. You mistreated a nice woman."

"Sally? She's a whore. I paid for her time. I didn't get my money's worth. So I taught her a lesson. No call to shoot me."

Cort reached for the sonofabitch but his arm swiped at air. Another man caught him and yanked his arms behind his back. Cold metal clicked. A new voice said, "Son, I can tell your eyes ain't good. I'm Marshal Tom Vale. Gotta take you over to the jail till I sort this out and see if they're right. Calvin and Mark tell me you still owe time in prison. Looks like you could use a bed and food. Just come along peaceable."

Another voice. "Just a minute, Marshal. My son had his say. Now I'll have mine."

Whoever held Cort swung him around so he could face the new speaker . . . the man who'd gotten him arrested back in

Ogallala. Cort squinted at what looked to be a tall, looming form in a dark gray suit. A fancy dresser. And a powerful man with revenge on his mind.

"Go on. I'm listening," Cort gritted out between clenched teeth. "You would be Calvin?"

"Calvin Tenner. And I know more about what went on with Judge McKenzie and Sienna Harris than you figure. You broke the deal. Unless you have a written pass from your *wife*. You'll serve the rest of your time. I'll see to it."

Cort was jerked into a stumbling walk. His eyes fogged while he blinked, trying to see where he was going. Chairs slid aside, and he lurched when he slammed into one. A few people laughed. Time in a prison where he couldn't see to defend himself sank in. Suddenly, someone jerked him to a halt. Another man unbuckled his gun belt.

"I better find my gun in the marshal's office," Cort snapped.

"It'll be there." The marshal's voice held an honest kindness.

A hand at his back nudged him forward. "Your horse and gear at the livery, son?"

"Yeah. Can you look after my horse and bring my gear to the jail?"

"That's what I plan on doin'. You got a wife or family? They might want to know you're in trouble. The judge this politician fellow is roundin' up is tough. I'm afraid you'll be sent to prison. And you can't see much, can you?"

"No, my sight comes and goes. Had a knock on the head down in Wichita. Guess I won't last long in prison if I can't defend myself."

"Sounds like you been there before."

"I have. For a different charge. I was a dumb kid back then."

Cort heard a long sigh. "Well, careful stepping through the door. Got some loose boards underfoot."

A breeze against his face told him they were outside. Cort

was led along a boardwalk and through another door, into what felt like a hallway and then into a room of shadowy light. Nothing took shape.

The marshal clutched his arm and turned him. "Sit down. I'll be back in here with some food and coffee in a bit. Got to see to your things first."

"How about taking off the cuffs?"

"Stand up. Turn around. What did you say your name is, again?" the marshal asked.

"Cort Enders." The shackles came free, but then the marshal locked one to Cort's wrist. "Sit down. Gotta fasten you to the bunk. Orders from Tenner. I don't like those two anymore than you do. But I got to keep my job."

"I understand." Cort laughed.

"What's so funny?"

"You said you have to see to my things. Seeing anything would be good right now. I'd do some things different."

Cort sensed the marshal studying him. "Maybe that judge will let you off, Cort. I hope so. Seems like you already lost somethin' important."

"Yeah. More than just my sight. You and I know I won't survive in that Lincoln prison."

"Don't talk like that. Things will work out. Even if they don't, you look like you can fight if you have to. They say a year ain't so bad. You sure there's nobody I can contact for you?"

"Maybe one person. Can you send a telegram to Fort Randall, and maybe Fort Leavenworth, to Gus Quaid? Tell him I could use a visit as quick as he can get here."

"I'll do that." The marshal stood and squeezed his shoulder. Cort peered through the watery haze. Tom Vale had white hair. An older man with maybe a kindly face.

"Tom. Somethin' else funny."

"What's that?"

"I'd just made up my mind to go home to my ranch. And Tenner found me."

"Nothin' funny 'bout it. I hope you make it back there. You have a written pass, accordin' to Judge Pelton. Where is it?"

Cort thought back. The pass had been in the pocket of his Levi's. The pair that had been ripped apart when he was dragged. That mistake was going to cost him. He shook his head.

"I was dragged by some no-accounts. Pass is gone. Not that you'll believe that."

"Sure as hell would be a good thing to have about now."

"Got one more favor. In my saddlebag you'll find a green ribbon. I know it seems strange to you, but I'd like to have that."

"Don't seem strange. I had a wife and kept her locket with me. Sure you don't want me to let your woman know?"

"No. Best this way. If I get out of this, just get me on a train to Ogallala."

Cort closed his eyes and the door clanked shut. The jangling of keys and the steady footfalls of the marshal faded. When he opened his eyes again, his world was dark, from either loss of all light outside or loss of vision. His wool coat gave him some measure of warmth. If Gus got here, Cort would make it clear that Lark was not to know where he was. He stretched out on the bunk and waited for fate.

A clatter of a cup against the bars sent him to a sitting position. Someone stood on the other side of the bars. For a moment, a blurry form appeared and then fell into blackness. "I see Tom listened to me and kept you in cuffs."

The voice belonged to Calvin Tenner. If Cort got out of here, he'd love to beat the man into the ground. No matter the consequences.

"So, you've come to gloat. Didn't bring your worthless son with you?"

Cort heard the man's boots as he moved closer. Calvin must be close to the bars. A tin cup clattered against the stone floor. "If I had the choice, I'd see you hang. Unfortunately, Judge Pelton can't go that far. Still, you will serve time in a brutal prison and I'll enjoy every minute thinking about it."

Cort's first thought was to pitch himself toward the bars and grab the bastard between the thick iron shafts. But his wrist was fastened to the bed. "At least I let your spoiled kid live after what he did to Sally."

"The whore?"

"You are a low-down smug son of a bitch. Get the hell out of here before I puke."

"You're blind. That just makes this all the better. I'd send the man who thudded you on the head a letter of appreciation. Want to tell me who he is?"

Cort managed a grin. "He's dead."

"Pity. See you at your hearing. Smells rancid in here. Like piss. It'll be worse where you're going."

Cort yanked at his wrist. He was weak from lack of food and water, at the mercy of circumstances, and blind. The only thing he had left was Lark's face in his memory. *Ah, Lark. What are you doing now? Don't be crying over me. I'll keep the green ribbon.*

Chapter 25
Dark Spring

"Jesus Christ. I got back here as quick as I could. I'm sorry you had to put up with that vulture. Saw him strolling toward the saloon, wearin' his cocky grin."

The sound of keys brought Cort out of the dark dreams he'd rather not have. "Appreciate it if you'd remove the cuff. Can't feel my hand. Hard to sleep."

"Surely will. Sorry about this. Had to have you bound while Calvin Tenner wallowed."

The lawman hunkered beside him and unlocked the cuff. Cort winced and rubbed his wrist where the iron had chafed into his skin. Mostly from tugging to get his hands on Tenner.

He would stake his life that Tom Vale wore a gun. In a minute, Cort could have it drawn on the old man and lock him down in his own jail. Seeing, and finding his way to his horse, were obstacles to that. Besides, he didn't want to cause the marshal embarrassment.

"You just settle on that bunk," the marshal said. "I'll be right in with some mighty good fixin's from the hotel restaurant. How are your eyes? I can bring a doc over to check you."

"I'll settle for food. Not much anyone can do about my sight. Maybe the doc tomorrow?"

When Marshal Vale turned away, Cort looked toward where he expected the man to be standing. "Tom. Did you send those telegrams to Gus Quaid?"

"Sure did. I'll let you know if I hear back."

"Thanks."

Suddenly the man stopped. "Almost forgot somethin'. I got your gear all stowed and I'll keep it safe at my house. Your horse and saddle will be here waitin' for you when you get out. Or some family might come along. Anyways, here's somethin' you wanted."

Tom handed him the green ribbon. While the marshal's footsteps receded, Cort slid the ribbon between his fingers and savored the feel in the darkness of his world.

A short time later, footsteps sounded again, and Tom set down a large tray on the end of Cort's bunk. The food smelled like he was home in his own kitchen, right down to the apple pie. Tom put a fork in his hand. Helpless, Cort had to accept what he couldn't change. As he clumsily shoveled the food into his mouth, he thought that in a few days or weeks he'd be eating beans and bread. At Christmas he might get an apple. For the first time, panic started to take hold. Cortland Enders in his youth might be tempted to throw this tray across the cell in frustration. Instead, he mulled the idea of a year and a half. What would he look like when he got out? He didn't know what he looked like now.

Late April 1877

Her first full day *home*. The Circle H was no more. Instead, the gate sign proclaimed it the Double E Ranch in scorched letters. Juan, Theresa, and Jude had met her and Tangle at the train depot. She hardly remembered the rocking, jolting ride home while Theresa peppered her with questions, the chatter of mundane events hardly sorted in her head. Her mind was numb and her heart cold. She now knew what Sienna had felt.

Nita and Theresa fussed over her, promising they'd help her sew new clothes to replace everything she'd lost in the fire in

Wichita. They'd put too much food out on the table, but she picked at it. Food had no appeal when Cort might be out there and hungry.

After leaving the table, she mindlessly wandered to the long porch, where she sat in a chair and leaned her head back, staring at the distant hills. The cattle were dark splotches against the waving Indian grass and bluestem. She truly loved this place. Could she love it as much without Cort at her side? A whisper of wild indigo and Virginia mint drew her attention and she thought about picking some.

"Sunflowers not out for another month or two. Recollect you liked them."

Zeke. She turned her head to see him sitting about ten feet from her on the other side of the doorway, slouched in the deep shadows of late morning. "Didn't hear you, Zeke. How's your leg?"

"Doin fine."

"You didn't come to breakfast today."

"Figured I'd let them yackety women do the talkin'. Besides, Tangle was in there and I can't get a word in edgewise when he gets to jawing." Silence fell between them and spoke more of their mutual worry than words ever could.

After a while, Zeke broke the stillness. "Herd looks good so far. Took care of ranch business and the graves. Like I'll do as long as I live. The books are fine."

"You miss her."

"Like the air isn't quite enough to fill my lungs."

"I miss Cort like that."

"Tangle filled me in on the doings in Wichita. Gus Quaid stood by you. And I'm glad Cort killed that mad dog, Cardin. You both been through more than you should."

"We were married. Cort and me. In case anyone questions that. Cort made sure I got the marriage paper before he took off. He wanted me to have proof."

"Do you think I'd question something like that?"

She gulped back a sob. Her tears ran over her cheeks and she wiped them with the edge of her coat. "No. But some might. Truthfully, I don't deserve this place. You should have it. I'll leave if that's what you want."

"Cort figured on what *some* might think. No one on this ranch will think less of you for staying here. I have a place to live. And that's all I need. As far as running this place, well, that's another matter. You'll learn and I'll be here to help you along until my old bones give out."

"I need to find him."

"Gus Quaid's a good man with a hard past. If he said he'll look for Cort, consider it done. I'd bet Gus is trailing him. Besides, knowing that mule-headed husband of yours, he's probably on his way back here."

"Do you have any idea where he might have gone?"

"He lived the outlaw trail after prison in Texas. He knows where to hide so no one can find him. Except for Gus."

"His eyes. He's going blind, Zeke. He can't stay out there alone."

Zeke stood, wobbling slightly. He walked to where she sat and hunkered in front of her. "Now you listen. You're gonna see that man again. He loves you and this ranch. Everywhere any of us looks, Cort is still there. And tomorrow, I'm sitting beside you to go over the books. We got a job ahead of us. Hirin' more hands and building the herd. Already sent some men down to Dodge City to run some cattle up here. Just so you know, one of the men is Mason Lanning."

"Mason. Cort fired him for no good reason. I'm glad he came back."

"Well. I hired him back when he came along. He's a good drover and we needed him. 'Sides that, Cort fired him only because he was jealous when Mace was trying to court you right under his nose. Fact is, Mason sent us a telegram to tell us where you were. Trouble was, Cort had already left to find you."

She laughed, surprising herself. "Jealous? I figured that. I didn't quite know what to do about it."

"Best not do a blessed thing. Let the bulls charge at each other. You go on inside before you catch a chill. Don't need no sick women around. I got to go help with rounding up what stock we still got."

She reached for his hand and squeezed it. "You are the kindest of men."

"Now don't go mushy on me. And don't say that in front of my ranch hands. I got my pride. He'll be back, lady. One day you'll see him riding up the road."

She watched while Zeke stepped down off the porch and strode toward the corral. Lark couldn't imagine this place without Zeke. He did a fair job correcting for his limp, but she couldn't forget how his search for cattle during a downpour had been disastrous for him and his horse. That same day, she had fallen into the Blue River where Cort rescued her.

Cort. She reached into her apron pocket and withdrew the wrinkled letter she wasn't sure she could read without shattering into a thousand pieces. Zeke had reminded her that there was hope. Lark opened the folds and saw Cort's boldly scrawled words. And began the task of reading them.

Dearest Wife,

By now you've found I've left. I'm hoping you will keep me in your prayers and know you'll always be with me no matter where I go. With a steady hand and your intelligence, you'll do me proud and run that ranch. Zeke will guide you. You were right. That head injury must have done something to take my sight. It has been fading and I fear I won't see much longer. If I can find a doctor to fix this, I'll be back. I didn't want to saddle you with my problem. You'll be with me no matter. For now, I have to do this alone. Being helpless isn't what I want. If you decide to marry again, I won't stand in your way. For now, know that my love and longing are with you. Always, Cort

Lark lifted the creased paper and pressed it against her heart. How would she endure knowing that he was suffering inside a dark world? She tucked the note under her coat and lifted her chin. Looking out over the wind-blown grass while it shifted in swirls, she imagined seeing him riding toward her. *Cortland Neil Enders, I will find you.*

Cort lay on his bunk staring into the dark nothing of his cell. Whenever he heard the outer door open, he caught sight of a faint glimmer and the vague shape of Tom Vale. Both the marshal and Cort's lawyer, a local man, had insisted that Doctor Trevor have a look at his eyes. The doctor was from some big medical school in Philadelphia. An Easterner. To Cort, he sounded young. And smart in new things. The doctor gave him assurance that this loss of sight might be temporary and that it most certainly had been the result of the whack on his head. He said something about bleeding inside.

The swelling had all but disappeared, though his headaches still erupted without warning. Without dangerous surgery, there was only one prescription, according to Doc Trevor. Long bed rest. Cort knew that hinged on Judge Pelton and Calvin Tenner. A few words from Tenner and the judge might send him to hard labor. A blind man hacking away at rocks would amount to torture. Cort had to put that thinking out of his mind.

"You look as helpless as a cow in quicksand! What will you get mixed up in next, Cort?"

Gus Quaid's booming voice could never be mistaken. Cort

widened his eyes until he could make out the vague outline of a buckskin clad man. He swung his legs over the edge of the bunk and stood. When he took tenuous, ill-guided steps toward his visitor, he heard Gus's mumbled curse. "Those eyes need tendin'. They got a damned doctor in this town?"

"Already been here. Maybe they'll clear up. Maybe they won't."

"After leavin' that pretty wife of yours in Emporia, I don't plan to leave here without you. She pleaded with me to find you. I'm here. Never met a more stubborn mule than you. How did you get into the hoosegow?"

"That kid I shot in the arm. The one who beat Sally to a pulp. The kid's father is Calvin Tenner."

"That politician I heard of?"

"The same. Mark Tenner's arm is paralyzed. They want my blood."

"He deserved worse. How'd they find you?"

"Just happened to be in a saloon, planning out where I was going. That's when Mark noticed me. He was likely gamblin' and looking for a whore. I couldn't make out faces."

"Go on."

"Damn. Gus, I can't see my hand clear. I'd already decided I had to get back to the ranch when I was arrested."

"You should have listened to us."

Silence fell, no sound except breathing. Cort stumbled back to his bunk and sat down. "I already had a hearing. Calvin Tenner is powerful. No one in that courtroom thought a whore deserved justice. After I helped Sally up and got her tended, I called Mark out. Challenged him to a gunfight. Pulled my shot enough to wing his arm. Everything got turned around in that court."

"And that's where the ranch comes in?" Gus asked.

"I worked for Wade and Sienna Harris on the Circle H. A

cocky young gunslinger from Texas with three years of prison behind him for bank robbery. You know all that."

"Thought you might get in trouble, the way things stood back in Texas. What happened in Nebraska?"

"Wade Harris made me foreman. Found Wade dead beside his horse in October 1875. The next March, I got into it with Mark Tenner. Sienna rode into town and brokered a deal. I exchanged prison for three years workin' her ranch. Trouble was, she wanted to keep me loyal and keep the respect of the ranch hands. She was dying of cancer and I didn't know it until she told me. The deal included marriage. Her and Wade had no heirs. Guess this was her way of keeping the ranch under my control. I owned it."

A loud whistle nearly pierced Cort's ears. "Seems like you go up one mountain and down twice as fast. Just like you to cross paths with a prick like Mark Tenner. Maybe I can beat the crap out of the pissant and get him to change his tune."

"I don't want you landing in jail. Maybe my luck will turn. If not, I keep telling myself prison won't be too bad the second time."

"Jesus Christ. This ain't fair. I might have to see this Judge Pelton in person. That prison wagon is already outside. I aim to speak on your behalf if they give me a chance."

"My lawyer thinks I'll have to serve eighteen months. Tomorrow I'll hear the sentence before they take me to prison."

"Don't sound like much of a lawyer. I'll see what I can do."

"Don't tell her. Don't tell Lark or anyone at the ranch where I've been sent. I don't want her to come here and see me behind bars."

"Damn. You're as wound up as a bale of barbed wire." Cort heard shuffling feet. Moccasins. Gus loomed on the other side of the bars. "I'm not goin' to let this go. If it means takin' this up to the Governor's office, I will. I won't promise about Lark, either. That woman's heart is splintered. She must be worried sick. I should've knocked you out at the train."

With that, a door squeaked and Cort sensed he was alone. After a while, the marshal arrived with his breakfast and kind words of encouragement. Cort picked at the food. Time had no meaning in the darkness. A while later, he was led by the marshal and a deputy into the courtroom. His ankles were shackled, for which Tom apologized. In the dim light, Cort could just see vague shapes in shades of gray. He stumbled amid laughs and gasps as he was led to a seat, where Tom grasped his shoulders firmly and directed him to sit.

Someone proclaimed the court in session. Mark Tenner shouted an obscenity while Gus shot back with his own objections and threats before he was led out of the courtroom, promising to bring back a new lawyer.

Cort rubbed his eyes and the judge ordered him to stand. A firm hand clutched his right arm. The mumbles behind him faded. His body shook with rage because he hadn't been accorded a chance to defend himself. His lawyer shouted above the tumult that his client hadn't given his testimony. A rap of the gavel sent the room into silence.

"You already told the marshal at your side, Mister Enders. I heard all I need to hear. All the evidence I've seen shows that you were the one to call out Mark Tenner. Not the other way around. As to this Sally woman, she never reported this event to the marshal in Ogallala. Besides, women of that sort know full well what is expected of them. Since you already served time in the jurisdiction of Ogallala, I will have you finish your term in the prison at Lincoln for eighteen months."

The judge paused. "If you could have produced the required pass from Sienna Harris Enders, then I would dismiss this case. Since you admit you don't have it, you've broken the terms set out in Ogallala. A warning. If you give them trouble in prison, you will finish out the entire three years. As to your blindness. I understand they have a mighty good doctor in Lincoln. I'll not have you assigned hard labor. Marshal, take the prisoner to the conveyance. Make sure he has a coat."

Another rap of the gavel. Cort felt a tug on his arm. He walked along silently, angry and defeated. For a good while, he'd have to live with the shame, emptiness, and mistakes. When he got out, he'd most likely be a hardened man. Bitterness would eat away at him inside. And Lark would be out of reach.

Chapter 26
The Fight and Redemption

Fresh-baked bread, fried eggs, and bacon filled the big kitchen with aromas, drawing Zeke, Tangle, and Mason in from out back where they always figured out the chores for the day. Since she'd returned from Wichita, Lark had made it her practice to listen to the men talk around the table about ranch workings. Mason and ten drovers had brought a herd up from Amarillo.

Things had settled a bit, but her heart was broken without Cort. Few talked about him in front of her for fear of causing an upset. She'd confided in Nita and Theresa about the baby coming in November, but no one else knew. This was something she wanted to tell Cort when he came home. She was holding on to that hope.

"Nita, I'm going out to the porch for a breath of air." She stood and left the men to their discussions.

"You try to eat something later," Theresa called after her.

Lark walked down the long hallway to the front door that had been left open for the soft breeze. She hesitated at the office, imagining Cort seated behind that big desk, scrawling notes and giving his grin. Outside on the porch, she cupped a hand over her eyes to look out over the hills. The sky was a splendorous azure blue without a cloud to be seen. The wind blew dust along the ridge line where the new cattle had been rounded up for branding.

As she moved down the stone steps to walk through the grass, another dark plume of dust caught her attention. That meant a rider. Something drew her forward, ever faster until she nearly ran, wishing she could make out the figure riding at a gallop. When the man got closer, recognition settled in. Everything inside of her went still like the quiet before a storm. *Peter Varnum. The marshal from Ogallala.* It had to mean bad news.

He reined in his horse and dismounted, and tipped his hat to her while Juan trotted over to take the marshal's horse. "Just water him. Won't be long." Varnum gave his full attention to her, his mouth turned down. "Good to see you Lark. The place looks mighty nice."

She took refuge in manners, needing to hear whatever tidings he'd brought but terrified of them at the same time. "Thanks. Surely you can stay to have some breakfast."

"Don't mind if I do. Some coffee would taste fine."

"What brings you out here? It's a long ride for coffee."

Gravel crunched beneath boot heels as Zeke, Tangle, and Mason hurried to her side, forming a protective circle around her. Zeke was blunt. "What's this about? Maybe I should hear first?"

"Zeke. If this is about Cort, I need to hear, straight out," Lark said, even as her lips quivered.

"All right," Varnum said. He reached into his vest pocket, pulled out a telegram, and handed it to Lark. "Rode out yesterday, early afternoon. Had to bunk overnight at your way station. Wanted to get this to you as soon as I could."

She scarcely heard what he was saying while she read the telegram. At first, she wanted to scream. Then she reread it. With a shaking hand, she passed the telegram to Zeke.

"What does it say, Zeke?" Tangle asked.

Zeke glanced at Lark and swallowed. "Jesus Christ. We got to put our heads together."

Mason snatched the telegram and scanned it while Tangle read it over his shoulder. Mason's face reddened with what

Lark guessed was the same fury she felt.

"He's in prison in Lincoln," Varnum said. "Gus Quaid was at the sentencing until he got himself thrown out. Eighteen months. And Cort's eyes aren't good. He's nearly stone blind."

For a while, no one spoke. Then the marshal broke the silence, the first to offer advice. "Gave this some thought all the way here. We got Sally, Gus, and me in Cort's corner. As well as all you folks. Heard Cort saved a train load of passengers and a payroll on the Santa Fe. He killed a vicious outlaw that terrorized trains and banks, whom the lawmen couldn't capture. What we need is a delegation to talk to the Governor and get Cort out. Then we'll worry about doctoring."

"I want to go today," Lark said. "Gus sent this at least a week ago."

"Sorry, ma'am. That telegraph operator tried to find me with it. I was out at Falls Point lookin' for a lost kid. Could've been sent more than a week ago."

"You eat somethin' first, Lark," Zeke ordered.

"I'll eat with you, Mrs. Enders. Since we all can't go along, I'll put together letters of testimony for the Governor. He's a stickler for justice."

"I'll tell him what I saw in the gunfight and the train robbery," Tangle snapped.

"Looks like Cort has more friends than he thought," Zeke said. "Mason, you stay behind. I need somebody in charge here."

"I'd rather go along. But I'll keep this place in one piece. You can count on it. Send a telegram when you bring him back and I'll be at the depot."

Lark turned and walked beside Zeke and Tangle toward the house, listening to their plans for supplies and gear. Guns, horses, food, clothes. She stopped in the hallway and allowed her dear friends to move on to the kitchen while she rested the back of her head against the wall, tucked her chin, and sobbed.

Early June 1877

The city of Lincoln bustled with wagons, horses, and large rectangular brownstone buildings that reminded Lark of gloomy castles she'd read about. She hadn't seen so many sorts of stores in one place since her riverboat days along the Mississippi. The saloons looked more like audacious hotels. Zeke spoke to her but she barely heard, so entranced was she with the comings and goings. Almost enough to forget briefly why they were here.

They'd brought Juan along to handle their gear and horses while they concentrated on Cort. The prison loomed above the city, an imposing stone fortress that sent shivers through her. One section was erected with a large square tower, while another section sported a row of tall, impenetrable barred windows. That building was three stories high and most likely where Cort was held. Around the perimeter was a massive wall. Soldiers in uniform rode past their buggy, barely giving them a glance. In the distance, soldiers stood sentinel at the large prison gate, apparently watching their approach.

Between them and the prison, a man mounted on a big sorrel horse sat high on a knoll. Behind him stood a riderless bay with a black mane and tail. Tangle brought the buggy to a halt and waved his hat in the air. Zeke reined up his white horse beside the buggy.

"That's Gus," Tangle said. "Coming toward us with Cort's horse trailin' behind."

When Gus reached them, Lark was surprised at how different he looked. He'd cut his hair and trimmed his beard, and changed from buckskins to a clean gray shirt and Levi's. Leather boots had replaced his moccasins. He nodded when he pulled up beside the buggy, his black eyes fathomless as he studied her.

"Gus," she whispered. "Have you seen him?"

Gus dismounted and tied Cort's horse behind the buggy. He said nothing, as if he could find no words to describe the horrors Cort faced within the stark prison walls. Blindness made the ordeal much worse. She figured Gus didn't want to alarm her with crude details about Cort's condition, but she had to know what to expect if she was going to do him any good.

He leaned against the buggy, facing the prison. "He can't see anyone. He blinks. Hardly wanted to speak to me except to find him a better lawyer. Still has a little fight left. Don't rightly think he'll appreciate your visit, Lark. You can expect him to be angry you came. He gave me orders not to telegram you. Course, I did anyhow. Not the first time I broke my word."

"I'll find him the best doctor. And a lawyer if he'll need one after I finish with the Governor. I'm not leaving till the Governor hears his story."

As Gus turned to face her, she lifted her chin, ready for an all-out fight. "He's prideful," Gus said. "Won't like you gettin' into this."

"I'm worried about getting my husband out, and his pride be damned."

"So be it. Let's get this part done."

"Is he well? Eating?" Lark asked.

"Don't like to say any of this. Brace yourself. I'm warnin' you so as you don't make a fuss when you see him. He's scruffy and his hair's unkempt. He's lookin' a mite gaunt. Says he don't have much appetite. They don't have him in a work party 'cause he's blind. But layin' on a bunk, not knowin' day from night, must be tearing into his gut somethin' awful. Probably enough to drive him mad in the head if he stays much longer."

"I don't think you need to tell her all that, Gus. She's already upset enough," Zeke chided.

"If I didn't give her the picture, this could go bad," Gus retorted. "Lark, don't get riled if he shuns you. Seein' him like this cuts a man. That pride is what he hangs onto."

She lifted her chin. "I'm ready. I know what I need to do. Tangle, let's get going."

Gus mounted his horse and followed them toward the fortress on the hill.

Once the group was given permission to enter, the guards collected their weapons and Lark's reticule. The men dismounted and the guards led the buggy and saddle horses toward a large wooden shed. After they'd all been escorted into the reception office, the three men were advised to take seats and wait for the lady. With a last look in their direction, Lark followed a guard through a barred doorway. Gus swallowed hard. Zeke ran his hand across his mouth and Tangle clenched and unclenched his fists.

"She goin' to be all right seeing him?" Zeke asked no one in particular.

"I'm bettin' on her," Gus replied.

"Ain't fair. I'd like to bust him out," Tangle added.

"Well, don't be sayin' that too loud else we'll all be in the hoosegow," Gus muttered.

With every step Lark took along the long stone corridor, her heart pounded more furiously in her chest. The guard was a tall, stoic looking fellow with black hair and a mustache. His blue uniform looked clean and crisp. She was glad he hadn't struck up a conversation. Deep down inside she hated each guard on a personal level because from her perspective, any guard here might have locked Cort away.

While she fantasized about reaching for the man's gun and

shooting him, she reminded herself that he was just a soldier doing his job. They passed rows of closed oak doors. Except for their quick footfalls, there was an odd serenity within this corridor. It almost felt like a fancy back-east school until she took in the long, barred windows to her left. Light cast the shadows of the ghastly iron rods against the whitewashed walls.

Finally, they stopped at the last door. The guard politely opened it for her and directed her to sit on the chair situated on one side of a long oak table. When he closed the door behind her, she heard the distinct click of the lock. Feeling trapped, she was tempted to return to the door and test the knob, but fear kept her frozen to her seat. Folding her trembling hands in front of her, she waited. A wall clock ticked off the minutes. The far wall held several barred doors. The seat on the opposite side of her, she supposed was for the prisoner. She wanted to scream that Cort wasn't a prisoner. He wasn't a prisoner, just a victim. Her husband.

The sound of footfalls and the clanking of chains cut through the nervous solitude and sent more violent tremors to her lips. The expectation of seeing Cort after more than four months made her grip the edge of the table. Another guard unlocked the door opposite her. When it swung open, she could clearly see a tall, haggard man dressed in a loose striped shirt and baggy striped pants.

Cort shuffled toward the seat across from her, the guard's hand clenched around his arm. He didn't speak. He blinked repeatedly but his stare told her he hadn't seen her. His rugged handsomeness was gone. Instead, he was a defeated man. Humiliated by a flawed system. No. This wasn't Cort. She flinched at the jangle of the chains draped from his wrist manacles. He took the seat and sat stiffly while the guard locked a length of the shackle to a ring in the table.

"I'll be back in a while. Take your time. You got a lot to talk about and I'll look the other way. Be in earshot." The guard left them.

She stared at those blue-gray eyes looking at her, unseeing. As long as she didn't speak, the ticking clock would be all that settled between them. Gus was right in his description. He'd left out how thin Cort's face was. And the striped uniform was meant to shame the lawless. What she wanted to say wouldn't come to her tongue.

"You my lawyer?" he asked hoarsely, breaking the quiet.

"No. Your wife."

He started violently at the sound of her voice. "Jesus Christ! I told Gus not to tell you where to find me. I can't trust him. You've wasted your time coming."

He tried to stand but the shackles kept him in place. He yanked at them. "Leave. Leave now!" He roared the words like a man possessed.

She didn't move. "I deserve to be heard. Even if just once. Please, Cort."

He lowered his voice. "This is no place for a lady. If you come again, I'll fight the guards before I'll face you. That'll get me into solitary. Say what you got to say."

"Fair enough. Cort, you can't see anything, can you?"

"No. It all went dark. The doctor gave me some headache medicine. That helped. I sleep. But I don't know morning from night. Satisfied? Did you find out what you came to?"

"There are good doctors and a new hospital going up in Omaha."

"I'm here. Not there." Abruptly, his tone softened a little. "How's the ranch doing?"

So he was still interested in the ranch. She took that as a partial breakthrough. "Better if you were there. Everyone is pulling their weight. Zeke is teaching me about ledgers and herd counts and beef prices. Everyone misses you." She leaned closer and whispered, "They'd all like to form a brigade to break you out."

When he grinned, her heart lightened. "Sounds like Tangle in charge."

"Well. Him, Nita, and Theresa. Doesn't matter. Get ready. You're going home."

"Yeah? How you going to make that happen? And don't tell me you plan to break me out. Lark, just go home."

"We're meeting the Governor tomorrow. He needs to know your side and the way you were treated in that courtroom. When we leave Lincoln, you're coming with us."

"Who's *we*?" he sighed.

"Gus, me, Tangle, Zeke, and Juan."

"Jesus Christ, *Lark*. Don't get your hopes up. Things like that happen to men with political ties and more money than I got."

"I'm determined. I won't go home without my husband. You are not a prisoner. You are a victim."

"A husband who's blind. Do you know how much help I'll need? I can't even get my clothes on without help. Finding my way to a privy? Who'll be assigned to that duty?"

"I love you, Cort. That's all that matters. If you love me like you said, we can work all that out once you're free."

Silence fell between them. He squinted and when he tried to raise his hand, he was brought up short by the length of the chain. Lark slid her hand across the table to cover his. He turned his over and grasped hers between his fingers.

"Just so you know. Before Tenner found me, I had already decided to come home. Maybe look for doctors someplace. You should know that. Don't come again, darlin'. I may not see you, but my heart aches for not holding you. Touching you. Hard for me to sleep because it's always night. That makes it easy to spend my time remembering making love with you. I'm tormented, shamed, and a lot more. Having you here just stirs things. Reminds me how much I lost. How much I miss you. Please. If your plan doesn't work, don't come again."

"Cort. Believe we're getting you out. You're tough. I'm going to be a force to be reckoned with."

He shook his head. "Guard! Guard! I want to go back to my cage. Now!" he shouted.

The guard's keys jangled against the metal bars. Lark stood up. She ignored the guard's warning look and marched to the other side of the table. Leaning over Cort, she touched his lips with hers and felt his tremble. Then his mouth took hers with a deep, searing kiss. Neither of them cared about the warning cough beside them.

She straightened and backed away. The guard unshackled Cort and led him away without another word. And if she could remember anything about that long walk back down that quiet corridor, it would be her sense of profound loss and Cort's haunted, pitiful glance in her direction as though he had said goodbye. She imagined him lying on a bunk in ever present darkness. He most likely knew he was unkempt, but no longer cared. She wondered if he kept count of the passing days. And she knew he hated the thought of depending on other people.

Zeke, Tangle, Gus, and Lark put on the best clothes they had with them. For the men, that was Levi's and cotton shirts. Lark wore a light green dress with an overdress of dark blue silk that Theresa had pieced together from Sienna's wardrobe. Lark fashioned her hair into a neat chignon, befitting a forthright woman on a mission.

The four were admitted to the Governor's new office by a soft-spoken, older woman with a cheery smile and courteous demeanor. Four seats were made available in front of a commonplace desk. The Governor looked up from his scribbling. At first, she thought they were about to be dismissed. Then a short grin beneath his long beard gave her hope that he was about to listen. When he set down his pen, his intense eyes pierced each one of them. Lark waited. When he didn't speak, she drew breath and began.

"I'm Lark Enders. We're here, Governor, to right a wrong. My husband is in prison here in Lincoln and we aim to take him home. He is not the wrongdoer you assume. He is a victim."

"I already have an idea what you aim to get from me before you leave, ma'am. And I've read Judge Pelton's opinion. I'm not happy with lawbreakers. That's why we spent time and considerable money on the new prison where your husband is housed. But since you came a long way, I'll give you the time you need to convince me he should be set free. And, please refer to me as Silas. Since that, in fact, is my name. Don't hold much with titles." He smiled and winked at her. "Please continue, Mrs. Enders. I have other appointments."

"Lark. Please."

Two hours later they left the Governor's office, a signed and sealed pardon in their hands. Cort was to be released immediately and his eyes tended to at Nebraska's expense, given that he'd single-handedly brought Will Cardin's gang to an end and lost his sight in the process.

Relief was slow to sink in. Their exasperation at having to wait until morning tempered their jubilation. Moreover, they still had Cort's blindness to deal with. He wasn't going to accept his vulnerability easily. All they could do was hope for a reversal of the fates that had plummeted him into darkness. Or hope he learned to accept his blindness because he had no choice.

Chapter 27
Freedom from Darkness

Was it time for breakfast? Cort was abruptly shaken from his dark dreams. He opened his eyes slowly, wishing as always for the surprise of light. Anything that would give him hope.

"Cort Enders." A familiar voice, one of the friendlier guards. "You're a free man. Got your clothes, boots, and coat here. Your friends have your other personals. Appears you're going home. I'll bring you a little breakfast so you can eat in here and be on your way. Ain't no sense in stayin' any longer than you need."

Cort shook his head to clear the cobwebs. What was the man saying? *Free?* Was he dreaming? Was this a trick? Maybe he misunderstood? He felt around his bunk, and his hand touched pants and a shirt. Next, his fingers slid over a leather belt. Reality started to sink in. He felt as if the floor might cave in beneath him. If only he could get into his own clothes. He'd been wearing this prison getup for so long, he'd almost forgotten what real clothes felt like.

"Can you stay and help with . . ." Cort caught himself. He hated admitting he was dependent on others. An invalid.

"Sure. Never did like them lockin' up a blind man. No sense to that. Glad you're getting out."

"Yeah. Guess today I *am* free." *Lark. My wife and friends.* They'd gotten him out of here. How?

Once he was dressed, he stuffed a biscuit and some bacon into his mouth and chewed as fast as he could. Getting out of here before his freedom was somehow deemed a mistake and the door slammed again made him move swiftly, blind or not. He felt around for the green ribbon, then tucked it into his pocket. The ribbon had been his salvation, taking him to another place.

Two hundred and seventy-two strides beside the guard brought him to the next door. The exit swung open and a draft of spring air hit him. Warm, clean air. The smell of piss and crap left behind, while the scents of sunlight, grass, and leather filled his nostrils.

The guard released his arm and bid him farewell. Then Cort stood alone.

"Cort. If I wasn't a tough, mean old man I'd bust out cryin'."

Zeke. "I wish I could say it was good to see you. But I'd know that voice anywhere."

Zeke laughed. "You'll see again. I'm a betting man."

Zeke took his arm and led Cort through another door and out into a space filled with movement. Boots crunching over gravel, plodding horses, snorting. Thuds, clanks, rolling wagons, and a distant whipping of a flag in the wind. A new world of senses he'd have to learn to depend on.

"Come on. That guard handed me your coat. Let's get you into it. A bit of a wind today. We got a buggy waitin' just outside this wall. And a pretty gal sittin' there about to bust with happi-ncss."

As Cort slipped his arms into his sleeves with Zeke's help, he said, "My horse, saddlebag. My guns?"

"Gus took care of them. He has Lincoln saddled and geared up for you. Gun and holster with Gus and your rifle in the saddle boot."

"Think I should rename my horse?"

"Nah. No sense in confusin' the animal. He got all jittery when you disappeared. Glad you've kept some humor."

"Wasn't easy. Nothin' amusin' inside that place. I'm damned

if I ever go back." Cort sighed. "Before I see her, tell me how she's been doin'. The truth."

"Lark is strong. Puts on a good front. But she was miserable. All I could do was keep tellin' her you'd come back in your own time."

"Almost did. Till I got stopped by Tenner."

"That's over now. You two got a lot to say to each other. Let's get to it."

They started walking. Somewhere ahead of him were his friends and his wife. He had no way to gauge where or how far. All he could do was follow along. "Zeke. Before we get to them, I owe all of you my thanks."

"We didn't do all that much. Stuck by your Lark. All of us together made quite a force. But Lark made a damned good case. She deserves thanks and more."

"I wasn't very pleasant when she showed up inside. I love her. I hated her seein' me like that. Tore me up into a thousand pieces. Didn't think she'd pull off a pardon."

"That's over. You two got mending to do. We're almost to that buggy where I see a woman running this way. Bet she plows into you. Brace yourself. I'm steppin' away."

Cort stood frozen. His hand went to his scruffy beard. When he ran his fingers through his tousled hair, he had a pretty good idea what he looked like. The sound of boots racing in his direction sent a kind of fear through him. How should he react? He hadn't been at his best when Lark showed up, yet he loved her with every breath he took. Why was his tongue tied into a knot? He wanted to *see* her. That was part of what made him a man. A man who could protect her from trouble. Keep her safe. Read her every thought in her eyes. In his world, everything was black. The sun felt warm, but he wanted to see the sun.

She stopped. Her breathing near him, the scent of lilies, and her hands curving around his neck nearly sent him to his knees with her in his arms. "Careful, Lark. I haven't had bath water in more than a few days."

"Do you think I care? You'd stand beside me no matter what I looked like. You've proved that."

"Guess you know me pretty well. I hope you know I love you. I'm sorry for what I said in there. I deserve a tongue-lashing."

"You won't get anything from me but devotion. Besides, I'd have used stronger terms if you'd been my visitor. That place put even me in a bad mood. I'm just so sorry we didn't get here sooner. Please don't ever leave me out of your decisions again. You mule-headed, contrary, loving man."

"You sure get through my crazy mixed-up head when I need it the most. Zeke told me you were plucky in that Governor's office. I owe you thanks. Got to hand it to you."

"I'm cashing in."

Her breath touched his face and his lips found hers. Whatever he'd thought to say, he forgot as his mouth urged hers open. Their kiss deepened, promising more to come. His nostrils filled with the scent of sage and a gentle breeze lifted the tendrils of her hair beneath his fingers. His arms wrapped around her and he held her firmly against his chest. The feel of her shattered the wall he'd built to dam up his emotions. His eyes closed. He didn't want to ever let her go.

Someone coughed. "Maybe you lovebirds can get reacquainted at the hotel tonight. We got a train to catch in the mornin," Gus admonished.

Lark's arms dropped away. She clutched Cort's hand and tugged. "Let's get some food and a good night's sleep."

He let her guide him, and briefly looked up. Something was different. A sliver of foggy light. He blinked. His feet kept pace with her, but the cloudy light stayed. Glancing behind him, he thought he saw a brilliant red glow. The horizon? He blinked again. It was there. *Some light.* A trick of nature? He wanted to shout for joy at this small thing, but he didn't say a word. Tomorrow it could be gone.

Once he'd been led to the buggy, he hesitated. A nicker sounded nearby. *Lincoln.*

"Take me to my partner." Using Lark's arm for guidance, he moved forward and ran his hand over his horse's sleek mane. The big animal nodded under his touch. *Would they ever ride together again?*

"Gus. Thanks for taking care of him and for everything else you did. You too, Tangle. And Zeke. Can't see you, but I know I'd still be sittin' in that hellhole if it wasn't for all of you."

"Just so long as you don't slip away again," Tangle said. "Ain't had a good night's sleep for worryin' about you, boss. Theresa and Nita acted like they'd been drinkin' sour milk most days."

"That sounds like them. I sure missed my women's cookin'." Everyone chuckled, and Cort accepted a hand-up from Tangle into the buggy.

They made their way to the hotel. After a meal of beef stew, fresh bread, coffee, and apple pie, the men headed for the saloon to celebrate, leaving Lark and Cort to some time alone. The two of them were sipping coffee, talking about the ranch and their future, when someone approached their table. "Mister and Mrs. Enders?"

"Yes." Cort stiffened. A man's voice, nervous. Blind men listened to the sound of voices. He wasn't practiced in that. He was used to reading the eyes. Keeping Lark safe wasn't going to be easy unless he got his sight back. He wore his gun, but he couldn't see to shoot. Damn. His fingers slipped around the grip anyway.

"Sorry to bother you both. Got a note here for you. I was told to give it to you before you left."

"Thank you. I'll take it, if you don't mind," Lark said.

Cort heard the man's footfalls move away amid the chatter of other diners. A rustle of paper told him Lark was reading whatever had been delivered. Another reminder of life without his eyes.

"What does it say?"

"Oh, Cort." She leaned forward. "This is from the Governor. He sends along his best wishes, and he paid for our dinner and stay at the hotel. Says here that he thanks you on behalf of the State of Nebraska for putting an end to Will Cardin and his gang. He'll see that Rozzie and Wes in Wichita get part of the reward. He's sending along the rest to you."

Cort leaned back in the chair and rested his hands on the table. "You must have impressed him. Never thought about a reward. Glad for Rozzie to get it."

Her soft hand smoothed over his. "*You* impressed him. There's no one better with a gun and no one kinder. You'll see again. I just know it."

He squeezed her fingers. They made their way to their room where he promptly felt at a loss. The only clothes he had were those on his back. Sleeping beside her in a clean bed felt wrong. While he longed for her body against his, had imagined having her beneath him over and over again, the time didn't seem right. Would he be gentle or too demanding after waiting so long? Worse, he couldn't see her reactions. He'd learned to give her pleasure from the longing in her green-gold eyes. Now everything was dark.

She guided him to the bed. He sat stiffly on the edge. The sound of a match strike told him she'd lit an oil lamp. Mercy. He could see the lamp glow. The shape of the lamp was distorted, and he blinked. The light inside the vague globe kept him focused, afraid to look away for fear it would disappear.

A swooshing of cloth, a thump as shoes clunked to the floor. His fingers fumbled with the buttons of his shirt. Lark moved his hands away and finished his undressing. Piece by piece, she removed his clothes and boots. Pride was forgotten; her touch was too sensual to deny her, the pleasure too great to ignore her fingers wherever they brushed against him.

A slow joining. A gradual step toward his new normal, and proof that not all of him was torn apart. They lay beside each other, and he turned his head toward that dim lamp. It held his attention. Afraid. If he closed his eyes to sleep, tomorrow the light would be gone. Her hand found his, their fingers laced together on his chest. He knew she watched him.

"What are you thinking, Cort?"

"I want to make love to you like before. Every inch of you. Not seeing you tears across every piece of what makes me a man. Why is that?" he said hoarsely.

"Because you have to find your way back to the man you were before prison. He's still inside you. Until you let go of that awful place, bitterness stands between us. I know. Not so long ago, my fears of getting too close to you and bringing you harm almost made me lose you."

"I want to be your husband in every way."

"For now, just hold me. I've missed you." She turned down the lamp. He couldn't tell her to leave it. He wasn't ready to admit what might just be a trick.

He leaned over her and she held his face between her hands. His fingers touched her lips, and then his mouth followed. They kissed deeply. Some while later, the night sent her into sleep, curled against his body. While her breathing soothed his soul, he peered through the darkness. Moonlight danced on the far corner of the wall, and his eyes found a new hope.

When he turned his head toward his wife, her watery, vague shape beneath the blanket sent shivers of revelation through him. He wouldn't close his eyes. If he did, he might never see her again. All night, Cort fought a war with sleep, keeping watch over the elusive light until weariness overtook him.

The next day found Juan waiting at the train depot with saddlebags and guns stacked around a bench. Tangle and Zeke hefted their gear and stepped into the passenger train that would take them toward Omaha, where they'd take the Union Pacific on to Ogallala. Gus walked toward Lark and Cort with his loose stride and a grin on his face. His sorrel horse plodded behind. Gus was leaving them here.

"Lark. Cort."

"Are you sure you won't consider coming with us, Gus? I can use a good hand," Cort said. "You proved yourself in Wichita."

"That's God's truth. You know I ain't much at stayin' put. Gettin' back up in the Dakotas along the Belle Fourche. My cabin needs tendin' afore somebody takes root in it. You know where it is. Things settled some with the Indians so I best get up there and do some thinkin' about where I'll settle in. Still have some renegades up that way to watch for."

"We'll miss you. You're a good friend. Watch out. Keep that gun handy. You'll have a place at the Double E when you get to thinking."

"Plan to." Now Gus's full attention turned toward a sad-faced Lark. "Good thing you wanted to marry this mule-headed gunslinger or I might've decided to take you away with me."

"You'd have a fight on your hands, mountain man," Cort declared.

Gus chuckled. "Take care of yourselves. May come see that big ranch one day. 'Sides, Zeke and I like to play poker."

Lark released the hands she clutched. Gus leaned down and she planted a kiss on his cheek. "I ain't much for cheek-kissin'," Gus growled. With that, he pressed his mouth to hers and then stepped back.

"Did you just kiss my wife?" Cort asked.

"Surely did. Better get your sight back afore I see you next so you can punch me in the nose."

The two men laughed. Gus shook Cort's hand. "Already said goodbye to Tangle, Juan, and Zeke. Good men. They'll keep you two outta more trouble. Got a wagon waitin' in Ogallala. Horses and gear aboard the train. You best get goin'."

When the train jolted and moved sluggishly past the depot, Gus sat atop his horse and waved. Lark was one of a kind. Cort was not only lucky to have her, he was damned lucky Gus Quaid hadn't seen her first. Cort Enders was a helluva good man. Gus hoped he'd see them again. That baby she carried was surely going to be a surprise when Cort finally figured it out.

Chapter 28
Joyful Dawn

At the stop in Omaha, the gear and horses were moved to the Union Pacific for the last train leg of the journey to Ogallala. Blurred shapes, dim light, and frosty images couldn't be blinked away. The thought of living the rest of his life in fog churned inside Cort. Having to be led by his wife to the restaurant prickled. Made it easy to think about sinking into self-pity. Instead, he resolved to rely on hope and relish the little improvements. And maybe even a trip to an Eastern doctor. Distorted colors and shapes were dangerous for a man who'd learned to live by his gun.

Once Zeke and the others joined them at the table, jovial chatter erupted. Most centered on getting back to the ranch where they all had to pitch in to get branding done. Cort clenched his teeth at the realization of all the things he couldn't do. They talked around him while he sat in stoic silence, seething inside.

Finally, he spoke. "How many head did you buy?" Though he said it quietly, he couldn't conceal his resentful tone. Forks clattered against the dishes, and he knew he'd unsettled everyone, but just now he didn't care. The loss of his sight was bad enough. Damned if he would be treated like he'd lost his intelligence.

Zeke spoke up. "We had a lot survived this winter. Figured we'd need five hundred head. Mason brought 'em up from Amarillo and then up from Dodge City."

"Mason! He's back?"

"Sure is. Doin' a hell of a job. Left him and Jude in charge."

Cort knew a spurt of jealousy, even though he understood it was unfounded. Still, would Lark find another man, someone like Mason? Jesus. He had to get his wandering thoughts under control. Lark loved him. He loved her. And he trusted her more than anyone.

"Who made the decision for five hundred?"

"I did. Along with Mason and Damon. They've been doing most of the roundup with about ten other hands."

"A thousand would've improved the herd in case we get a hard winter." Everyone fell silent at that. "When we get back, I want everyone here to know that, blind or not, I plan to figure out how to work the ranch. That clear?"

Zeke sighed. "Look, Cort. We're all goin' to help you. Don't forget you got a wife beside you. She's part of this."

"Back home, it'll all be familiar," Lark added.

Cort set his fork down. He'd gripped it so tightly he figured he'd bent it. These folks deserved better than his whining. "Sorry. I'm rattled. If everyone's finished, why don't we head for the train. I'm anxious to get going."

Aboard the Union Pacific, Cort sat beside Lark and gave thought to telling her that he was seeing snatches of light. Then he thought better of it. He didn't want to get her hopes up, or his. The train lurched and they were underway with a loud whistle. The sounds around him were of ordinary folks, talking about money, children, land, and the dangers that lurked out on these plains. He touched his holster and knew he'd be of no use with a gun. Resentment rose like bile inside. Maybe it always would.

As though she had read his thoughts, Lark leaned against him. Her quiet voice washed over him. "You'll use that gun again, Cort Enders. You'll ride the range land and tease your cowhands beside a campfire. It will happen."

"Wish I had your confidence, sweetheart. When I can see. Really see. If I ever do, I'll dance. I'll pick you up and swing you in my arms. Right now, I can't shoot, ride, or button my shirt. Or dance with my wife without stumbling. And it kills me."

"Cort. Can you see anything?"

He leaned his head back and closed his eyes. When he took her hand in his and rested it on his lap, he counted himself the luckiest man to have found her. Gentle, loyal, kind, and intelligent. She didn't deserve his problems. And she didn't deserve lies.

"No." Until he could see her face plainly, he would keep this to himself.

The wagon jolted and bounced over holes and ruts. The air was warm in the June light, sinking over the distant hills and fragments of mountains to the west. The horses snorted. Mason tried to keep the wagon to a steady pace. Lark noticed how Cort sat straight on the seat beside her, his left arm behind her along the bench. The two men had kept to cordial comments about weather, cows, and the excitement at the ranch.

Zeke, Tangle, and Juan followed on their mounts. Mason headed them toward the newly repaired way station between the ranch complex and Ogallala. Before they got to it, they'd have to ride under the Double E gate.

"Look! The Double E. We're halfway home, Cort," Lark declared excitedly. Too late, she realized she'd said *look*. An insensitive mistake. "I'm sorry."

"Can't be watching every word. I have some things to get used to again, myself. Theresa's biting tongue. Nita's frittering around with a feather duster. My gun at my side when I can't shoot it. And just overlooking every time somebody forgets I can't see."

"Anything else?"

He looked in her direction. She saw that grin, so quick to appear and quicker to melt. Since he'd agreed to a haircut and shave in Ogallala, he looked more like himself. Except for his pale skin and drawn face, the Cort she remembered was emerging. A lot of good cooking would fill out his bones.

"Oh. You mean our bed?"

She slapped him playfully on his arm. Mason took that moment to join the teasing. "Don't go talkin' about that in front of me or you'll have me blushin' and that won't do my reputation any good."

"Close your ears," Cort chided him.

"That'll be the day."

"Mason. I been meanin' to apologize. I got my tail in a twist and you didn't deserve that. Glad you're back. You're one of my top hands. Always were. Missed having you here. I'm relyin' on you to make decisions. Five hundred head should work out."

"Let's just say I got over it. Hooked up with Cardin after I left the Circle H, but that didn't last long once I figured he was crazy. Lucky, I got out of his circle before he shot me."

"I'm beholden to you for sending that telegram to me. Zeke told me."

"So that's how you found me," Lark said.

Mason said, "I think my telegram got to the ranch too late to do much good."

Cort turned his head toward Lark. "No matter. Between Gus, and Will Cardin's trail of blood, I was able to track you down. Damned sure glad I got there when I did."

"Was Cardin the one who hit you over the head?" Mason asked.

"Probably."

Lark's head rested against Cort's arm. All three of them wandered into their own thoughts. Cort looked toward a rim of red sunset. Light was all he could count on for now. He said a silent prayer that it would stay.

That night, Lark helped Juan with the meal. They set up a large coffee pot on the grate. Theresa had sent along frizzled beef sandwiches, cold potato salad, and biscuits in the buckboard. While the men talked about wolves, Indians, beef prices, and fencing, Cort took in the emerging but distorted faces around him. Maybe tomorrow there would be more. He heard Lark's soft yawn before she took his hand where she sat beside him at the fire.

"Why don't you go on to bed?" he told her. "I'll be along."

"Think I'll do just that."

Cloth rustled as she got up and went inside the line shack. Without her nearby, he stared into the blazing fire. Flames danced amid the charred wood while the hiss and pop entranced him. After a time, the quiet struck him. The men had stopped talking.

"You're seein'," Tangle snapped. "Lordy. Did you get your sight back? And don't hem and haw about it."

Cort looked toward the shadowed figures across the fire from him. They had been studying him as he studied the flames.

"Don't go celebrating yet. Not clear. But better than yesterday. I'm afraid that if I sleep, I might wake up blind again."

"Pshaw! Boss, this calls for a drink," Tangle said. "Got me a bottle in my saddlebag."

"Maybe you better tell Lark, Cort. This is pretty important," Mason said.

"I'm not ready to tell her until I'm sure. Till I see her face."

"Don't know how I'll be able to keep my mouth shut," Zeke added.

Tangle guffawed. "The rest of us is too plug ugly for you to want to see."

The dim light in the line shack did little to help him toward the bunk where Lark's hazy form lay curled beneath a blanket. The potbellied stove sizzled. The orange glow offered more than heat. He viewed Lark as if in a watercolor without clear lines, the vague outline of her hair hanging over the bed. With each day, he held out more hope that his vision was returning.

She sat up abruptly and lurched from the bed. "You should have called me."

"I'm here. Lay down beside me."

That night, they touched and kissed. That was all they needed. Exploring deeper needs would come when they were finally in their own bed and away from the others. For now, tender whispers celebrated today. Her heartbeat made him happy to be alive.

As his fingers followed her outline beneath the blanket, it struck him that her breasts seemed fuller. Unless he'd forgotten the feel of her. He thought back to Emporia. Had he been so filled with his shortcomings that he'd overlooked this? His hand moved over her stomach and he heard her intake of breath. His hand stilled. He froze.

"Lark?"

"I was hoping you wouldn't notice till we got home. In a real bed."

"My God. A baby? *A baby.* I must be dumb not to have figured it out."

"Not dumb. I've been doing my best to hide this under a coat and fuller dresses. No one else knows. Except Zeke and probably Gus. I think they guessed. And I told Nita and Theresa after they figured it out."

He sat up and cupped her face between his hands. "When?"

"Sometime in November."

"How?"

"Wichita, I'm guessing."

"Thank you." He leaned toward her and kissed her deeply.

She pulled away. "Can you see me?"

He sighed. "In a watery blur."

"Oh, my God! Prayers have been answered. You're going to see! Cort!"

He grasped her arm. "Don't say it. Not until I can see your face and my land clear. I want to be able to see my own baby and keep you both safe."

She exhaled a relieved breath and wrapped her arms around his neck. They kissed until they fell into restless sleep. *Home.* He wanted to get her home where he could show her how much he loved her.

CHAPTER 29
VISION OF TOMORROW

"Boss!" Tangle shouted. "Look over there!"

Cort squinted into the blaring sunlight, not seeing anything but light and watery looking grass.

"Christ's sakes, Tangle! Watch what you say!" Zeke barked. "Wait here."

Cort made out the shapes of the horses as the men rode away. The sounds of the wind, the creak of the harness, and snorts of the team filled him with the urge to blindly follow them atop Lincoln's back. He looked over his shoulder, considering his horse tied to the rear. "Tell me what's going on."

"Vultures," Mason said. "We've found a few beeves shot up. Funny thing. They leave most of the cow and take enough for a meal. Makes no sense."

Three loud shots rang out, followed by two more. They waited.

"Have you trailed them?" Cort asked.

"They disappear upriver and we lose them."

"Son of a bitch." Cort rubbed his eyes, willing them to see. The sky looked blue through the haze. He couldn't see Zeke or Tangle with any clarity.

"Hand me a rifle, Mason."

"You can't be thinkin' of riding." Mason's chastisement sent a burn down his gut.

Cort took the proffered rifle and eased from the wagon seat, shrugging from Lark's grasp. He'd just mounted his horse when Zeke and Tangle rode back.

"What do you think you're doin?" Tangle asked, and spit on the ground.

"Nothin' any of us can do for now, Cort. Dead cow," Zeke snapped.

"Who would do this?" Lark asked from the wagon seat.

"Whoever is doing this is either stupid or planning to destroy my herd. Drawing in wolves. I want men sent back here to trench that carcass."

"Will do, boss," Tangle replied.

"Cort? Want some help getting back in the wagon?"

The horse was beneath him and Cort wasn't about to give that up. In fact, he had every intention of riding up to his house. "Lark."

"I want to watch my husband ride home."

Cort nudged Lincoln into a slow walk. Before long, the big house came into his hazy view.

Cort dismounted and lifted Lark from the wagon. Theresa ran down the steps to hug her, and Nita led her into the house. Cort took tenuous steps to reach the porch. From there, he followed the smells of pie, coffee, and cooked meat and the sounds of happy chatter. For him, things were not all normal, yet. He had a lot to forget and a lot to overcome.

Lark had watched her husband withdraw. Instead of joining wholeheartedly in the celebration at having him home, his face looked taut. He'd gone someplace deep inside. She imagined him building a wall against people rather than allowing them to see his weakness. When the women realized he was blind, they'd become overly accommodating. Eventually, Cort stood and found his way to the front door, where he stared out at the distorted, unfocused range land he loved. She followed and stood behind him, resting her forehead against his back. He turned, grasped her hand, and tugged her toward the stairs. She led him to the room that had been hers before Sienna's death. He squinted into the waning light from the window.

"You didn't move into the big room?"

"Someday. When I don't feel Sienna in there."

He nodded in understanding. "Order new furniture and whatever else you need. We're making that room ours."

Lark felt heat flow from ear to ear. She imagined her face blooming as red as a rose. Before she could protest his extravagance, he picked her up and walked to the room at the far end of the hallway. A room that had been a symbol of Sienna's possession of him. A little stab of jealousy would always live inside her.

He shoved open the door, carried her through, and kicked it shut, then dropped her onto the bed before sitting down beside her. "This is our bed. Our bedroom. No one else matters. Ever."

Lark watched him yank off his boots and strip down his pants. She unfastened his shirt buttons, exposing his broad chest to her view. She removed her blouse and chemise, yanked off her shoes, and tossed her skirt onto the growing pile of clothes at the foot of the bed. The curtains lifted on the breeze from the open window. Dying rays of sunlight played on the walls and touched their skin. They knew each other's bodies.

Now they explored deeper needs. Finding new ways to please and be pleased. He touched her swelling stomach while she ran her fingers over his many scrapes and bullet scars, knowing he was lucky to have survived. They tumbled with each other onto the bed. He rolled her above him.

Her fingers traced his mouth and stroked his throat. Her hands moved over his chest, and she felt him shudder. Suddenly, she was beneath him. His hands cupped her full breasts, while he blinked to clear his vision. His hands smoothed over her hips and along her inner thighs. She leaned upward and kissed his mouth, eliciting his demanding growl from deep inside his chest.

When his hands wandered from her legs back to her stomach, they froze. His mouth left hers. He lifted his head and stared at her, squinting as if her face was still lost in a foggy haze.

"Lark? Are you sure we can do this?"

"This is my first baby, Cort. But I have it on good authority that we can do this."

"Whose authority?"

"Nita's and Theresa's."

"Jesus."

"They've had children. They should know these things."

"I won't be able to look them in the eyes. Even if I can't see them."

He rolled her to his side. His mouth met hers in a fiery kiss that nearly took her breath away. Lark stretched her arms out to give his mouth access to every part of her body. His lips trailed kisses over her scar and then along her throat to her breasts.

He touched her in places that sent spasms pulsing through her skin. When he returned to her mouth, he looked into her eyes as though he saw deep into them. "I memorized you. I saw you through the darkness. I held you close to me in that prison."

"Shh. I'm here."

Cort raised himself above her, his arms supporting most of his weight. His mouth took hers and he took them to heaven, swallowing her cry. In the aftermath of their joining, they lay in each other's arms while his hand roamed over her rounded stomach. She rubbed the sole of her foot along his calf and heard the rumbling deep within his chest.

When their breathing slowed, Cort pulled her against him, their mouths barely touching. Joy at the feel of his pounding heart beneath her hand and his satisfied sigh filled her with abiding love. His gaze stayed with hers as they descended into a peaceful sleep. The ghosts of Sienna and Wade were gone.

She woke alone. She lurched to a sitting position, ran her hand through her tousled hair, and searched the sunlit room. Cort stood in front of the window, just watching while light spread over his rangy body. He was still shirtless, but he'd pulled on his Levi's. Lark swung her feet to the floor and padded toward him. He said nothing, just stood tall and silent. She wrapped her arms around his middle and rested her head against his back.

"How long have you been standing here?" she whispered.

"Quite a while. I want to see everything. Hard to explain. I'll never take this sight for granted again."

It took a moment for his words to sink in. She followed his gaze to the corrals and the open range where their cattle grazed peacefully. The Indian grass blew in swirls beneath the touch of the wind as though parting for the smaller creatures that made it their home.

"What do you see?" She couldn't hide the hesitation in her voice.

He turned to face her. A smile lit his face. "I see what you see. The horses and men heading out. My cattle. Even those wild roses and sunflowers you like so much. And right now, I see your gold-green eyes looking into mine. Searching. Filling with tears."

"Oh, Cort! You can see?"

"Clearly. Every little strand of your love-twisted hair. Your rounded stomach and the breasts that I'll share with my son or daughter. The pink of your cheeks. Everything."

She reached for him and he lifted her against him. Their mouths met. They kissed. And kissed again.

"I love you, Lark. With every breath I ever take." He set her on her bare feet.

"Do you remember when we were stranded in that shack?"

"Yes," he said distantly. "Nearly drowned both of us."

"Do you know that's when I knew I loved you."

"How's that?"

"You could have taken me that night. Instead, you were honorable. Noble. Some men wouldn't have cared about a wife they didn't love."

"I loved you before then. I keep my promises. Sienna was an imperfect promise. But a promise all the same."

"And I love you for being loyal and true to what's right, Mister Enders. What are you thinking?" she asked when he looked toward the window.

"I don't think I'll ever forget losing my sight. I've been gifted with a second chance. I'm making this place into something even Wade never dreamed. And I'm doing it with you beside me. Have to admit, I've been scared. I've been in dozens of gunfights, had run-ins with Indians, and been in drunken brawls where I thought I'd busted every rib. Nothing was as bad as losing my sight."

He reached into the pocket of his Levi's and withdrew a tattered green ribbon. She slowly looked at it and then up into his face. "You've kept that all this time?"

"Yep. Got me through lonely nights when I couldn't have you."

Lark struggled to find something to say. There were no words to describe the poignancy of this moment. A hard man bound by his promise to a dying woman while yearning for love out of his reach. Held by a ribbon. She leaned her head against his shoulder and felt his arm tuck her close. Tears ran over her cheeks.

He lifted her chin with a finger. "None of that. How 'bout we get down to the kitchen and scrounge up some vittles?"

"I'd say we better put some clothes on and get to it because I might just want my husband again. Right here. In that bed."

He winked. "That's a promise."

Epilogue: Three Weeks Later

Three fiddles, two banjos, and a clacker provided enough music. The dancing was held inside the swept-out barn. Tables of food were set in front of the porch. At least seven wagons had arrived by late morning to celebrate the marriage of Cortland Neil Enders and Lark Marie Garrin. Cort had decided that before tongues wagged, he'd make sure there were no whispers about his wife. Not that he liked proving anything to anybody. Still, Lark deserved a wedding celebration after that hurried affair in Wichita.

Glory and Macon Sanderson arrived in time for the nuptials, with Pastor Micah Jeffers presiding. No one was more surprised than Mason when Cort asked him to stand as best man. Zeke was more than happy to step aside. Afterward, the guests filled their plates near where a beef roasted over the firepit. Once the eating was finished, the drinking and dancing commenced. More than a few were corned by the time they tried to mount their horses and wagons to head home.

As evening drew on, Damon and Tangle picked up their banjos while Jude, Zeke, and Jeffery Landon set their bows and fiddles to a raucous round of music in the barn until campfires burned low and folks either camped for the night or made their way toward outlying farms. Jeffery hadn't won his wife's heart at the Ribbon Cotillion, but he sure played a mean fiddle. Some guests were invited to stay at Zeke's new house. Theresa and Nita fluttered around the food tables, refilling coffee tins. Folks applauded when Cort and Lark Enders danced to "Softly Tread, My Nelly's Sleeping."

Dan, Billy, and Adoeete were assigned herd duty but food had been set aside for them. The laughter faded into the air and the music ended. The bunkhouse lanterns were lit. Cort and Lark made their way to their bed where they would speak with their hearts and once again remove the green ribbon from her hair.

Over the next two months, the ranch expanded by degrees. Corrals were built. New ranch hands were hired on. And a porch was added to Zeke's house so he could look out over the graves of Sienna and Wade Harris. Zeke's arthritis grew achy and he took on a new role as office and personnel manager. Mason Lanning relished his new position as foreman.

The cow killer taunted them from time to time. They didn't spend much time looking for the culprit after they discovered a child's toy near one of the kills. Cort had no inclination to leave a kid without food in winter. Sooner or later, the day would come when he and the cow killer would meet up, and then Cort would exact punishment.

A late November snowstorm blanketed the ranch. The main house was busy with the birth of the baby. Cort paced while Zeke handed him a glass and a bottle of whiskey. Theresa and Nita tended to Lark, who screamed in distress. Cort swigged whiskey and muttered something about finding a doctor to live at the ranch.

When he finally heard the baby's cry, he took the stairs two at a time to find a squirming bundle cradled in Lark's arms. She smiled adoringly and offered him their baby to hold. "Your son. Bryce Wade Enders."

Tucking his little boy in his arms, he felt both joy and worry. What kind of father would he be? Lark's eyes trailed to the gun at his hip. He guessed she'd never quite get used to that. Right now, his eyes were on this light-haired boy that sucked his tiny fist and kicked his feet. Bryce Wade Enders. Cort's brother, Bryce, had most likely died during the war. He might never know for sure. And Wade had been like a father to him. The names were fitting.

"Bryce Wade Enders," he murmured to his child. "You have big boots to fill. This land is big. You'll learn to be bigger."

ABOUT THE AUTHOR

After a fulfilling career in science teaching, an awestruck visit to the Rocky Mountains led **Susanna Lane** to uncover stories from history and write about the frontier. While writing about the Western settlement of the U.S., she has learned to ride horses, fit into a cattle drive, and hike into remote regions of the West, absorbing the details and getting a feel for the settings of her books.

Married for forty-one years to an avid gardener and traveler who shares her interest in historical locations, Susanna loves to visit new places, read, and spend time with family. In addition to her spouse, she has two grown sons and three darling grandchildren who fill her life with delight.

The employees of Five Star Publishing hope you have enjoyed this book.

Our Five Star novels explore little-known chapters from America's history, stories told from unique perspectives that will entertain a broad range of readers.

Other Five Star books are available at your local library, bookstore, all major book distributors, and directly from Five Star/Gale.

<u>Connect with Five Star Publishing</u>

Visit us on Facebook:
https://www.facebook.com/FiveStarCengage

Email:
FiveStar@cengage.com

For information about titles and placing orders:
(800) 223-1244
gale.orders@cengage.com

To share your comments, write to us:
Five Star Publishing
Attn: Publisher
10 Water St., Suite 310
Waterville, ME 04901